# AN

By
Yvonne Arlott

To Steve
9.12.2016

Yvonne Arlott

Ruthern Valley
Publishing

Copyright © Yvonne Arlott 2014

This novel is a work of fiction. All characters, events and places in this publication are fictitious. Any resemblance to real persons, living or dead, is purely coincidental.

All Rights Reserved.

No part of this publication may be reproduced, stored in a retrieval system, or transmitted in any form or by any means, without the prior permission in writing of the publisher, nor be otherwise circulated in any form of binding or cover other than in which it is published and without a similar condition including this condition being imposed on the subsequent purchaser.

Published By Ruthern Valley Publishing.

ISBN: 978-0-9929920-1-9

Printed and bound in Great Britain by TJ International Ltd

# Acknowledgements

I would like to thank Neil Clift and Norma Till for their helpful comments and time spent reading through earlier drafts of this book. Also I'd like to thank the staff at TJ International Ltd for all their advice and guidance which was much appreciated.

To my parents, Ray and Claire, for their endless support and encouragement.

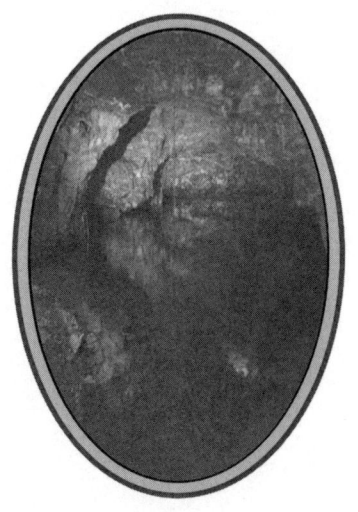

# Part One

The Unknown

## Chapter 1

The bright light glistened off the many small streams that cut their way through the massive, thick green forest. The sound of the clear water trickling downwards rose into the air; it was the only sound that could be heard. A strange stillness hung over everything, giving the impression it was deserted of animals but in the dark hidden depths of the foliage, the rustling of leaves gave away the presence of life.

Two men frantically pushed their way through the thorny undergrowth, sweat dripping off their red faces. The green t-shirts they both wore left their arms exposed and they were now covered in deep scratches and streaks of blood. A shaft of light, that had managed to penetrate the matted canopy, illuminated the fear in their eyes as they forced themselves relentlessly onwards, along the dimly lit trail. They looked at each other in relief as at last the trees and shrubs thinned out to reveal a cliff wall ahead. It spanned some distance to the left and right to form an impenetrable barrier. They seemed unconcerned by it as they plunged through a muddy patch of ground, exhaustion beginning to overcome them. Every so often, they nervously glanced backwards, as though expecting to see some dreaded thing behind them but there was only the still forest.

Both panting heavily, the shorter of the two men risked further exertion on speaking to his companion.

"Can you see it?"

"Just keep moving Patrick." The other man snapped "We've got to get this thing out of here." He nodded down to a fairly large and obviously heavy black box that they were dragging between them. Patrick seemed to understand and redoubled his efforts.

As the men approached the cliff face, a jagged opening in the base of it became apparent, which they now headed towards. A sudden rustle of leaves and cracking of twigs behind them caused Patrick's face to drain from its rosy red to a colourless white, as they both abruptly stopped. The taller man let go of the box and spun round, the gun he was carrying, raised, shaking slightly in his grasp.

"Get it out of here quick." He shouted to Patrick as his wide eyes surveyed every inch of the forest about him. "I'll try to hold it off for as long as I can." There was no reply. He heard the box being dragged backwards. He wasn't sure if he could hear a dull thudding or if it was just his racing heart beating violently inside his chest. With the sound of twigs snapping his search of his surroundings grew more intense as he waited in nervous anticipation for it to loom out of the fading light. Several uneventful minutes passed and still nothing happened. Silence prevailed. He couldn't even hear the box being dragged. He turned to see where his companion was but there was no sign of him or the box.

He gasped in surprise and fear.

"Did he make it out?" The question haunted his mind as he realised that maybe the hell they had been through was all for nothing. Dread gripped him as he felt his lonely and vulnerable situation. His only chance would be to make a run for it.

The sound again. He turned back to see a branch shaking before coming to rest. He froze. The air was still; there was no explanation as to what had disturbed the branch, except one. All looked normal but now he knew it was close to him. His hands began shaking uncontrollably as he finally made himself turn and run for the cliff face.

It was too late. He felt something make a grab at his leg and in the next moment he was violently thrown forwards onto the ground, as his leg was pulled away from under him. The gun had been jerked out of his grip as he had fallen and with despair, he saw that it now lay out of reach. He knew there was no escape but instinct took over and he began desperately struggling to get away. His fingers clawed the muddy ground before him but he was being pulled backwards by a much stronger force.

Slowly the still struggling form disappeared into the dark depths of the forest. As it vanished from sight, a deathly scream rang up into the air and over the treetops, disturbing nothing but the stillness for a second.

## Chapter 2

The darkened windows filtered out the bright sunlight's dangerous rays while still allowing enough light through to illuminate the entire room beyond. Under the suns gentle warmth an old man sat dozing in a soft leather chair placed in the centre of the room. With a sudden start, he woke, glancing around in confusion until his eyes properly focussed on his surroundings. A slight satisfied smile touched his wrinkled face as he settled back in his chair, feeling the safety and protection that the four white walls about him offered. From his position he had a clear view out of the window at the great expanse of skyscrapers and other large buildings. Concrete as far as the eye could see, even though he was on the top floor of a mile high skyscraper.

Bright flashing signs were seated on the tops of many of the buildings, advertising various products, while large greenhouses filled with brilliantly coloured flowers had been created on others. As he watched, a mist descended over everything obscuring his view. Slowly it sank lower until it hung dense, just below the window, giving the illusion of solid ground. As the mist disappeared out of sight, the man turned his attention back to his own dull room, the only furniture being the armchair he sat in, accompanied by two sofas, all of which were white.

"Computer. Run programme CountryRoom4." His voice echoed round the bare room shortly followed by another voice that though clear had an unmistakable monotone to it.

"CountryRoom4 programme is now running." As the voice spoke "now" the room was transformed. The bare white carpet and walls turned into a rich cream. Opposite the man a large fireplace had taken form, flames flickering upwards into the blackness of a new chimney. Pictures of rural countryside hung on the walls, while thick oak beams spanned across the ceiling. Holographic projections had advanced considerably over the last few years. Though it had taken him a while to get used to all the new technology, he now loved it. The one drawback was the computerised voice, which he found incessantly irritating and he still had trouble getting the computer to do what he wanted.

"A special news report is just starting" he cringed at the sound but his eyes had suddenly widened with interest as he sat forward.

"Show the report" the man said urgently. Nothing happened. He groaned, as he remembered it wouldn't respond unless he said "computer" first. A mistake he had made many times before.

"Computer show report."

"Showing report now." He breathed a sigh of relief

as he settled back slightly in the chair, listening to the voice that had begun speaking.

"This is a special news report brought to you by the IGNC (Interactive Global News Corporation). The company created to bring you the latest news at any …" he ignored the rest of the introduction. His attention was absorbed with his room, which had again transformed. Now he was surrounded by large skyscrapers, above which a gigantic disc floated. Using his hand controller, he zoomed in towards the black circular object, studying its dimensions and at last coming to the conclusion that it was some 800 metres in diameter.

"One week ago, an alien spaceship arrived in orbit around the Earth and sent radio messages to the government, demanding that they hand over the "device" within a week or the whole of the human race would be destroyed. Government officials have since said that they have no idea what the "device" the aliens were referring to is and though they would like to, are unable to comply with the demands made.

There has been much talk that everyone should seek refuge in one of the many underground shelters that were built back in the 1960's in case of nuclear war. So far the government has assured us that the aliens pose no threat, despite their warnings. Several miscellaneous reports are circulating, which state that the government did not build large enough shelters to accommodate everyone, in an effort to save money. When questioned, the government spokesman replied that there was absolutely no truth in the allegations and they would evacuate the entire population to the shelters immediately if they thought there was any real danger.

We are now going live to the alien ship." The scenery about the man changed. Though the giant ship remained motionless above his head in mid-air, vast numbers of people had gathered in every available space, staring upwards at the unbelievable sight. They had been told to stay at home but the chance to experience a once in a lifetime event had driven them here.

A new voice started speaking. "This huge alien craft has been drifting slowly across the skies of Earth for the last week, until yesterday when it came to a stop here in New York; one of the most heavily populated areas on the Earth's surface and has remained motionless since.

We have spoken to the government in the last 10 minutes and they have confirmed that they will inform the aliens that they cannot hand over the "device". Also the government stated that should the aliens try to attack, they will fight back with whatever force is necessary.

The countdown to the deadline from a minute is beginning. As you can see everyone has fallen into a trance at this magnificent, incredible sight. History is about to be made here today and they will all be part of it." The old man looked round at the people all standing with their eyes transfixed upwards at the ship.

Silence was all he could hear. Even the voice of the reporter had stopped, as a large red counter, appeared in front of him. 10 seconds. Earth stood still as they slowly ticked downwards. His thoughts raced. If only he could stop the relentless progression of time. With dread he knew the inevitable zero would come and perhaps with it the destruction of mankind.

No one had paid any real attention to the threat, they were all too happy with the realisation that they were not alone in the universe. That's what all the talk shows had focussed on; the thrilling sensation of meeting other life forms and what they might look like. The mention of the aliens destroying the human race had been quietly overlooked, everyone preferring to believe the government's reassurances. But now with an overwhelming fear, reality hit him. He realised the images he saw before him might be the last he would ever see. If only his son could survive it all he would be happy. Thankfully he was over in England, miles away from the ship. He had made the right decision telling his son to stay put at the University.

"This is it." His eyes focussed harder on the counter, willing it to stop. An instance and it had hit zero.

He was still alive. He looked up at the spaceship still motionless, as was everything about it. Suddenly a deafening noise tore through his brain, making him grab at his ears in an attempt to block it out. He watched, terrified, as the people about him jumped with fright and then turned to face the same direction.

He turned also, unable to believe the sight of an enormous skyscraper toppling downwards into a pile of rubble, crushing those people that stood around its base. A giant dust cloud rose up into the sky, blanketing the entire city, and obstructing his view. As the noise began to subside, more explosions rang out, bringing the sound to a continuous unbearable level. Ignoring it as best he could, he squinted through the thick cloud, able to just see the forms of buildings crumbling and people running in all directions. Those nearest the ship seemed to vanish. He adjusted his view trying to get a clearer image of the people. With horror he watched those close to the ship stop, their faces contorted with pain and their eyes searching as if for help. Without warning, their bodies exploded and he turned his view away, unable to bear the sight.

"This is terrible" the news reporter broke in "we never expected this. It looks like the military have taken action, since we can see hundreds of our missiles closing in on the ship." A pause ensued as the man sat forwards eagerly, trying to reposition his viewing point to focus on the rockets. With difficulty he at last succeeded and could just make out the black outlines through the wall of dust. The reporter began speaking again. "We've just had a report from the government that states that they have also authorised a fleet of our latest military aircraft, the G9 Hawks, to attack the spaceship and so they see no reason for panic." The man was hardly aware of the voice as he watched the outlines of the rockets growing larger.

The distance between them and the ship rapidly disappeared and he gripped his hands together in anticipation of the impact. He heard fresh blasts of sound before they had reached their target and the outlines seemed to disintegrate. More dark objects became visible on the horizon, flying in formation at speed towards the ship.

"It can't be!" he whispered to himself, beginning to realise what had happened. "Those rockets were state of the art …"

The dark objects became clearer and he could make out the forms of the G9 Hawks closing in on the ship. He watched aghast, as the aircraft exploded, unable now to hear the noise due to the continual eruptions of sound as buildings crumbled earthwards. Metal fragments that had once formed the skin of the high tech aircraft, spiralled downwards into what was left of the crowd. "They didn't stand a chance, no one did." He thought as he watched the radius of death and destruction from the alien ship steadily increase.

At last the reporter began talking again, his voice sounding distant and full of despair. "We've just had a report in from our scientists who at this stage believe that the aliens are using … sound! … to destroy everything. Somehow they have sent out sound waves in all directions that cause objects to explode due to resonance. As yet the scientists haven't worked out how they have managed to do this."

"Sound?" the old man repeated in amazement.

Suddenly the scene was disturbed by a door bursting open and a tall man in his early 30's entered the room. The Stetson he always wore had slipped and now sat at a rakish angle giving his face a somewhat comic appearance whilst partly hiding his features.

"Dad we've got to get out of here now." His British accent was tinged with fear, as he looked around desperately before finally spotting the old man amongst the holographic backdrop.

"No!" The old man looked like he had seen a ghost, "you should be in England away from all this."

"I couldn't stay there I had to come here to make sure you were ok."

"You knew I was, I told you."

"Quick hurry up." He shouted as he grabbed his father's arm and almost dragged him out of the room.

"Josh calm down, I'm coming as fast as I can and luckily that ship is miles away." As if in protest the holographic ship lurched forward becoming a blur as it sped from the ruined city and across the skyline before coming to a stop within seconds over the White House in Washington.

"And getting closer by the second." With effort Josh dragged his attention away from the holographic projections. "Maybe Pittsburgh is next on its hit list and we need to get into an underground shelter before it arrives here. The streets are packed with people, crammed so tightly together, that it was almost impossible to get through and that was before the attack. I dread to think what it is like now." The White House crumbled in a pile of dust.

"Ok I'm coming. Stop pulling me." The old man tried to yank his arm free but failed.

"Dad if you don't hurry up we'll both be killed and before you say anything, you know I won't leave you."

The building was already deserted and they were able to quickly make their way to the elevator, situated on the side of the building. As it descended its glass walls gave them a clear view of the pandemonium down in the streets below. Order had completely broken down and people ran screaming in all directions.

"I'll never understand why you chose to retire here." Josh said as he watched the scene below. "It's just a jungle of concrete." The old man was about to answer when one of the G9 Hawk fighter planes roared past, so close that they could clearly see its underside as it banked. The noise it made was deafening and its movement caused the whole skyscraper to shake in the same way as it did in very strong winds. The swaying was a necessary evil in the design, since a ridged structure would have broken and the engineers still hadn't found a solution. Josh felt his stomach churn as the resonating downward motion of the lift continued, until at last it met with the ground and he could once more feel solid concrete beneath his feet.

As they exited the building they were hardly able

to believe their eyes. The whole of the horizon was carpeted in a dust cloud, through which a tiny black dot was slowly travelling. A deep rumbling noise was so loud that they could feel the ground vibrating. All around them was a mass of people pushing and shoving, each seeming to want to head in a different direction. The weaker individuals were trampled in the mad stampede, their screams unheard, as they sank beneath the sea of bodies.

"Have we got to go through that crowd Josh? Isn't there another way into the shelter?"

"You know there is only one way in or out of each shelter and we haven't got time to get to another one, besides which there's bound to be as much trouble at all of them. Just stay close to me. Ok?" The old man gave a timid nod. Josh looked down the wide road, trying to work out exactly where the shelter was. At last he saw the familiar large yellow sign, about 100 yards down the road, indicating the entrance. They had been lucky to have a shelter so close. He sighed deeply and then smiled back at his dad.

"Let's go then" Josh said as both men crashed headlong into the mass of bodies. As soon as they entered the crowd they could feel the weight of the people crushing them. They seemed to fight endlessly, trying to push their way through towards the sign. The force of the people fleeing in panic soon separated them and in a short while the old man was exhausted. A final shove sent him flying to the ground. He struggled weakly, feeling pain curse through his body, as ceaseless numbers of feet stamped down on him. His senses began to fail as a numbness passed over him. "I have to get up" the words repeated in his mind as he slipped into unconsciousness forever more.

Through the crowd, Josh could make out the shape of his father disappearing from sight.

"No …" he couldn't even hear his own voice as he fought desperately to get to his father but the weight of people pushing on him proved too much and he was swept along. He was already close to the sign and he could see the people pouring into the door. Struggling he somehow managed to remain on his feet and in a matter of minutes he passed from daylight down a very long steep escalator, encased in a dark tunnel that seemed to extend downwards forever, and into a large cave beyond. He was now free of the crowds as they spread out. He turned and tried to force his way back out but more people were still tumbling into the cave. It was hopeless.

The dull roar had become even louder and the ground had begun to shake violently. Suddenly red lights on the rocky ceiling started flashing madly. At the same time, the thick metal door at the cave entrance automatically began to shut. Slowly it swung to, disregarding the people who were still trying to enter. Nothing could stop it, and it snapped into place, crushing anyone in its path and condemning those left outside to certain death.

His head pounded and he covered his ears, trying

to keep his balance on the shaking ground. He found it difficult to work out what was going on, everything seemed a blur as though nothing was real. At last the noise began to subside and his senses returned. He looked about to see 3 or 4 thousand people standing silently in an enormous cave cut out of brownish, red rock. Off to one side a large concrete platform had been built, which a short, balding man was now making his way onto.

The relief of silence was more than he could take and Josh leaned back against the nearby rocky wall. He couldn't believe what had happened, it had all seemed so unreal like he was just a spectator in a dream watching events unfold and the strangest part was now he didn't feel anything. Somewhere deep down though he knew it was real and that his father was actually dead.

Quietly he stood and listened to all the commotion about him, lost in his thoughts. Not even six months had passed since they had celebrated his father's retirement from the GP practice that had taken him more than 50 years to build up. He had invested his life in helping others and had been looking forward to finally relaxing and enjoying life but that dream had now been cruelly snatched away from him, as it had been from Josh's mother some years before. Josh played through the events of the past hour in his mind, struggling to suppress the nagging doubt that he could have done something more.

Outside, above the chaos and devastation, the alien ship briefly hovered for an instance, as though it were scanning the ground in search of something. There was nothing left though but a broken city where not even the song of a bird rang out to break the deathly silence that had begun to envelop it. Satisfied the giant ship moved on in its systematic annihilation of every trace of human life.

The dust still hadn't settled as the sun dropped down behind the crumbling skyscrapers of the once grand city, the orange glow it threw out fading into night. Between the remnants of the buildings, the pavements lay shattered in fragments, while great cracks ripped their way through the tarmac roads. Scraps of metal lay shattered everywhere, torn from the numerous vehicles that had lined the streets, as smoke rose up from the smouldering ruins, shrouding the city in a black choking fog.

## Chapter 3

Shocked silence filled the air as the short balding man came to an abrupt halt in the middle of the concrete platform. He shifted his weight uneasily, drawing himself up to his full height in an attempt to give his short stature every ounce of authoritative manner that he could. His attention was seemingly unconcerned by the traumatic events that had just passed but instead focussed intently on the agitated faces before him as he opened his mouth to speak.

"Seth" a woman screamed, the shrill panicked tone of her voice cutting him dead, as she barged her way through to the door. "He's still out there" tears streamed down her pained face as she turned appealing to the rest of the crowd. "Help me, we can't leave him out there."

"Michael"

"Mum" the shouts from different people came thick and fast as they joined in the assault on the door. Order rapidly began to break down into chaos.

"We have to open it." They were the last coherent words before the crowds desperate shouts deteriorated into hysterical screams, as they continued their frenzied but ultimately fruitless assault on the solid door.

Others fearful for their own lives or those of loved ones with them tried to pull people away from the door, fearful that they might succeed in their attempts to open it and doom them all to death. The pushing and shoving intensified, threatening to turn into a full-scale fight.

"Anyone outside is dead." The voice boomed and echoed round the chamber, projected by countless hidden speakers. Immediately most of the crowd stopped, turning to look round for the source of the voice, as they tried to grasp the enormity of what that single word "dead" really meant. No one could believe it was true but even so it still raised a cold chill in their spines and left them feeling sick to the pit of their stomachs.

"We would all die if we opened that door." The amplified voice of the man on the platform continued. Several members of the crowd grabbed the last couple of hysterical people who continued to scream and fight wildly before at last breaking down into fits of sobs.

The man on the platform looked nervously about, his ears picking up the sound of children crying in amongst all the other hushed noises. He had trained for years for this very scenario when the city's population would have to retreat to this underground shelter for whatever reason but he had never expected it to really happen. All that training didn't seem enough to get them through the coming days or even the coming minutes. The reality was so much harder than the mock tests he had vigorously undergone. He knew the procedure inside out but having to see the pain of so many people, to tell them their loved ones outside were almost certainly dead and they were fighting for their very survival was more difficult than he ever thought.

"There is nothing we can do for them." He continued quietly, his voice sounding strained and full of false conviction despite his best efforts to portray an air of confidence. "I know it's a lot to take in but we would all die if we went up there. I can assure you that in here we are safe."

"We've had countless assurances from the government and look where that's got us." An angry, raspy voice from the crowd argued. The man on the platform shifted his weight nervously as a worried frown spread unbidden across his face.

"You can trust me when I say you're safe down here." The effort of trying to make his voice sound sincere proved too much and his worried frown deepened.

"Trust you? We don't even know who you are?" the raspy voice retaliated.

"Mike Hawkins." The bald man responded bluntly. "My sole responsibility is the running of this facility and the safety of its inhabitants. I don't have anything to do with the government beyond my appointment here and I certainly have nothing to do with their decisions."

"Great just what we need, another leader to throw us to the wolves." The raspy voice intensified to shouting as the individual gave full vent to his anger. Murmurs of agreement swept across the cave.

"Please." Hawkins raised his hands defensively and waved them down in an effort to reduce the noise levels, all the while his eyes scanning the crowd trying to pinpoint the owner of the raspy voice. Angry shouts rang out from the traumatised people as anger started to take hold of them. "This isn't helping anyone" Hawkins persisted gently and compassionately despite realising panic had set in "you need to calm down." It was too late. Order completely broke down as the crowd disintegrated into a mob of angry people, their yells and screams sounding inhuman in the confined space.

The children huddled, paralysed with fear, some crying, as their parents tried to protect them against the violence that had erupted as the mob lashed out. In the space of a few minutes normal ordinary people had turned into a horde of raving mad yobs, punching and shoving at anyone close. In their frenzied state no one but Josh noticed the small nod Hawkins gave previously unnoticed blue uniformed security guards who complied instantly, stepping forward and drawing concealed guns.

"I don't want anyone to get hurt." Hawkins entreated once more, trying to settle them. If anyone had heard him no one showed any signs of it as fights broke out all round the cavern.

One of the security personnel close to Josh aimed his gun into the crowd, his finger twitching restlessly on the trigger. Without even thinking it through clearly Josh launched himself at the guard, managing to deflect the gun upwards as the shot went off. The red beam narrowly missed the top of the crowd as it struck the rock wall sending out a loud crack and causing small pieces of rock to fall away. Josh barely slowed, his momentum carrying him forward, as he slammed the guard up against the wall, one arm pressing up under his chin while the other hand snatched the gun away. The crowd stopped, turning to watch.

"What do you think you're doing?" Josh harshly asked giving the man a shake as another guard fired at them in an automatic response. "Hasn't there been enough death." The blue light from the guards gun hit, their muscles and nerves screaming in protest before buckling and sending them both sprawling to the ground. The white-hot pain Josh felt was excruciating as he tried to regain control over his twitching and convulsing body. He never thought in his wildest dreams he would end up experiencing the effects of a stun gun and it was one thing he never wanted to repeat. A full five minutes passed before he could at last slowly drag himself up. The crowd remained silently watching the events and he couldn't help noticing the tear stained face of one small boy amid the sea of people.

"Stand down." Hawkins ordered the guards as they aggressively approached, "and as for you Phelps." He glared hard at the unsteady guard tottering around. "I gave strict instructions you were all to use stun only." Phelps arrogantly shrugged in response. "I'll speak to you later." Hawkins threatened, turning to address the crowd.

"That ship was systematically taking out each city in turn and we felt it pass overhead just now. You all must have seen footage of the devastation left in its wake. Nothing could have survived."

"But it seems so wrong to do nothing." A woman murmured in utter disbelief and shock.

"There's nothing we can do for them." Hawkins reassured. "We have to concentrate on ourselves now. We are safe down here. These shelters were originally built to withstand nuclear bombs and are completely impenetrable both from any radiation or direct attacks."

"How can you be so certain?" A man asked.

"I know everything there is to know about this facility. After all it's my job to ensure this place runs efficiently and to safeguard its inhabitants." He paused trying to find the right words and the worried frown returned to his face. "There is one small draw back though. Unfortunately some, like this one, were built in a rush and they never got round to hard wiring lines between all of them, so there is no way to communicate with anyone on the surface or in any of the other shelters." Hawkins hesitated, unsure of the effects of his next words. "Just so you know the last message we received was that we are now officially at war."

"War!" a stunned voice echoed. It was obvious that they were at war but it was the first time the word had been said out loud.

"It doesn't really affect us for the time being." Hawkins hastened to add. "All we need to focus on is this place. In fact things might seem a whole lot better if you see the full extent of this base. People always say it's nothing like they imagined." He nodded to the 30 or 40 uniformed guards standing round the edge of the cavern. "Styne, McCauly, Stone, if you could organise everyone into smaller groups. You know the procedure." The guards responded, shuffling amongst the crowd, giving orders to the other security members as Hawkins continued. "If you just follow the blue uniformed people's instructions we can get you all settled in as soon as possible." Satisfied that the guards were doing their jobs efficiently, he turned and made a silent exit. Behind him a whirlwind of commotion erupted, as confused people were ushered all ways by the security personnel.

At last a number of groups were formed, each made up of 100 or so people and led by a security guard, down one of the twisting tunnels of rock. All were subdued and the air was heavily laced with a depressing gloom.

Josh followed the rest of his group as they filtered into one of the passageways, partially shrouded in darkness. In a short time they rounded a bend to arrive on a ledge, a path from which sloped steeply down into a massive cave, far larger than the first one they had entered. The view was breathtaking, as they looked out across the open area, unable to see the far wall clearly.

"This is the main city where most of you will live." Josh heard O'Callaghan, the guard say, as he examined his surroundings, noting how light the whole place seemed, even though the same dark rock formed the walls. As you can see most of our food supply will be grown here. There is an ever ready supply of water from that stream over there." O'Callaghan pointed to a fast flowing stream that ran through the centre of the cave into the very distant walls at either side of them. Large fields positioned in the centre of the cavern surrounded the stream. Somehow they had managed to lay down softer earth over the hard rock floors. Already crops of wheat and other things were springing up from this soil. Round the fields were rows of houses, constructed from metal and stone. From a distance they looked very modern and out of place in the rock cave.

"How is this possible?" someone gasped.

"We have everything we need to grow any crop we like." The guard continued. "Water, soil, plant food, light, the latest farming robotic equipment and we don't have any problems with pests or at least not at the moment." At the mention of light Josh looked upwards to see huge shining discs of light, suspended below a white canvas that lined the entire roof. The brightness hurt his eyes and he had to turn away.

With images of light still blurring his vision, he looked over to the sides of the roof, for the first time noticing the large black discs hanging there.

"What are they?" The guard looked towards where he pointed.

"Fans. They circulate the air underground and ensure a fresh supply of oxygen is always present by adding it to the air when needed." As Josh's sight returned to normal, he still had trouble focussing on the huge discs, perhaps some hundred feet above him. "Only problem with them is the noise." O'Callaghan was right. Somehow Josh had failed to notice the ever constant clamour, as air was forced through the giant blades that turned at speeds, fast enough to give the illusion that the fans were solid black discs.

O'Callaghan paused to give them a chance to take it all in "The designers were worried that people living down here might find it claustrophobic and so they tried to keep the whole place as open as possible. There are a number of tunnels leading from this cavern to other caves that house things such as the games facility and the medical labs but you will be shown all that at a later time." He seemed deep in thought for a moment. "I guess the rock walls make it all look a bit primitive but everything down here is as or nearly as high tech as you're used to on the surface, including the accommodation. I think there was a rush to build these shelters and so they didn't have time to make it look as nice as they could have. In fact I'm not sure they even built them as big as they originally intended but as it is there is more than enough room for all of us and we have digging equipment so that we can expand the base." As he stopped talking the strange stillness returned, like the calm after the storm.

Josh heard someone begin to cry, followed by hushed voices. O'Callaghan must have heard it too because he speedily moved on. "You'll see more of the shelter later but first I need to get your names and ID numbers and then I can assign you accommodation and appropriate jobs. If you could form an orderly queue." He pulled out a small hand held computer and began logging in each set of details, before issuing the person with a piece of paper and sending them off in a particular direction. Slowly the queue shrank as people moved off down the slope into the main cavern towards their new homes, all of them now looking too tired to argue with anything they were told.

"This place is an extraordinary feat of engineering and I should know." Josh turned to see a tall lanky man not much older than himself, talking to him. "I'm Steve Evans by the way."

"Josh" he said as he shook the hand offered, wondering how this man could look so calm and almost cheerful, after what they had just been through.

"British?" Josh nodded.

"My dad retired here, so when the trouble started I came out as soon as I could to be with him." Evans looked round questioningly. "He didn't make it." Josh said in answer.

"Oh, sorry." Evans paused awkwardly. "I guess it won't be so bad living down here." He continued, examining his surroundings as he spoke. "Not quite what you'd expect, considering we're deep underground."

"No, I suppose not. Hopefully we won't be here for too long"

"I wouldn't count on it. I reckon we're going to be down here for quite some time. Even they're expecting it." Evans nodded towards O'Callaghan. "I mean they've made it so we're completely self-sufficient down here. We even have digging equipment to expand this place. We could live here forever if we had to."

"No, they're just being cautious, making sure we're prepared for the worst."

"Well I can't see it getting much worse than it already is. Stuck down here for lord knows how long. The government. I'd like to … " He scowled, anger rising to the surface before quickly vanishing and his good-natured look returning. "Well not much we can do about it. They put us in this situation and now we have to make the best of it."

"Name and ID number" Evans looked round, surprised to see that he had reached the front of the queue. Josh's attention was drawn back to the diminishing crowd, while he waited for him to finish.

The struggle to get into the shelter had taken its toll on them and they now stood, a bedraggled group, caked in dirt and dried blood, their clothes filthy and torn. Evans was one of the few people that still had a fairly tidy appearance; even his fair hair was smoothed down. Josh glanced at his own clothes, unsurprised to see that they had not fared so well. The blue trousers had great rips through them, surrounded in dry blood. His own from grazes and knocks he had suffered. The white shirt was now almost black and in the same tattered state and for the first time he felt the scratch and scab on his cheek just above his short beard. He hadn't even noticed any pain.

Somewhere back in the struggle to get into the shelter he had lost his beloved Stetson that had travelled everywhere with him, shielding his face from the often intense tropical climates he had been obliged to endure on some of his fieldwork studies. He ran his hand through his dark hair, noting its rumpled condition but then it was always like that. Not messy but naturally dishevelled, no matter what he did to it. All his life everyone had joked about it but that had never worried him. He didn't even mind the fact that he was known as the nutty professor at university because of it. The university. He thought back, recollecting its ancient walls, surrounded by the well-maintained gardens. Probably a pile of rubble was all that was left of it now.

"... But I'm a structural engineer." Evans was saying. Josh turned back to see his face flushed with anger and indignation.

"I know you are but like I said we have no use for them down here. You'll have to work on the digging machines." O'Callaghan appeared unconcerned. His voice sounding tired.

"I do not operate digging equipment" Evans said, more proudly than he had intended.

"You do now." A satisfied twinkle flashed in the guard's eye.

"But what about all my qualifications, just to waste them like this?"

"I'm going to have to ask you to move along. As much as I'd like to, I haven't got all day to discuss this with you."

"I want to talk to someone more senior."

"I have full authority in this matter." O'Callaghan barked beginning to sound annoyed. "You have been assigned a job and that is the end of it. Now go."

"But …"

"Good bye" O'Callaghan looked past him to Josh.

"It's like talking to a brick wall" Evans thought, deciding against arguing further. "Good luck" he said to Josh as he passed, giving the guard a sideways glance full of contempt.

"Name and ID"

"Joshua Forbes. ID number 55283961." He waited while the guard keyed the information into the computer.

"It says here you're a lecturer at Cambridge university. You've got a degree and masters in Biology. Is that correct?"

"Yes. I only recently got back …" the guard cut him short.

"So you studied the human body then"

"Well only the basics but then I branched out into other areas. I specialised in botany for part of my masters."

"Well you'll have to do." O'Callaghan said absently, handing Josh a piece of paper.

"Go stand over there." Josh looked in the direction he pointed to see 5 other people clustered in a group. He walked towards them across the now deserted tunnel entrance, reading the slip of paper as he went. "Accommodation number 1425, possible candidate for training to become a doctor." He turned back thinking that the guard had giving him the wrong piece of paper but then the questions he had been asked began to make sense.

Life it seemed, as always, was filled with cruel irony. He was being forced into the very profession his father had wanted him to pursue. When Josh had refused it had caused countless rows, which only got worse when he declared he was going to become a Biology lecturer instead. Josh could still hear his father's voice reciting that old phrase as he had so often "Those who can can, those who can't teach." His father had never been able to understand how satisfying and rewarding teaching could be, especially when the students were enthusiastic and had gone on into good professions. Every day Josh felt satisfied knowing that his teaching had played a part in the lives of some of the most prominent people in society and hopefully contributed towards their success. His job at the University had also given him the opportunity to study rare species of plants and even financed fieldwork in the protected Amazon rainforest, where discoveries of new plant toxins, that could cure various diseases, were still being made.

His mother had understood his passion for plants, having realised long ago that he had more interest in plant physiology than human. She had supported him all the way, her only concern his happiness and it was her intervention that had finally persuaded his father to accept his chosen career and even become proud of him for it.

Josh had always hoped that his research would perhaps help the medical profession one day but that seemed a distant dream after the attack and destruction on the surface above.

As he stood waiting with the others he tried to make sense of why they had chosen him when he had no previous training and virtually no knowledge about it. There had been several thousand people in the cave and with such a vast number there had to have been more suitable candidates.

With the last few people logged and dismissed in various directions, O'Callaghan now approached Josh's group, which had failed to grow in size from the six it numbered.

"If you could follow me please."

"Just a second." The guard completely ignored Josh as he disappeared down another tunnel away from the main city. Their route led them down a maze of unmarked tunnels, until they had lost all sense of direction but still O'Callaghan marched onwards, unfazed by the seeming complexity of interlocking passageways.

"If you could all wait here." O'Callaghan's somewhat large frame moved away from the tunnel exit to reveal that they had emerged into a smallish cavern, where other similar groups had already congregated. He withdrew to the left hand wall, where all the other guards had retreated and now stood chatting amongst themselves.

A few minutes later, Hawkins appeared, the worried frown that had seemed to be a permanent fixture had now gone.

One of the guards, his uniform adorned with decoration, stepped forward to meet him. "Everyone has been logged in and this is the group requested." He motioned to Josh and the others. "It doesn't look very promising." He held out a hand held computer which Hawkins took and began examining.

"Are you sure this is right." The guard gave a curt nod of his head. "Ok then." As the guard returned to the others, Hawkins mumbled something under his breath, the frown once more appearing for a moment before he regained his calm and addressed the group.

"I'm sorry to have kept you all waiting." He glanced at the weary faces before him. "You've probably all seen the jobs assigned to you by now and some of you may be very surprised, since you have no expertise in the particular field of work. I'm afraid we've had no option though. This shelter already has a medical team of 4 doctors and 20 nurses assigned to it. The government assumed that some of the people seeking refuge here would be medical staff, unfortunately their statistical probabilities turned out to be wrong, since there are not as many of you as we had hoped. Therefore we have no option but to ask the qualified doctors and nurses amongst you to train others. We have only selected possible candidates that already have degrees in Biology, so they should have some of the anatomical knowledge required and hopefully be intelligent enough to learn the rest. I have selected" he stopped to look down at the hand held computer "Erin Campbell to be in charge of all the medical staff and so you'll be responsible for organising the training.

If you'll follow O'Callaghan he'll show you the medical labs before you go to your new homes." Hawkins pointed at the same burly guard who had been leading Josh's group round. O'Callaghan nodded at Hawkins before marching off down a path leading through the cave and into yet another of the monotonous tunnels. Before they could get the chance to ask questions, Hawkins had gone.

Not far on, they came to a series of doors on either side of them.

"All the medical facilities are located in this area." O'Callaghan said, as he dived through one of the doors, marked ward, into a very clean, fresh looking room. White tiles covered all the walls, ceiling and floor. The room was long but not very wide, allowing a row of beds to be pushed against the walls down either side.

"Medical supplies are kept through that door there under lock and key. You'll be given the security codes at a later date." O'Callaghan pointed and then led the way back out and into another room like the last, decorated in the same white tiles but large tables replaced the beds around the walls. Research equipment was neatly placed on various tables, while larger equipment stood up against any bare wall space that remained.

"As you can see we have fairly good research facilities here. The lab is equipped with some of the latest equipment. Who knows maybe you lot can research something to get us out of this mess." He moved out of the room. "Operating theatres and recovery rooms are through there. You'll find them almost identical to the ones in hospitals on the surface." He nodded to the doors at the end of the corridor, before heading back to the main city.

"Excuse me." The guard stopped, surprised to see a short man, with wiry ginger hair and thick glasses, addressing him. "Is there any way we can get hold of our research data stored in our accounts on the Internet."

"We have no communications with the surface or any other underground communities. Besides which most of the Internet servers have probably been destroyed along with any backups." He started to walk off and then stopped. "We downloaded as much information off the net as we could just before the attack. We hardly got a fraction of it, the sheer amount of data held on it is phenomenal but if you give me your name, I'll see if we downloaded your account."

"Thanks. It's Dr Rob Kolinsky."

"Well don't get your hopes up." O'Callaghan led them back to the city. "All your accommodation is in the main city, just down there. The numbers are on the doors." As he left, the main thought on everyone's minds was just to find their new homes.

In seconds Josh found the door to his, the modern hand scanner set on the wall besides it. He slapped his hand onto it and the door opened to reveal a reasonably sized, comfortable looking room. As he entered the door hissed shut behind him. The room he was in was obviously the main living room, complete with sofa. An old fashioned screen hung on the wall, which displayed TV programmes or information all in the standard 2D format, which had not been used for more than 30 years. These days programs were usually displayed as holographic images; giving the viewer the sense that they were in the scene they were watching. They could even choose they're viewing angle. Obviously the 2D screens had been used, since they required a lot less power than the holographic projections.

He headed for the shower realising as he went that there were no programs to watch since all the entertainment and news companies had been wiped out like the rest of the world. Maybe there was absolutely nothing left up there and even if they escaped this prison they would have nothing to go back to.

The first and second rooms he tried had been the kitchen, filled with all mod cons, and bedroom respectively but on his third attempt he located the bathroom. The 2D screen on the wall flared to life as he entered and the face of a woman with the appearance and manner of a flight attendant began talking.

"Please be aware that water underground is more scarce than on the surface. We ask that where possible you use water only when essential, that is for drinking. For general hygiene SoniCleaner Systems have been provided on the shower and washbasins. We can assure you these are as effective as water and soap despite the irregular sensations you may experience during use. Thank you for your attention." The face smiled sweetly before disappearing as the screen turned off. The entire message grated on him but he was too tired to do anything but shrug out of his tattered clothes and enter the shower. Instead of water what felt like warm gentle jets of air surrounded him, creating a strange bubbling sensation as they made contact with his skin. The dried blood fizzled and split into dust that crumbled away from his body along with all the dirt and grime. The shower automatically switched off after a pre-set time and refused to turn back on. Like everything else underground it was no doubt rationed.

Josh left his old clothes where they lay scattered over the floor and headed to the cupboards he had seen in the bedroom. Inside were new clothes in a range of sizes. The shelter authorities had managed to think of everything. He made the effort to pull on some clothes before giving into the exhaustion he felt and collapsing onto the bed, too tired to even bother about eating. So much had happened in one day and all he wanted to do was to forget about all of it.

## Chapter 4

Rob Kolinsky sat facing the far end wall of the research lab, into which was set a glass window that, despite appearances, was very thick and the material it was made from able to withstand almost anything. It made carrying out any experiments almost risk free, despite whatever harmful chemicals, radiation or viruses were being used.

Kolinsky's gloved hands moved through the air before him, the patterns he made causing corresponding actions of the two mechanical arms positioned behind the glass. They were inside what was little more than a large, amazingly well lit box, with rough brown rock making up the other walls. In the centre of the box stood several different glass containers, which the arms now manipulated with a certain deftness, despite their cumbersome look.

Josh sat at the other end of the research lab, his head bent over an old tattered medical book. He passed his hand through his hair unconsciously, as he screwed his face up, puzzled. Something didn't make sense. It was as though all the books he had been given to study were years out of date. He had stumbled upon conflicting methods of treatment for various ailments more than once. He glanced over to Kolinsky but decided straight away from the intense look of concentration on his face, now was not the best time to ask anything.

It had been two months since they had been forced to move down here and Kolinsky had been assigned his tutor. Over that time Kolinsky had become the joke of the whole team for his eccentricities and obsessive research, but at the same time they all recognised the genius in him and respected him for it. Josh suspected Kolinsky had received the same treatment all his life, shunned yet silently idolised, resulting in the distant and remote man Josh had come to know. It seemed to be the case with all the very clever people Josh had ever met. The very essence in their psyche that gave them the ability to approach problems, as well as all other things, in a different way to the majority also caused strange quirks in their personalities. Most never seemed truly comfortable in society and like Kolinsky threw themselves into their work to the exclusion of all else. In Kolinsky's case that meant Josh's tuition and so he found himself left to his own devices, the old collection of medical books being the main source.

It would have been easier to get the information off the main database but there weren't many useful files on it. Apparently some idiot in the government had decided that the shelters should download the information off the Internet at the latest possible moment, so that they would have the most recent files. Though some people suspected it was more to do with cost saving, since keeping all the databases up to date could get expensive. It had turned out that the latest possible moment had been too late and now they had to suffer the consequences. Perhaps the whole of the government were crazy.

Josh shut the book, deciding to try another one. He stood up, accidentally knocking the stool over as he did so. His heart went cold as he made a grab to try and steady it but it had gone too far and clattered loudly on the tiled floor. Kolinsky's hands in mid air had the arms holding one of the glass containers but the sudden noise made him jerk his hands awkwardly. The mechanical arms shuddered slightly almost recovering before, in a moment of horror, they had dropped their precious cargo.

The vile plummeted downwards smashing into pieces on the floor, the tiny drop of liquid it held spilling out freely. Stunned silence followed.

"The whole experiment ... lost." Kolinsky's voice was barely audible. "You stupid fool! Do you realise what you've done?" His face reddened in anger, to match his hair, as he turned to face Josh.

"I'm sorry. It just went before I could stop it."

"I was on the edge of a breakthrough and now thanks to you I'll have to start all over again. Not to mention the fact that I have to keep stopping to treat patients with imaginary ailments."

"I'm sorry they're such an inconvenience to you but they have just lost everything. If nothing else they're still in a state of shock and a little sympathy wouldn't go amiss."

"You don't understand. This research could save millions of lives."

"You've found a way to stop the aliens attacking us, have you?" Josh said sarcastically before a vague hope began to form that he had.

"No, of course not but my work is still very important."

"I think we've got bigger problems at the moment other than whatever it is you're trying to find a cure for."

"You've got no idea what you're talking about."

"Well maybe if you told me." Kolinsky looked away in a somewhat pompous attitude.

"You'd never understand. How did I ever get lumbered with you anyway…" The research door smashed open and a security guard rushed in breathless and struggling to speak.

"Hawkins wants … medical help … right now. Got to come."

"Get the bag of medical equipment" Kolinsky shouted to Josh, regaining his composure amazingly quickly, as he tried to get more information out of the guard.

"Accident" The guard managed to say as he rushed off with the two men in pursuit. His breathing increased heavily to gasps as he raced back down darkened passageways on a route that bypassed the town and took them into newly constructed tunnels.

The maze narrowed to just one tunnel, at the entrance of which stood Hawkins, looking worried but otherwise unhurt.

"Stay here" Hawkins shouted to the guard, who gratefully collapsed to the floor, as he led the way down the tunnel, talking to them as he did so.

"We've just had a radio message from one of the digger teams. There was an accident in one of the tunnels down here. The man in charge somehow got hurt we think, but his co-worker wasn't very coherent. The accident site became visible in the distance ahead of them.

Josh's attention was drawn immediately to the huge digging machine, filling up most of the end of the tunnel. Beside this metal monstrosity, a man kneeled bending over another figure, lying still. He looked back at the digger, noting the damage that had been caused to the giant blades at the front, now a tangle of bent metal. He could see that some of the blades had been ripped to shreds. Metal that had obviously flown outwards at speed and now lay imbedded in the rock around. As they approached the figure on the ground, the metal sticking out of his thigh became apparent.

"Thank god you're here." The man next to the figure turned his face towards them, his hands still held firmly around the wound in an attempt to stem the flow of blood. Josh recognised Evans at once, despite the paleness of his face and his blood soaked clothes.

"Give me some room" Kolinsky said as he almost pushed Evans out of the way and began attending to the injury.

"I think some rock or something hit him in the head at the same time because he's been unconscious. Is he going to be ok?"

"Should be" Kolinsky said moving a hand held computer over the patient. "What's his name?"

"Johnson, Kip Johnson."

"Well I can't see any damage to the brain and removing that metal from his thigh shouldn't present too much of a problem. It'll be as good as new in a day or so. We better move him back to the hospital now." The man groaned and twisted slightly as he began to wake up.

"Just hold still. You're going to be ok. Josh give me that bag." Kolinsky grabbed it and tore it open, pulling out a tube, containing liquid. He placed one end on the man's neck, holding down the button on the other end as he did so. There was a hiss of air "There that should kill the pain and keep him quiet for a while. You can move him back to the infirmary now." Kolinsky said to the two guards that had just arrived with a stretcher.

"What happened Evans?" Hawkins asked as they walked back to the infirmary. Evans looked down at his hands, covered in blood as he answered, shock beginning to hit him.

"I don't know. I was in the driving compartment and everything was going like normal." He paused shakily as he remembered back. "I saw someone approach. I was just about to stop the digger when there was some kind of explosion. It all happened in seconds, the noise and then the metal flying out and buckling. I just don't know what happened ... If only he hadn't been there. He shouldn't have approached the digger while it was working."

"An explosion?" Hawkins asked concerned.

"I don't know. Maybe it just hit something very hard."

"But I thought those blades could go through any known material on Earth" Hawkins said startled.

"I know. They are supposed to. I just don't understand what happened."

"What are you saying, that you hit some new material?" interrupted Josh.

"Maybe" he hesitated confused. "No it can't be. We knew about every material on this planet."

"What so it's some kind of alien material?" Evans shrugged, his face still deathly white.

"Don't be stupid" Kolinsky gave Josh a look full of contempt. "It couldn't be this far underground. It wouldn't make sense."

"You heard what he said."

"He doesn't know what he's saying. He's still in a state of shock. Just look at him." Evans was walking along still staring down at his now shaking hands.

"I want you all to forget this ever happened. It's not your concern now." Hawkins intervened.

"It's all our concern, especially if it's alien."

"Just let it go Josh and I don't want any of you speaking about this again. The last thing we need is a panic." They had reached the hospital and Hawkins was about to leave when he turned back threateningly.

"If I hear any of this has reached the others I will hold you all responsible." This time he left abruptly, not waiting to see what their reaction was.

Silently they entered the ward "I don't know what it was" Evans continually muttered, still traumatised by it all.

## Chapter 5

The next morning Josh entered the research lab to find Kolinsky still working at his experiments, oblivious to everything about him.

"Any change?" Josh asked. They had left the hospital late the night before after ensuring all foreign bodies had been removed from Johnson's thigh and that his condition was stable.

"What?" Kolinsky looked up frustrated.

"Johnson. How is he?"

"Fine. He'll be on his feet in a day or two."

"And Evans?"

"Nothing more than shock, now can I get back to this?" Josh shrugged as he settled down to yet more reading.

Several minutes later Josh looked up from the book wearily, feeling sure it wouldn't be such a tiresome learning process if he had have been on the surface. He knew for a fact that all the medical schools had virtual simulators where students could actually practice different procedures in a realistic setting but without any risk of harming any one. From what he'd heard even performing operations felt real when you were doing it and for beginners there was a choice of virtual doctors who could talk you through every step. They had one of the simulators down in the games facility area but because it needed so much energy its use had been restricted. Each of the new students had been allocated a time slot and his was in two days time, for a whole hour. It was ridiculous for them to think they could become fully competent doctors with so few facilities. He had even found out that one of the other trainees was petrified at the sight of blood but he was still being forced into the profession.

Josh's thoughts drifted back to the blood at the accident as they had done many times and the question of what had caused it. He had tried to see Hawkins but the security had been tighter than ever and he had been turned away.

"Curse it." Kolinsky snapped as he peered at something on the computer screen, his blues eyes narrowing.

"What's up?" Josh approached.

"Look why don't you just take a break or something."

"Fine" he turned back before leaving. "What are you researching that's so important?" Kolinsky sighed, glaring back at Josh.

"I've been working on this for a long time, and I'm not about to let you or anyone steal my work."

"It may have escaped your notice but there aren't many of us left to steal it and I doubt anyone cares about it enough to even try. We have got somewhat bigger problems." Kolinsky frowned. "Ok I promise I'm not trying to steal your work." Kolinsky remained silent. Josh sighed. "And I won't tell a soul about it."

"I suppose if I don't give you any details," Kolinsky muttered before raising his voice. "Nanobots."

"But I thought there had just been a breakthrough in that field and the first few had already been made for the first time in history."

"Oh yes but it was astronomically expensive to do. I'm working on a new way of manufacturing them that will be much cheaper." Josh nodded at the screen.

"I take it it's not going to plan."

"Unless you call the nanobots taking each other to pieces successful then I'd say it's not."

"What!" Josh half laughed but the look on Kolinsky's face made him quickly suppress it. He could see by the slight twitch of his eyes that Kolinsky was about ready to explode in another one of his temperamental moods.

"I can manufacture them more cheaply and quicker but the connection paths are screwed up somehow. I don't know what I've done wrong. Instead of repairing damaged tissue, as intended, they're regarding other nanobots as a threat and are going round trying to destroy each other. Look." He stabbed at the screen. A magnified image of the rapidly diminishing nanobots was displayed on it.

"Maybe I can help."

"I doubt it very much." Kolinsky sat back in his chair dejectedly. "I'd rather just some peace and quiet to work in."

"If that's what you want." Josh left heading for the hospital. Possibly nanobots could do a lot but they weren't going to be much use against the aliens. He pushed open the door, almost slamming it into Evans.

"Sorry. How are you?"

"Fine till you showed up." Evans answered with a nervous laugh, almost back to his old self.

"And Johnson?"

"Take a look." Evans gestured to a bed opposite from them, in which Johnson was propped up on, beaming at them.

"I take it you're feeling better" Josh said approaching.

"No work and I'm being waited on hand and foot." Johnson's grin grew wider. "I'll survive."

"Glad to hear it." Josh turned back to Evans. "Have you heard anything more about the accident?" Evans shook his head.

"To be honest I don't even want to think about it."

"I know but it's important we find out what happened."

"I guess."

"What do you do with the soil and rock you take out?"

"Why?" Evans asked puzzled.

"I was thinking that maybe there's some clues in it. Maybe you hit some kind of gas pocket and there may be clues such as certain minerals in the rock you took out just before."

"I'm afraid you won't be able to check it"

"What do you mean?"

"I think I'd better show you." Evans headed off down deeper into a maze of tunnels away from the medical area. All about them, the very walls themselves seemed to be running with water and constant drips echoed round. Deeper in still, the air felt colder and the tunnels became less uniform and more natural looking as though they had entered caverns that were already there. The lights were dimmer too.

"In front of you." Evans suddenly blurted out. Josh stopped, transfixed to the spot with awe for a moment. Before him lay an emptiness expanding into dark eerie depths.

"Natural fissures in the rock." Evans explained. "We've been filling them up with the material we dig out."

"So it's down there." Josh said in disbelief.

"Apart from a very small amount left at the accident site, the rest went down here. You see we'd only just emptied it."

"Well I guess that means that plans out the window." Josh said peering down into the darkness. "It looks pretty deep."

"I wouldn't recommend falling down it."

"Maybe I could abseil down."

"Whatever you may or may not be able to tell from that soil, it's definitely not worth the risk. Besides I'm not sure we'd even have ropes that are long enough."

"There must be a way."

"Josh, please respond." His radio burst to life.

"What is it?"

"It's Kolinsky. We're to meet Hawkins at the accident site straight away."

"What about me?" Evans asked disappointed.

"He just ordered Josh and myself there. He didn't say anything about you."

"Have they found something?" Josh asked.

"I don't know but it sounded urgent."

"You'd better wait with Johnson, I'll fill you in later." Evans scowled, annoyed.

The lights in the tunnel leading to the accident site seemed brighter than they had remembered, as Josh and Kolinsky made their way down it.

"What do you want down here?" Two armed guards were stationed up ahead. A fairly robust looking uniformed woman moved towards them, levelling her gun as she did so.

"We're here to see Hawkins. It's Joshua Forbes and Rob Kolinsky."

"What's you're ID numbers" she pulled out a hand held computer and typed in the numbers, meticulously checking the photos against the men who stood before her.

"Is this really necessary?" Kolinsky asked. The guard looked up from her screen fiercely, studying Kolinsky's face more intently. He began to cower under her penetrating gaze; it was the first time Josh had seen him back down. The guard appeared satisfied.

"Hawkins is waiting for you two." She said as she stepped aside and nodded to the other guard to do the same.

They could see movement of people in the distance. Not far on, the tunnel opened out into the now large cave, where the accident had been. They stood for a moment trying to take in all the changes. The digger had been removed and the rock it had hit had been carefully chipped away to reveal a circle of some kind of blue metallic material. The material spanned about eight feet in diameter and looked as though it went back into the rock a fair way.

Evans appeared behind them, grinning insanely. "Got a call to get myself down here," he explained, "and I thought I was going to miss all the fun."

"You're welcome to it." Kolinsky offered, glaring uneasily at his surroundings.

"It wasn't an explosion" Hawkins said as he approached them. There were other people in the cave, besides Hawkins, some of whom were busily working on the uncovered material.

"What is it?" Josh asked.

"We don't know. I've had scientists working on it non stop but we haven't got good enough equipment. The most they can tell us is that the material doesn't match anything we have in our database and we did manage to download information on all known materials."

"So it is alien then?

"Who knows! We hadn't explored every square

inch of the Earth so maybe we just stumbled across some freak of nature. An unknown material that looks like it has been moulded into a specific shape. It seems a more reasonable explanation, than aliens putting it this far below ground. After all what purpose would it serve, since it doesn't seem to pose any threat." Hawkins rubbed his chin "I'm baffled as to how they got it into solid rock like that. What's stranger still is that Dr Dennis Jenkins, one of the scientists, believes that it is a door. We had no other ideas and so I gave him permission to continue his experiments at opening it."

"Not that I think for one second that it is a door" Kolinsky began hesitantly "but if it were then it could lead to some kind of alien base. It could be dangerous opening it."

"Well if there were an alien base, it couldn't have been in recent use since there was thick rock this side. Any aliens would have been trapped in there, unless they could walk through rock, in which case why bother with a door. It must be deserted. This could be an opportunity for us to find out more about them."

"You're forgetting these aliens only just arrived on Earth. Any base they built would be in frequent use." Josh said.

"Well I've got a small security team here and of course yourselves, in case of any medical problems." Hawkins said.

"We're there." Jenkins kneeling at the door

shouted. "I think it should just come free when you pull it open now."

"Good work" Hawkins said. Jenkins began gathering up his equipment, which was strewn about all over the floor, helped by his assistants. He scrambled up, pulling armfuls of stuff with him as he backed away from the blue material, now clear of people.

"Get to work" Hawkins motioned to the security team, at the same time as explaining to Josh and Kolinsky. "That material is fairly magnetic whatever it is. Jenkins reckons we should be able to pull it open with magnets, now that he's freed it."

Eight guards picked up two metal blocks with handles on, each and placed them on the door, with a clank. Awkwardly they adjusted the position of their feet, trying to get more grip on the hard floor. Perhaps somewhat unwillingly, they started to pull back. Silence fell as everyone involuntarily held their breadths; even the grunts of effort from the guards were low. Suddenly a groan of metal against metal echoed down the tunnel, as a faint movement of the door alerted them of success. The noise of the creaking grew louder as the door slowly swung outwards on its strange looking hinge. In seconds it had fully opened to reveal a large tunnel, the diameter of the door. Many lights lined the greyish coloured walls, allowing the onlookers to see that it descended downwards at a steep slant. The tunnel appeared to continue onwards for miles, the same monotonous walls spanning into the distance.

Josh felt the adrenaline rush through his body. Something important lay at the end of it, waiting to be discovered by them. He was sure of it. The only question was what.

## Chapter 6

"Appears to be all clear." The plump guard was standing where the door had been, peering down the tunnel and all about him, looking for signs of trouble.

"Thank you Henderson" Hawkins said approaching a little closer though still wary. His worried frown returned to his face contorting it more than usual as he stared at the grey walls leading downwards. "What's a tunnel and door doing underground?" he mused barely loud enough for the others to hear. "Obviously it has been made by something but why bother when there's only thick rock this side." He raised his voice addressing Henderson. "Do you think it's safe to leave it open?"

"If it is the enemy I would have thought there would be some detection system in place and we'd be dead by now." Henderson paused to raise a plump hand holding a handkerchief and wipe the sweat from his brow. "With the unknown materials used I don't see who else could have done this other than the aliens, although it doesn't make sense and since we're not dead this could be our one opportunity to gain the upper hand. We might be able to find out what they're up to."

"You mean send a team down there?" Hawkins asked.

"It's the only way." Henderson nodded solemnly.

"You can't do that you could end up getting us all killed." Kolinsky interrupted. "We should just shut the door before they realise we're here."

"And live down here for the rest of our lives too scared to return to the surface." Kolinsky fell silent at Hawkins words. "Something is not right here, surely the scientist in you can see that and is curious about all this. We need to find out what's going on, especially if it could help us destroy them." Hawkins switched his attention to Henderson. "I take it you would volunteer to lead the team?" Henderson nodded.

"There is one problem." Hawkins raised his eyebrows. "There are not enough security staff to send a decent sized team down there and retain a suitable security force here."

"As it happens I wasn't intending to send just security personnel."

"But surely we need trained military people in case we run into any hostile forces."

"Force doesn't seem to have worked against them so far." Hawkins momentarily thought back to the attack. "No I've decided if there are aliens down there I want a team consisting of scientists to take surveillance and gather as much information as possible before returning here undetected."

"They'd see them coming a mile off. It would be a suicide mission."

"They haven't detected us so far and if they're not expecting us then maybe just ..." Hawkins voice trailed away.

"And if it's not aliens."

"Either way I think on this occasion brain over brawn is called for." Henderson drew back trying to suppress the mortified look that spread over his face. People always had the same notion that if you'd served all your life in the army, as he had done, you were automatically thick. There was more to being a soldier than just shooting people. Lots of situations called for brains but still the same prejudices were held by the public.

"I'm sure we could handle the surveillance." Henderson began.

"We need to keep a security force here and besides which I've already selected the team."

"Shouldn't we discuss this?"

"No need."

"Who's the lucky people then." Henderson sighed deeply, admitting defeat.

"Look about yourself with the exception of me of course."

"Of course." Henderson grimaced.

"Now hold on a minute." Kolinsky burst out. "You can't seriously mean me?" he asked in disbelieve. "I need to stay here and continue with my work."

"Forget you're research, if that's what you're referring to. This is much more important."

"But you can't force me."

"Actually I can. When war was declared it gave me the right to call up anyone I choose and order them to fight or go down strange tunnels in this case. If it makes you feel any better I wouldn't have chosen you if it weren't for the fact that you were the one who attended the accident, so it makes sense that you are the team doctor rather than letting more people know about this."

"If we run into anything I can't fight." Kolinsky pursued stubbornly. "I don't know anything about fighting."

"He's right on that score." Henderson intervened. "You can't send these people down there. They're not trained. It's like sending lambs to the slaughter. Look at him he wouldn't stand a chance."

"He's the exception. Basic military training is taught in that game VSWAR (Virtually Simulated WAR), without the players even realising it. That game is the most popular one around. I'm sure everyone here has played it haven't you?"

"No" Kolinsky said cantankerously, as the rest nodded.

"Oh great." Henderson muttered to himself. "They've played a computer game. Now they're experts."

Hawkins shook his head, his patience beginning to wear thin with Kolinsky.

"How about you Josh? Have you played it before?"

"Yes, a lot when I first started university."

"Good. You can teach Kolinsky the basics then." Kolinsky sniffed, annoyed at the reversal of roles.

"I don't see why you're sending him? He's not a doctor." He retorted.

"His background in Biology could come in useful. And before you even ask it, I'm not going through any more of the reasons for my choices."

Henderson lowered his voice so that only Hawkins could hear. "I think you're making a mistake sending these people." Hawkins looked about himself.

"No I think there's a good mixture of skills to deal with anything they may have to face." His bright eyes once more focussed on the tunnel as he addressed the group. "The community will panic if they find out about this discovery and so whatever you do don't mention anything about this to anyone. You'll be leaving tomorrow morning, so get a good nights rest and I'll see you all here at 0700 hours." As Hawkins left, loud voices erupted as the people moved into groups.

"Can I all have your attention please?" Henderson bellowed. Josh quietly watched as the enthralling conversations all about him continued, oblivious to Henderson's request, who in turn silently fumed, his eyes bulging. "Listen up." Henderson roared, shocking them into silence. "Next time I talk you listen or we could all end up dead." He paused. "Line up in a row." His voice remained deep and loud. Josh and Kolinsky stood back as the others scurried in all directions accomplishing nothing. "Get a move on."

At last a none to straight line of people was formed, which Josh and Kolinsky joined the end of. "Well you certainly took your time about that." He glanced over, glad to see the calm looking man stood next to him. "As you all know I'm Greg Henderson and this is second in command Terry Styne." Josh had heard all about him, they all had. He had been one of the elite Seals until, on an assignment, shrapnel had caught him on the left side of his face badly scarring it and damaging his eye beyond repair. Styne had had it replaced with the latest electronic false eye available, which fed vague pictures directly into the brain but there were still some discrepancies in the images he saw and his actual surroundings. His altered vision had caused him to fail the medical and, with much resentment on his part, resulted in him being forced to retire from the job he loved so much. He hadn't wanted to become an instructor, as his superiors suggested, it would have reminded him too much of what he was missing and so instead he had taken the job of a security guard at the shelter. He had been bored stiff until the aliens had arrived and then his job had proved its weight in gold, since his wife and daughter, already living with him in the base, had survived the attack.

"If we run into trouble I'd advise you to listen to anything Styne has to say." Henderson continued. Styne made no movement, as he hadn't done all the way through. His brown eyes focused ahead of him, the only difference between them was the slight red tinge and glassy look of his false eye. "Just for the record we'll run through who everyone is." Henderson said gesturing to the man on the left end of the row. Styne pulled out his computer and began logging in the names.

Steve Evans elegantly spoke his name, his clothes as always looking immaculate. Next came Roberto Martinez, a man in a security uniform with a latino complexion to his face. Beside him the bulky form of Fredrick O'Callaghan shifted impatiently. Since the burly guard had first shown them the med labs Josh had learnt that he was the man to see if you were after any of the luxury items that had become scarce commodities underground. It was common knowledge that he had some kind of secret stash hidden away and was making a fortune, especially from the small proportion of smokers who would do anything for their daily nicotine fix.

The tiny form of another guard, Kieron Attwell was next in line, looking more like a dwarf in comparison. He lazily chewed his gum, a common fixture in his mouth, his attitude as laid back as always. Beside him stood Barry Lester. There had been rumours circulating that he had been in some kind of trouble with the law but Josh believed it couldn't have been that serious since Hawkins wouldn't want to risk jeopardising their surveillance. Whatever the truth Lester did himself no favours by constantly smirking, which combined with his close set eyes gave him a dubious appearance.

Josh knew nothing about the next two people, Adrian Sutton and Fiona Ricks though when she talked her voice sounded haughty and her manner seemed to back it up.

The scientist who had been working on the door, Dr Dennis Jenkins stood next with his two assistants after him, Meriel Ellis and a tall woman Sandra Bennett. Finally Rob Kolinsky and Josh or rather Joshua Forbes gave their names. Styne looked up having completed the list and handed it to Henderson, who examined it.

"Good you can go now but just be sure you are all here by 0700 hours tomorrow."

"I don't believe this." Kolinsky mumbled.

"We ought to get to the games facility soon." Josh stated. "So that we can go through it all before it gets too late."

"Don't bother."

"Trust me I'd be more than happy not to but if we get attacked and you don't know how to use the weapons …" Josh shook his head considering the outcome. He heard a sharp intake of breath from Kolinsky.

"If we must but you should know I've never liked guns."

"Who does?" Kolinsky raised an eyebrow. "Oh I forgot you Americans are obsessed with them."

"Not all of us." Kolinsky protested.

"Don't worry. The gun is so high tech all you have to do is pull the trigger. Dead easy." Kolinsky's face paled and his eyes went into a trance. Josh immediately regretted his poor choice of words. It was becoming apparent that despite his domineering, pompous attitude Kolinsky was petrified. What Josh couldn't fathom was why he felt so calm about the whole thing, even excited. Maybe it was because everything he had cared about had been destroyed and now all he was left with was a bitter hope of revenge.

"Have you ever been here before?" Josh asked as they entered into a circular cave. Seats lined the walls and descended in rows downwards to the round flat ground in the centre, similar in design to an old amphitheatre. Machines, slightly larger than a man and similar in appearance to coffins, stood standing in their own patch of ground in the arena.

"No. Why would I?"

"Well then, these machines are virtual reality machines. They're self-contained units that allow the occupant to experience any virtual environment that they want." He opened the door of one of the machines, to reveal a black interior. "Here put these on" he picked up a suit and helmet and passed it to Kolinsky.

"What for?" Kolinsky asked holding them suspiciously.

"The helmet detects your thought patterns and inputs images into your mind, while the suit monitors your bodies nerve impulses and heart rate. Basically it allows you to experience a virtual reality world that is all too real at some times. They had cases of people having heart attacks when playing murder mystery games or extreme sports, which is why they had to start monitoring the heart rate and shut the program down automatically if it goes above a pre-set danger level."

The suit was tighter than Kolinsky expected and he had a struggle to get into it. "Once you enter the machine VSWAR will start and take you through a training mission." Josh passed him one of the heavy guns on a rack nearby, which Kolinsky nervously accepted. "Don't worry." Josh reassured him, smiling. "It's only a mock gun for you to get the feel of. After all they couldn't have people blowing up their machines. Just select the mode you want with this button here and then pull the trigger. It's simple. The only thing you need to remember is that the explosives are limited to sixteen but the laser won't run out for a very long time."

"Why do we have to enter the machine at all?"

"It's to block your senses off from your surroundings so that, for example, you don't hear any erroneous noises in the virtual environment."

Kolinsky reluctantly entered, feeling twinges of claustrophobia trying to take a hold on him, especially as the door closed. It shut throwing him into darkness and panic overtook him. He threw his weight against the chamber walls, wanting to get out, when the blackness suddenly evaporated and he found himself in the middle of a lush green field in open air. Occasional trees and sheep decorated the landscape, whilst a baking sun shone brightly through the pale blue sky. He breathed hard, trying to get the air into his lungs and feeling relieved at the openness of his surroundings. A voice began coaching him, just how to move around at first and then the skills taught progressed. At first he felt totally disorientated by the realism of the world he found himself in but after a while he gradually became accustomed to it. Only slight glitches that appeared in the rendered images every so often, gave away the fact that his surroundings weren't real. The movement was strange as well since, although he had every sensation of moving his legs and feeling the ground beneath his feet, somewhere in the back of his mind he knew it wasn't really happening.

Outside the machine, Josh stood back to watch the massive holographic projection that had appeared above the arena, showing Kolinsky and his virtual surroundings, which had changed to a busy metropolis amidst which targets randomly appeared. Despite his reluctance he had learnt surprisingly quickly and was dispatching the targets efficiently with a lot fewer civilian deaths than most of the other first time players.

For a moment Josh almost felt he was back at the University attending one of the most crucial tournaments he had ever participated in. He had been selected for the Cambridge team in a friendly match against Harvard that eventually he and his team had succeeded in winning. He hadn't known at the time but a scout had been watching and afterwards offered him a position on the British team, to play professionally, in the World tournaments. It would have been a full time job and he had anguished over the decision for days but at last his love of plants had prevailed. He had turned down the once in a lifetime opportunity to continue his studies. He had never regretted his decision but he had often wondered just how far he could have gone, possibly even obtaining the ultimate elusive goal of World Champion, although that seemed a pointless title now.

Inside the virtual world, a voice cut into Kolinsky's head. "Training completed." The environment disintegrated into blackness, the door opening at the same time.

"See I told you it was easy." Josh was standing talking to him but the real world didn't seem real after the game. He stepped out in confusion, trying to readjust to his surroundings. "Wasn't so bad was it." Josh smiled, thinking back to his first time in the machine. The confusion and disorientation was the same for everyone but with practice you got used to it. "I think you'd better get back to your house and get some rest before tomorrow." Kolinsky nodded, still trying to grasp what was going on and finding it difficult to even walk. Inside the machine he had just thought about movement and it had happened but now he had to actually make his legs work again.

"It seems a fairly pointless exercise if it makes you feel like this afterwards." Kolinsky muttered.

"Most people find it's worth it for the enjoyment you get inside the virtual worlds."

"I'd be surprised if that contraption doesn't cause medical problems as well." Kolinsky prodded a finger at the machine, trying to pull the suit off at the same time.

"They have discovered that people using it for too many hours each day have developed several long term health problems, which is why strict guidelines were introduced limiting its use. It's no worse than any other luxury in life though. You know the saying too much of anything is bad for you."

"Any time spent inside that thing is bad for me." Kolinsky said in disgust, almost falling over as he tried to walk out of the arena. Josh's lips tightened as he repressed a laugh.

Josh left Kolinsky at his apartment still grumbling about the virtual world, although the effects had already worn off. As he walked back to his own house, he considered all that had happened. Maybe there were no aliens down there. The door and the tunnel had to have been made by something though. If it were humans, the fact that they had used this new unknown material meant it had to be top secret. But what were they hiding? And more to the point what would the consequences be? Nothing but questions and no answers, he thought as he entered his apartment.

## Chapter 7

At 0630 hours Josh left his apartment and headed for the accident site and the newly discovered tunnel. The city was only just beginning to wake up but already smells of freshly baked bread wafted through the streets along with the sound of children giggling and laughing. It was extraordinary how quickly they had all settled in but what was even harder to comprehend was the feeling everyone had of a close knit community. Above in the now devastated cities these same people had rushed to and fro in their hectic daily lives, never even taking the time to notice anyone else, let alone help one another but that had all changed when they had been forced underground. The same ruthless attack that had ripped the city apart and left them with a bleak future had brought them together and given them something they had never had before; a sense that they were no longer alone. They had to help each other if they wanted to survive. With a severe shortage of entertainment, they learnt to make their own and each evening the underground roof rang with sounds of laughter, more than Josh could remember ever hearing above. It was crazy but the truth was the attack had given them as much as it had taken away.

As Josh approached the accident site the sound of voices grew louder. The same two security staff guarded the tunnel but this time they let him through with only a quick check. He was ten minutes early but already many of the team were in the cave, going through equipment checks. Henderson was stood overseeing everything in his usual loud manner, with Styne at his side, watching silently, his gear packed neatly into a backpack on the ground before him.

The last few people came in behind Josh. Unsurprisingly Kolinsky arrived last, carrying two bags of medical equipment, one appearing considerably heavier than the other.

"I've sorted out what we need with us. Here." He tried to toss the bulkier bag to Josh but its weight was too much and he ended up almost over balancing, as it swung outwards in his grasp. Josh grabbed it just in time, surprised to find that it was nowhere near as heavy as he had expected, after seeing the way Kolinsky struggled with it. He swung the knapsack onto his back, as he followed one of the guard's instructions and gathered some other supplies and equipment, the most important, the AR Assault Gun.

He was busy checking his gear and making sure he had enough food rations packed when Hawkins arrived.

"Glad to see you all here." Was his first comment, with a pointed look at Kolinsky. "I hope you're all ready." Henderson looked despairingly at the shambles about him and Hawkins seemed to get the message.

"Remember it's surveillance only so try to stay hidden." He stared round as the fiddling with equipment had just about ceased. "Well I think that's all, except for be careful and good luck."

"We will be." Henderson's tone sounded more hopeful than full of conviction. "Is everyone ready?" There was no answer. "We should get going then." Most of the group appeared flustered as they were herded into the tunnel entrance, somewhat reluctantly, especially Kolinsky. Hawkins waited as they disappeared into the distance before leaving the two guards to watch the entrance alone.

Henderson's deep rumbling orders soon had them all moving at a fast pace, their leather boots pounding on the grey floor. The steepness of the tunnel meant the entrance was soon out of sight. With the last glimpse of home gone, everyone's attention focussed on the tunnel as they peered downwards, hoping to see a change.

It became clear most of the team was made up of academic people with little time for exercise when after an hour they were already tired out. Reluctantly Henderson let the pace slacken, biting back his urge to complain when hushed talking broke out amongst them. Some of the voices sounded shaky to Josh as they speculated on the tunnel and the strong possibility of aliens.

"If it's aliens I can't understand why they haven't discovered our presence yet." Dennis Jenkins was saying to his two companions Barry Lester and Fiona

Ricks. "I'm sure they would have guarded it somehow."

"What, with booby traps?"

"Just shut up Lester." Ricks flashed him an angry look. "This place is weird enough as it is without you suggesting things."

"Do you reckon it definitely is aliens." Lester continued.

"I'd rather not think about it."

"Oh come on."

"Leave off Lester." Jenkins interrupted. "This isn't the time to talk about it."

"Well when is the time to talk about it, when you come face to face with one." Ricks shuddered. "What scared?"

"No." She glared at him.

"Hey. Lay off her." Jenkins persisted.

"Ok, calm down, obviously she believes there are aliens down here."

"Do you really think they put traps in this place." Adrian Sutton joined in.

"Could have" Lester grinned inwardly at seeing Sutton's nervous reaction. "They certainly aren't very friendly so I don't suppose they would want anything traipsing into their … whatever this is." He gestured ahead of him with his hand. "We could be walking into some unseen trap right now."

"I think you've been watching too many movies." Martinez chuckled, causing Lester to frown.

"It's not like I've got much choice available to me

on that antique 2D screen they call the entertainment system in the underground shelter."

"I think we should remain cautious and alert." Jenkins interposed. "It would make sense for them to guard it."

"It's a tunnel." Ricks expostulated. "They're hardly able to jump out from behind or to the sides of us. It's just a concrete tunnel, what could possibly happen."

"Quieten down." Henderson warned.

"Look at this." Josh drew their attention to the wall on their left where a trickle of water was bubbling out from tiny cracks.

"Very exciting, a wall." Lester mocked.

"No look closer, round the water seepage." They approached taking sometime before at last realising what Josh was referring to. Faint patches of some green substance sparsely lined the wall in places round the crack. "If I'm not mistaken it's a species of algae though I don't recognise it." He placed the probes from his computer onto a patch and ran a program to test for the plant species. A blue bar slowly trundled across the screen.

"Is this really necessary?" Henderson asked impatiently as the bar reached the other side of the screen.

"That's odd." Josh checked the probes placement and the computer program.

"It's algae so what?"

"The computer can't identify it. I'm pretty sure

there's a database of all known species on it. I think we just discovered a new one."

"Great we've found a new algae." Lester complained. "Can we go now?"

"Is it an alien plant?" Burnett asked hesitantly.

"No its structure is almost identical to Pleurococcus but there are definite variations in its makeup. It would be highly improbable to find such similar algae on another planet."

"We should get moving then." Henderson encouraged with little interest in the algae.

"I've got to get out of here." Kolinsky's breathless voice sounded strained. It was warm in the tunnel but nothing accounted for the sweat that glistened on Kolinsky's red face. He looked very close to panic as Henderson glared questioningly at him.

"I think he's claustrophobic." Josh volunteered.

"I'm not." Kolinsky tried to deny it. "I just don't like being in this tunnel it feels like the walls are closing in on me." He added quietly.

"It's the same tunnel for a long way whether you go back or forward."

"Don't remind me." Kolinsky focused hard on the ground trying to ignore his surroundings.

"We need to make a move." Henderson's voice was full of frustration.

"Try walking at the front, at least you'll be slightly more in the open." Josh suggested.

"He can get blown up first that way." Lester

chuckled. Kolinsky moved to the front, ignoring Lester's jibes, as he walked uncertainly forward.

"As soon as there's any change I want you back with the rest." Henderson ordered.

"Don't worry I will be." Kolinsky said feeling a little more relaxed and not quite so boxed in.

Henderson shook his head, cursing under his breath. Why couldn't he at least have had a group of people able to walk down a tunnel without finding some difficulty? What was wrong with them? He would have had less trouble from a bunch of kids but then those he had taught in the military school had had discipline. During his time in the army discipline had been fundamental and without a chain of authority all hell would have broken loose. Thoughtfully he pulled out a cigar and began chewing on one end of it. He had given up actually smoking them a long time ago but there still seemed something comforting about having them.

Henderson looked at his watch. Five minutes had passed and Kolinsky was still moving forward, for now at least. He had spoken too soon.

Ahead Kolinsky abruptly stopped.

"Now what?" Henderson said through clenched teeth, trying to control his temper. Then he saw it and stopped dead, the cigar falling from his mouth. Lester ploughed into the back of him. "This doesn't look good." Henderson whispered to himself.

A click had resounded down the tunnel and Kolinsky had stopped immediately, his eyes tight shut.

"Oh God. Trip wire." He looked down gingerly to see his foot in the path of a red beam. "Wha…" He stopped in amazement at seeing a tangle of red beams spanning across the tunnel ahead. They had appeared from nowhere.

"What is it? A trap?" Sutton said, noticing at the same time Roberto Martinez staring intently up the tunnel from where they had come. "What?" he asked

"Uh" Martinez returned, half listening.

"What is it?" Sutton asked again, frustrated.

"I don't know, it's just this tunnel reminds me of something out of one of those old adventure movies. I was wondering if a huge stone ball was about to come rolling after us."

"Don't be so stupid. This isn't the time to mess around."

"Shut up both of you" Henderson ordered.

"Did you feel that Sutton?" Martinez said ignoring Henderson.

"Stop playing about."

"Shut up." Henderson repeated.

"No wait I can feel it too." Evan's face had gone white as he spoke. "The grounds shaking more and more."

"Ball or no ball, I say we run for it." Lester screamed.

"No wait." Henderson shouted. Most of the group had already followed Lester's example and were tearing down the tunnel.

"Come back." Henderson and the rest had started

to give chase, when they felt the floor crack beneath their feet. All down the tunnel, beneath the red beams, the ground began to tear apart, chunks of rock falling away. Great cracks appeared, with only blackness below. Trying to find a safe footing became increasingly difficult for all of them.

Beyond the red beams, the floor appeared stable but Lester and the others were still some way off. A whiplash of sounds resounded as more rock split apart. The situation was made worse by the ceiling starting to crumble, showering them in fragments of rock. The whole team were now at a distance from either of the end of the red beams, stuck in the middle of perhaps a deadly trap. Another chunk of rock fell away. There was a scream and they all looked round to see Sutton, faltering on the edge of a now massive opening. The ground gave a violent shudder, throwing Sutton off the edge and into the darkness.

Without warning the whole floor gave way and they found themselves plummeting downwards. Josh's heart pounded as he struggled to grab at anything. He dropped a short way before bouncing and rolling awkwardly off a floor of slanting rock. Pain cursed through his side as he fell still further. He hit more rock, this time his body coming to rest on the hard floor, sore and bruised, but otherwise unhurt.

He lay still for a moment before raising his battered arm up to adjust the light on his headband. The ray it threw out was bright against the darkness. Two other shafts of light appeared near him and more moved about not far above him. He traced the two beams of light back to their source, to find Kolinsky lying between him and a woman in the centre of the cave. He could see Kolinsky was ok, apart from being somewhat shaken but the woman was struggling to get up, looking dazed. Her slim frame appeared tiny in the beam as she turned towards him on her hands and knees, her long hair briefly parting to give him a view of her face. In different circumstances she would have easily had the glamorous, beautiful appearance of a model but, as it was, the makeup was gone replaced by dried blood and dirt. Even so the bone structure gave away the promise of her beauty and she looked sorely out of place in her unflattering surroundings. Josh thought back, her name eluding him for a moment before he remembered the line-up and the tall woman, Sandra Burnett.

"Burnett are you ok?" The woman turned her head towards him, the light blinding him.

"Yeah I think so." She sounded shaky but talking clearly otherwise. The beam spun back round to the floor as Burnett continued trying to get up. Josh watched her, deciding that she had probably knocked her head on the way down but not too badly and that she would be ok in a moment or two. His next thought was to find a way out.

Josh focussed on his surroundings, shining the light over the rock walls all around, noticing another shaft of light from Kolinsky flashing around also. He could only find one opening, into a misshapen tunnel, more like a natural fracture in the rock but large enough to crawl through. Josh moved the light back over the floor as he looked at the solid rock all around. He suddenly stopped, the beam coming to rest on a crumpled body, laying completely still. Kolinsky's light flashed onto it. Now Josh could see the pool of blood and more still flowing from the fractures in the skull. The whole head had been badly damaged on the rocks, making the face difficult to identify. Josh fought back a rising sickness he felt, forcing himself to examine it. Adrian Sutton. He looked away, there was no way he could be alive surely.

"I've got to go and check him." Kolinsky said as he started crawling forward. Cracking of rock issued from where Burnett was. Josh looked round. She was still struggling but her movements were more controlled. More fracturing resounded as he saw the rock beneath her part. It gave way and she lashed out, managing to grab the edge, her legs swinging down beneath her.

"Grab her." Josh shouted at Kolinsky as he scrambled towards Burnett. Kolinsky didn't move. He was rooted to the spot, staring intently at the tunnel and the shadow that crept slowly across the wall before disappearing. It was a twisted and distorted shadow, making it impossible to tell what it belonged to but he knew it wasn't any of theirs. It was the sign of an unseen presence, watching them.

The rock Burnett clung to loosened from the rest at the same time as Josh launched himself at her. He knocked Kolinsky over as he landed, his arm outstretched trying to grab her. The rock broke and Burnett fell away from him. Both men had landed hard and the fragile rock beneath them gave out under their weight. They were now falling for what seemed like an eternity, through the darkness, losing all sense of their surroundings.

A loud noise resonated, indistinguishable due to the repeating echoes. Josh hit something hard, feeling more pain and then he was surrounded in liquid. Water. He thrashed about disorientated; his head emerged at last, breaking the surface of the water. The backpack was weighing him down and he quickly pulled it off, letting it fall away into the watery depths below. The light on his headband cut through the blackness and he felt thankful that it was still working. They were in another cave, filled with water. He could see the lights from the rest of the group, now about 20 meters above him. The water was strangely warm.

"Are you all ok?" The radios they carried burst into life.

"Were they?" Josh thought as he looked for the others. Burnett and Kolinsky were near him, both treading water, looking ill with fright but by some miracle uninjured. Their backpacks were also gone.

"Yes, we're fine." He said into the radio, his eyes resting on Burnett. Small spots of blood showed up on her blonde hair and the water was blood coloured around her. Maybe she had had a fairly hard knock to her head but the water revived her to full consciousness. "No sign of Sutton at the moment though." He paused not wanting to say what he really thought, that Sutton was almost certainly dead. There had been just too much blood.

"Why didn't you help her?" Josh glared at Kolinsky, talking calmly, for fear of bringing more rock down.

"What like you did? Now we're all down here." Kolinsky thought back to the shadow, unsure if he had been seeing things. Should he tell them? No. It could have just been his imagination. It must have been.

"I couldn't just let her fall."

"The pair of you shut up." Burnett's voice sounded hazy. "I'm tired. I can't keep this up for long and I don't see any way out." She was right. Rock walls on all sides and nothing but water beneath them.

"Well at least the floor won't fall away." She chuckled as the world became surreal to her once more and treading water became more difficult.

"No sign of a way out." Josh said into the radio. "I'm going to see if there's an underwater tunnel out of here or something."

"Water?" the radio responded.

"I'll be back soon." Josh said. Kolinsky grabbed Burnett as she began to sink under the water.

"Don't be long I can't keep us both up for that long."

"We're sorting out some rope and gear now. We'll have you out of there in a little while." Henderson's voice came over the radio.

"You'd better not be too long. We haven't got the

strength to hold on." Josh heard Kolinsky say into the radio, as he dived beneath the surface.

Even with the powerful light, it was difficult to see anything beneath the surface. He fumbled about with his hands, his feet propelling him downwards, until he at last felt and dimly saw rock beneath him. It was warm like the water. He moved his way over it, feeling for any sign of a tunnel, eventually reaching a wall with no success. He needed air and returned quickly to the surface.

"It's no good." Josh heard Henderson say over the radio, as he gasped in several breaths of air. "The whole floors about to give way any second. We've got to move back down a tunnel that we've found up here. I'm sorry but you're on your own till we figure out a way to help you."

"Thanks for nothing." Kolinsky said angrily in to the radio, starting to panic when only static answered him.

"No wait. You can't leave us down here. You've got to help us."

"I can't risk losing any more people." The static resumed.

"They can't do that!" Kolinsky said shocked. "The roof's about to cave in any second, we're done for Burnett." She was still out of it and made no reply.

Josh dived back down to the wall and started groping his way along it. At last he felt what seemed to be like a large indentation in the rock. As he explored further, he found it receded some way into the wall, narrowing into a small tunnel. Maybe only three feet square. He pushed his way down it having to squeeze through places. He couldn't hold his breath for too much longer but he had gone too far to turn back now, in the tight space. He twisted and managed to pull his way through a very narrow section. The tunnel now headed upwards steeply. He followed its course, relieved to see the sparkling surface above. He broke through into the fresh air above, madly breathing it in.

A very tiny tunnel led off into darkness, just large enough to crawl down, provided it didn't get smaller further on. No point in seeing where it led. The rest of the roof back where the other two were would fall in soon. This tunnel was their only chance. He took a deep breath and headed back. He just prayed it led out of the mess they were in.

## Chapter 8

Burnett had regained consciousness but she was too weak to keep her head above water and Kolinsky had to help her. He was tired out and the only thing that kept him going was the adrenaline that rushed through him, every time another rock hit the water. More and more ware falling now.

"Where's Josh got to?" he mumbled. Burnett barely responded as darkness tried to take a hold on her senses.

"What was your life on the surface like?" Kolinsky asked, shaking her awake in an attempt to stop her losing consciousness.

"I don't know … I'm too tired to think."

"You've got to. Come on talk to me." He demanded.

"I don't want to think about it, about Eddy."

"Who's Eddy." She didn't respond until he had given her another shake.

"My husband. It's our second wedding anniversary soon." She groaned at an unwelcome thought, her head slumping forward.

"Where is he now?"

"Dead. A gang of yobs attacked us when we were

heading to the shelter after the alien ship attacked. I don't understand why they killed him. He was protecting me even at the very end. He told me to run for it. Why did they do it?" She appealed her mind slowly becoming more lucid.

"I don't know." Kolinsky answered tightly. Nothing was making much sense to him anymore.

Suddenly the largest chunk of rock so far plummeted into the water, making a loud splash and causing a wave that sent them bobbing up and down. Kolinsky stiffened with fright, his mind finding it difficult to cope any longer and something seemed to snap inside him, his concern for Burnett forgotten.

"We're going to die, trapped under tonnes of rock in a watery grave." It was one of the worst deaths he could imagine and the thought made him panic more. "The aliens are doing this, they're going to kill us all."

"What?" Burnett tried to look round.

"I saw it up there." Kolinsky raved. The world had become clear again to Burnett but now she wondered if she was dreaming.

"There's no one here. Only us."

"I bet they've already killed Forbes."

"Calm down."

"We're as good as dead." His eyes looked wildly about as more rock shards hit the water all about him.

The surface of the water broke, as suddenly something emerged. They drew back terrified with nowhere to run. The first thing they noticed was the green eyes, glinting red. Then they saw the face. It was

Josh. The light was reflecting of his normally blue eyes, causing the strange effect.

"There's a tunnel but I don't know where it goes, if anywhere." A load of rocks fell at once, as Josh spoke, causing an enormous splash. "It'll be tight but I think we can get through." He quickly talked into the radio. "We may have found a way out. Haven't got time to talk." Josh's voice brought Kolinsky out of his momentary madness and he managed to regain his self-control. "Is Burnett going to be ok to go?"

"I'm fine." She pushed Kolinsky away and with an effort, swam over to prove the point. "I'll make it."

"How tight?" Kolinsky asked anxiously.

"We've got to get going." More rock crumbled. "Just follow me." Josh dived, swimming straight to the tunnel. He pushed Burnett in and she began pulling herself through it with much more ease than Josh, due to her smaller size. Kolinsky followed hesitantly.

"Go, go, go." Josh thought as he brought up the rear. He felt the water hit him hard from behind and glanced back to see the roof cave in, rock landing in the mouth of the tunnel, sealing it of behind him. Kolinsky was too slow in front of him. They had to get moving quicker.

They squeezed through the final tight part and headed for the surface. The rocks had displaced the water and now it half filled the previously dry tunnel. Kolinsky hauled himself into the tunnel on all fours, relieved that his head was finally clear of the water. His fleeting happiness was short lived though, as his light illuminated the solid rock all around with the only hope of escape through a small tunnel. He felt a shove from behind as a breathless Josh surfaced, jamming into the tunnel next to him.

"I can't get through there." Kolinsky drew back, looking at the tiny opening.

"You've got to, rocks are blocking where we just came from, there's no way back." Josh encouraged gently.

"We're trapped!"

"Calm down Kolinsky."

"You know he's claustrophobic." Burnett said, looking much better now.

"If I can fit down there you certainly can." Josh looked at Kolinsky, he was small compared to Burnett even, though both Josh and Burnett were slim. "I'll go first." Josh pulled himself into the tunnel. He felt the rock scraping on his back as he dragged himself forward on his stomach. The water was up to his mouth, threatening to cover his nose. He had to ignore it and pretend he was somewhere else. The tunnel dipped and he could no longer keep his head high enough to stop the water covering his face. He felt the restricting walls, as he grabbed at the floor and pulled himself through, back above the water. The tunnel now headed upwards, looking even smaller than before. He didn't even have the room to look back to see how the others were doing.

"You ok back there?" No answer. Probably couldn't hear anything through the water barrier. He crawled on further, hoping to give them room this side.

"I think Kolinsky's coming, I can't see." Burnett's voice reached him.

"You ok?"

"It's tight but I'm getting through ok. I hope the tunnel gets dryer. I don't like all this water."

"Should do, it slopes uphill." Josh paused. "You there yet Kolinsky?" No reply. He crawled on further, wondering if there was enough room. He could hear the water splashing as Burnett followed. Still no Kolinsky.

Kolinsky struggled with his fear as he entered the tunnel, panic immediately gripping him. He could feel the rock all about him; he was entombed in it. He moved his arm to pull himself forward, his elbows hitting the wall. He had to get out but he was trapped, his movements severely restricted. The water felt suffocating round his face and his breathing became ragged. Maybe it was rising and he would be drowned, unable to move.

He struggled to get up, his back hitting the rock savagely, scraping against it, as he tried to claw his way out. The water rose over his face and he somehow managed to slide forward into the dip. He couldn't breathe at all. He tried to scream, violently throwing himself forward anyway he could. He emerged from the water, finding it almost impossible to breath in his panic.

"Kolinsky" he could hear Burnett calling his name. "Calm down you're ok." The water was still around him but not so near his face now. "It's not far now. Just keep calm." He crawled forward a little, relieved to be out of the water but knowing he was still trapped. He had to force himself to somehow ignore his instincts to get up but the thought of the rock all about him was petrifying. "Not much further and then we'll be back in the open."

"I can't."

"Listen. It's either stay here and hope the water doesn't rise or get the hell out of here." Burnett crawled forward after Josh, hoping Kolinsky would follow.

Kolinsky swallowed hard, feeling a lump in his throat, as he forced one arm after the other. He wanted to stand up, to hopelessly fight against the rock.

"Open air ... soon." He repeated, mechanically moving one arm after the other and dragging himself forward.

At last, the tunnel ended in an opening into a cave. Josh and Burnett were already standing in it waiting for him. He scrambled out, never feeling happier in his life.

"You ok?" Josh asked as he gave him a hand.

"Thank God" was all Kolinsky said. He didn't notice the blood trickling from the torn and bruised flesh on his back and elbows where he had struggled against the rock.

"We talked to the rest over the radio. They're

waiting for us. That tunnel should go to where they are, though they reckon it's like a maze down here." Burnett was wide eyed as she spoke, obviously having recovered from the knock to her head. With relief, Kolinsky saw that the tunnel was large enough for them to stand up in easily.

"I really want to get out of this place." Kolinsky looked round as they walked down the tunnel, dark except for their lights.

The rugged tunnel widened into a small cavern. The conical forms of Stalagmites jutted up from the rocky ground all around them, whilst the similar forms of Stalactites hung directly above. The two points of the rough cones nearly met on most of the pairs, indicating the long time they had been forming for. Even as they watched the salty substance dripped painfully slowly between them, each small drop increasing their size.

On one side of the cave a clear pool of water glistened in the light from their headbands. They peered into the still depths, watching, mesmerized by the trickle of water that ran down the wall behind. Directly above a narrow shaft receded into unknown heights.

"This looks like one of those antique mines in places, rather than just a natural cave." Burnett commented, tossing a loose piece of rock into the pool.

"I wouldn't know, I've never been to a mine. I don't know why anyone in their right mind would."

Kolinsky looked away disgusted. "Let's just get out of here."

"The tunnels do seem to be a constant size and shape", Josh said ignoring Kolinsky, "suggesting they've been cut from the rock rather than occurred naturally."

"So what if it is one of those old mines from the 19th century, that we managed to stumble across." Kolinsky said watching the stone disappear from sight.

"They didn't have the technology or resources to build a door like the one we found."

"We just fell out of that original tunnel and then found this place. It obviously just happened to be here and the rock collapsing caused a pathway through into it. We'll just have to find a way back to that first tunnel or better still a way back to the base."

"Something tells me this is all connected with that first tunnel on purpose." Josh gestured at his surroundings.

"Yes, an over active imagination." Josh scowled at Kolinsky.

"In the 19th century mines wouldn't they have shored these tunnels up with something, usually wood and wouldn't there also have been electrical cabling along the walls?" Burnett asked.

"Let's just get out of here." Kolinsky complained as Josh searched through the many pockets in his trousers for his hand held computer, grateful that he hadn't packed it with the rest of his gear in his now lost pack.

"This way." Josh directed them into a new tunnel,

its floor as uneven as its walls and they had to watch their step. The tunnel seemed to narrow in the distance.

"Are you sure we're going the right way?" Kolinsky asked nervously.

"I'm getting a signal from their computers in this direction." Josh looked back concerned. "Are you going to be all right?" Kolinsky grimaced in response as he felt the walls closing in on him once more.

"How about you Burnett?" There was a shuffle from behind.

"Better than he is." Burnett nodded back to Kolinsky who was recovering his balance after tripping over. He kicked out at the rock in annoyance only to discover it was attached. Burnett stifled a laugh as Kolinsky let out a yelp from behind. Josh looked back at the commotion.

"Oh very funny." Kolinsky's eyes suddenly widened. "Watch out!" Burnett grabbed Josh, roughly pulling him back. He stumbled into the wall on the side of him.

"What's wrong?" He gasped. Burnett nodded to the floor where moments before he had been about to walk. There was nothing except a deep darkness. He stared in shock.

"Maybe another mine shaft." Kolinsky suggested.

"That noise!" Burnett cocked her head to one side, listening intently. The faint mumble of talking was coming from further down the tunnel. "It must be the others."

Carefully they skirted round the hole and continued their route through their rocky surroundings. Soon the faint sounds became recognisable words, Henderson's deep baritones echoing in the confined tunnel.

"We've found them!" Burnett smiled thankfully.

"We're not out of here yet though." Kolinsky thought "and what about that shadow?"

## Chapter 9

An eight-year-old girl accompanied by a boy of six years, huddled in a small cave cut into the tunnel, leading to the restricted area. They had ignored the mass of red tape, warning of a cave-in ahead, the girl remaining certain it was nothing more than a deterrent to keep people away from the door. Her childish convictions for once had paid off and from their hiding place they could safely peer out at the two guards, who hindered their passage through the strange glimmering blue door.

"Is it time yet?" The boy whined, his face a picture of boredom. "We've been here for AGES."

"Shush, Nick" the girl whispered back "we have to wait until they are far enough down the tunnel, otherwise they will know that I'm following them."

"I don't understand why you didn't just ask your dad if you could go with them." The boy commented, much more inclined to go back and play in the caves near where he lived. The girl hesitated, unwilling to divulge to her companion that her father had strongly forbidden her to go when she had begged him.

She shrugged. "You know adults they never let us do anything that is even remotely fun." She still couldn't understand why her dad hadn't realised she had just wanted to keep him in sight, to make sure he was ok. "My dad would have probably just said that it was too dangerous for me to go." The boy could easily sympathise with this, after all only this morning his mother had forbidden him to go rock climbing with his friends, when he had asked. She had said that it was far too dangerous, "but all the other boys go" he had complained.

"Yes but they are much older than you, besides if I were their mother I wouldn't let them go. Climbing 20ft high rock faces, without safety equipment is very dangerous, if not suicidal, they ought to be stopped." His mother had replied.

Nick's thoughts wondered to the present situation, perhaps going down strange tunnels really was dangerous.

"Susan aren't you scared?"

"What do you mean?" Susan said with a look of surprise, though secretly her heart pounded with excitement and a little fear.

"This place is meant to be a secret but everyone has heard all those different stories about the tunnel. I heard there were monsters of some kind down there and they do horrible things to people, especially children." The tunnel had been impossible to keep secret in the close knit community and though at first Hawkins had kept up the false pretence that a team of people were busy carrying out work in a distant part of the underground shelter it wasn't believed for a second.

What Hawkins found strange though was despite knowing the truth his fears of a panic were unfounded and if anything the community had banded together more closely in their joint goals, helping families of the brave people who had gone.

"Oh don't be such a baby." Then after a moments thought she added "I've told you before, you shouldn't listen to those other boys, Nick, they're only trying to wind you up, besides which you have to stay here, that was our agreement." Nick looked much relieved as he answered.

"Well I'll help you if you keep up your end of the bargain." Susan sighed and took off the heavy backpack, she had previously packed and now wore. She rummaged around until finally she produced a small bar of chocolate, a rarity in their new life underground. Sighing again she passed her treasure to the eagerly waiting hands.

"Now you remember what I told you to do? Just create a commotion." The head opposite her nodded, all the while, the eyes in it, staring intently down at the chocolate bar. "Remember you can eat it later but first this." She hastily added, fearing he would devour it and then she would have to wait until he had finished.

Carefully the boy placed his prize in a pocket in his coat, fearful lest any misfortune should befall it.

"Ok go now." Susan urgently whispered as she shouldered the backpack. Nick stood up and walked forward towards the two guards. As he caught their attention, the shorter of the two smiled and walked forward to say hello, while the other guard looked away disgusted, murmuring under his breath.

"Now what are you doing here, you know you're not supposed to be here." The first guard, whose name badge read Pete Woodridge, asked. Nick responded with a demand to be allowed to go with the others. "Now let's be reasonable, it's not safe for you to go, you could get hurt. Now why don't you go and play with the other children?" As he finished speaking Nick rushed forward, his short legs carrying him faster than the guard had realised. He lurched forward trying to catch the little villain but the boy dived past him towards the other guard.

"Catch him Fred." The shout caused Fredrick Moore to jerk to and launch himself towards the boy, almost colliding with the other guard as he did so. Nick continued running as fast as he could towards the tunnel, enjoying the mayhem he was causing, though feeling a little trapped, with a guard coming at him from either side. As he made another dive out of the way of clutching hands, he felt his foot catch on a rock or something, sending him flying forward. He heard a loud thud as he hit the rocky ground and then seconds later realised pain was surging through his knee. It was too much for him and he burst into tears, sobbing that his knee hurt. The two men, taken aback for an instance, now rushed forward, unsure how badly the boy had hurt himself. Moore stood back, leaving the other guard to try and comfort the boy, feeling out of his depth. It appeared that he had only cut his knee but nothing seemed to console Nick and at last Moore stepped forward, his face full of concern as he produced a chocolate bar.

"I tell you what, why don't you have this and see if it stops your knee hurting." He passed the bar to the boy, who instantly stopped crying, surprise and delight, lighting up his face. He thanked the guard as he popped a segment into his mouth, the pain forgotten. He sat sucking it, feeling that overall things hadn't gone too badly.

"Hey wait." Woodridge made a run for the door, as Moore looked round to see him in pursuit of a young girl.

"What is this? have the schools shut or something" Moore cursed moving towards his companion who had caught the girl.

"Let me go" Susan screamed "I want to see my dad."

"You can't it's not safe."

"Let me go" Susan lashed out, struggling wildly.

"Now stop that, you'll hurt yourself or me."

"Looks like you've got your hands full." Moore laughed.

"Come on calm down."

"That's Styne's daughter isn't it?"

"You could give me a hand here." Woodridge said, trying to pin the girls flailing arms down before they struck him another painful blow.

"Thank heavens." A tall fair-haired woman had appeared coming from the direction of the main town.

"I was scared something had happened to her." The woman grabbed the girl hugging her. "I thought she was playing when she wanted the backpack to go exploring. I didn't realise she was actually going to try and go. Then when I couldn't find her I suddenly realised."

"It's ok she's alright they both are."

"Thank you." The woman said gratefully before hurrying both children back towards the main settlement.

"But I want to go down the tunnel." The girl was still complaining.

"You can't." Their voices receded into the distance.

"And I didn't think you liked kids" Woodridge laughed.

"It was only a chocolate bar."

"Yeah right." Great Moore thought, now I'll never live this down.

While all the commotion had occurred no one had noticed the dark shadow that emerged from the tunnel, slinking its way across the roof. It leisurely moved onwards and down to the wall, finally disappearing towards the main settlement.

## Chapter 10

"There has to be a way out." Henderson was saying as Josh and the others reached them, he turned a mixture of surprise and pleasure on his face. "I'm glad you could join us."

"No thanks to you." Kolinsky raged. "You left us to die." Josh grabbed him before he got the chance to take a swing at Henderson.

"Now hold on a minute we were trying to find a way to help you but the roof and floor were about to completely give way. I couldn't risk any more lives." Henderson reasoned.

"I see we were expendable."

"You made it out ok."

"Apart from Sutton."

"What do you mean…" Henderson's voice trailed away.

"I don't know if he's dead." Kolinsky fumed. "I couldn't get back to check because the floor gave way. We didn't see him after that."

"His wounds looked pretty serious" Josh added "and the whole roof caved in after we left. There's no way he could have survived." They stood for a moment in silence.

"We thought the rest of the rock had collapsed. We heard the noise from here." Henderson said.

"You should have helped us." Kolinsky grumbled.

"It looks like we have bigger problems", Burnett patted him on the shoulder soothingly, "such as finding a way out of here."

"You mean we're trapped." Kolinsky's face went paler.

"Styne and Evans explored lots of the tunnels and they couldn't find a way out. All of them seem to just lead to dead ends, back to the pit we fell down or back to this point."

"So there must be something here, perhaps a door or something." Burnett reasoned.

"Or perhaps, we're meant to die in here, trapped." Lester interposed.

"No, there has to be a way out." Kolinsky looked more hopeful. "That thing would have to be able to get out of here, back to the base or whatever. There must be a way out."

"What thing?" Henderson asked. Kolinsky stopped and then realised he didn't care what they thought, he just wanted to get out of here."

"I saw a shadow moving on the tunnel wall, when the three of us were on that floor that gave way. I couldn't tell what it was but I know it wasn't any of our shadows."

"Wait a minute." Burnett said, pausing from her examinations of the rock walls of the cave.

"What?" Josh asked.

"Look the rocks are different on this wall, it's much smoother. Someone must have put a wall in here, whereas the rest of the rock was originally here and they just cut out the cave from it. There must be a way through it."

"There is." Lester said, firing his gun at it.

"Are you crazy?" Henderson shouted, as the rock fell away, crumbling into dust, which dispersed to reveal a large cave beyond, filled with what looked like machinery.

"I cleared a path."

"And if there is anything down here they would have heard that a mile off."

They entered the room, staring round it in amazement. They'd never seen any human machines like these. They were made from the same blue metallic material used on the door, combined with other materials they had never seen before. They looked like boxes seated on the floor, with pipes connecting them. More pipes ran from the machines and disappeared into the walls. Steam rose up from the floor in places.

"What are they?" Ricks asked. Jenkins stood gazing at the steam for a moment before replying.

"Look steam vents. I bet they're using geothermal energy here and a lot of it to. This is how we generated our energy at the shelter but the machinery we used was nothing like this."

"Christ. I think it's safe to assume we might come across an alien base through there." Evans pointed to a single tunnel leading from the room. The walls in the tunnel were still made of rock but now they were smooth, having been cut more carefully. A sign they were nearing the base, perhaps.

"Styne. Check it out." Henderson ordered. Styne crept forward and disappeared from sight into the tunnel.

The rest of the group waited. Ten minutes passed and still nothing.

"What's he up to." Henderson said impatiently. Air suddenly jetted out of a vent somewhere with violent force, making them jump.

"It's just the machines." Jenkins remarked as the radio burst to life.

"My God!" Came Styne's breathless voice. Henderson felt scared, nothing had ever phased Styne before.

"Is it safe?"

"I think so, it's hard to tell."

"What is it?"

"I don't know how to explain …" Styne began.

"Let's get down there." Henderson said to the group, as he led the way.

The tunnel turned and twisted, continuing on for some time before at last turning back on itself again and then they were there confronted by it, all of them speechless as they stood next to Styne.

## Chapter 11

Meriel Ellis was still looking round at the machinery in awe, as the group moved off down the tunnel. She couldn't believe how the technology used by the aliens could all at once be so advanced yet based on the same principles as their own. But then again, thermal power was the logical choice, since it was free.

The voices of the rest of the team became unclear as they receded down the tunnel and only her single light was left to illuminate the large cave. She suddenly felt scared and made a move to follow when she heard a low grating sound. She turned back to the room, her eye catching sight of something glinting in the corner next to the tunnel. It wasn't the same as the rest of the blue metallic material; it was different. Hesitantly Ellis walked forward, her curiosity aroused. Strange. She bent down to take a closer look. A square block of silver material, jutting slightly out of the ground. Slowly she reached out, gently tracing over its smooth surface with her fingers, captivated by the rainbow of light reflecting off its surface.

One of the machines behind her let out a sudden hiss of air, making her jump and she felt her hand slam down onto the object. It sunk into the ground, a previously hidden door swinging open, allowing passage into the dark tunnel beyond.

Ellis pulled her hand back in shock, the object remaining buried in the ground and the door still wide open. She had stumbled upon a concealed door. As she stared into the blackness, she suddenly felt a chill come over her, as though the air had turned cold. She looked round wanting to tell the others but they had all gone after Styne. She was completely alone, even the voices of the group had left her.

The air was turning colder. Suddenly she felt a strong breeze and then something grabbed her round her neck, squeezing tightly. It had come from the newly discovered tunnel. She tried to scream but no sound escaped her lips. A warm liquid was running down her neck and Ellis instinctively new it was blood, her blood. She tried to look down but failed. Something was pulling her back into the tunnel, with overwhelming strength. She was like a rag doll in its clutches. Before she could do anything darkness had engulfed her.

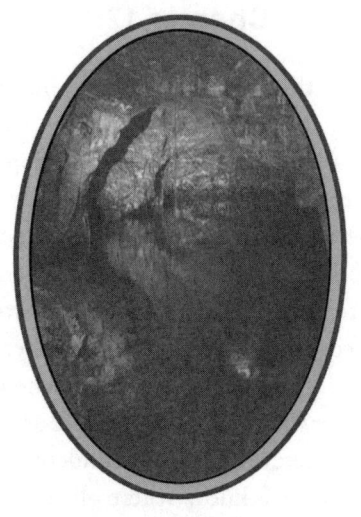

# Part Two

Discoveries Within

## Chapter 12

They were in the entrance to an enormous cave, dwarfing the cavern their shelter was in, by comparison. What was even more amazing was that it contained a tropical forest, of strange and exotic plants. Different species of trees, ferns and Cycads were the main population, a sea of greenery where even the walls next to them had creeping plants of some description, covering them. The overall effect was to give them the feeling that they were in the middle of a rainforest rather than underground. But what was a jungle doing underground, Josh wondered.

"Well I guess we know where all that energy goes to." Jenkins said after a while, looking upwards. Powerful lights were all over the roof, which was so big they couldn't even see the far sides of it. "They needed a lot more than our small community."

"What is this place?" Burnett whispered.

"What do you reckon that is?" Martinez had moved off left towards a circular object in the wall, not far from them. As he drew close to it, he found it was a circular tunnel, slanting steeply upwards. The walls were the same grey of the original tunnel they had first entered. "Hey do you think this is where we would have come out. I mean it looks like the other end of that tunnel."

"Has to be." Ricks was at his side as she spoke.

"I don't think we'd better take any chances. Kieron Attwell and Fredrick O'Callaghan, you two stay here and guard the tunnel. Any sign of trouble, you tell base to shut the door, whatever the consequences." Henderson said, feeling confident he could rely on O'Callaghan and Attwell. "Forbes, you're the biologist aren't you?" He didn't give Josh time to reply "What do you make of this? All these plants!"

"Well obviously plants don't grow underground. They were put here." Josh paused thinking hard, as he heard a sharp intake of breath from someone who had apparently failed to notice the obvious. He looked round again, suddenly seeing the plants in a whole new light. Sparsely dotted in amidst the green foliage was the very occasional brightly coloured flower, looking somewhat out of place. "But what's even more fascinating is that virtually all these plants are Gymnosperms!"

"What?" Henderson asked.

"Gymnosperms. They're seed plants, not flowering. Look. There's a whole range of plants from the cycad family. This is unbelievable it's just like going back in time to the early Cretaceous period."

"What do you mean?" Burnett interrupted.

"I mean Gymnosperms dominated all through Jurassic and early Cretaceous period, although by then

Angiosperms, that is flowering plants had started to appear."

"Cretaceous Period?"

"It was a period in our history from about 144 - 65 Million years ago. If I didn't know better I would say that this forest is exactly what it would have looked like, except there would have been animals."

"You're right." Burnett said. "There are no animals. It's really quiet. I'm not sure anything lives down here."

"You're wrong about that." Ricks screeched slapping at some flying insect that was trying to gain a purchase on her neck. "These insects have got some bite to them." She briefly stared at the remnants of its mangled remains on her hand before brushing it off. "Wasps or something."

"With all these Cycads it's no wonder there would be insects about." Josh commented staring at the palm like plants in awe. They looked questioningly at him. "They don't have flowers but cones which are pollinated by insects." He explained.

"The question is what eats the insects?" Evans jokingly asked.

"Maybe nothing since if there is a limited area and therefore limited food source they will automatically be restricted to a certain number."

"We better try and find out for sure." Henderson said, repositioning his backpack to a more comfortable position. "We'll start by heading down one of those paths, that thick foliage should keep us hidden." He pointed to several paths, winding their way into the depths of the forest. "Keep your eyes open you two."

"Yes sir," O'Callaghan answered as Attwell nodded.

The rest of the group followed Henderson down the crude track trying to walk silently on the noisy undergrowth. Soon they were in the heart of the forest. The thick canopy above blocked out a large amount of light, making the plants about them look gloomy and sinister. Without Henderson asking a hush had fallen over the group. The path had all but disappeared and they now had to fight their way through the giant ferns and other shrubs. It was hard going.

They had come a long way but now exhaustion was beginning to overcome them and some had dropped back, straggling some distance behind. Henderson knew he would have to let them rest soon.

The only sound, of the leaves being pushed aside, was slowly replaced by a low murmuring. The sound grew louder and louder, turning into a roar. The forest suddenly gave way to a massive clearing, divided by a fast flowing stream, running across in front of them. Their attention was immediately drawn to the rocky wall on their right, by a thundering noise. From high up in the roof, a hole allowed water from some underground stream to enter, cascading in a mad rush, over a rocky outcrop into a pool, halfway between the ceiling and the floor. Another angry torrent of water gushed from this pond to a large, deep pool of churning water, at the base of the waterfall, from which the stream originated. As the water hit the pool, large sprays were sent up into the air, shrouding the whole wall in a fine mist, through which they could see images of greenery beyond. The whole effect was breathtaking and frighteningly awesome all at once.

They would have to rest before finding a way across this monster. That Henderson knew for sure. "You can all take a break, just keep together and close into the trees. I don't want anything that may be down here to see us. We're like sitting ducks if we're out in the open." Most of the group sighed as they threw themselves down, too tired to care about anything. After a moment low talking between the team members started.

Josh couldn't resist studying a Cycad he was sitting close to; his normally calm face lit up with interest, as he became absorbed in the task.

"So were you in research then?" Burnett asked approaching.

"Pardon", Josh started, "I mean no I was a lecturer. Kolinsky's the researcher." His attention was attracted to another fern. "How about you?"

"Computer programmer." Josh looked up for a second.

"Unusual isn't it?" Burnett nodded.

"There are more all the time but for some reason most women have never been that interested in it, so it is still one of the few professions dominated by men." Josh remained silent, too engrossed in his beloved plants. Burnett couldn't hide a laugh. "You look like a kid in a candy store." He sheepishly looked up reminded of her presence.

"Sorry, I've just never seen this many species of Cycads in one place before, not to mention the fact that most Cycads are incredibly rare these days. This is unheard of. I couldn't even begin to name all of them there's just so many." His gaze fell onto a tall plant with a slender branching trunk at the top of which sprouted simple trim fern leaves. He moved closer, his eyebrows knitting. In between the leaves were growing very delicate cones that had such a close resemblance to flowers that it was difficult to be certain which they were.

"What one is that?" Burnett asked over his shoulder.

"I'm not sure but I'm certain it doesn't look like a Cycad should." He pulled out his computer. "This should tell us." Josh said waving it in the air before pulling a leaf from the plant and placing it in a hidden compartment in the computer that functioned as a mini lab for fieldwork.

"What are you doing?" Burnett asked with interest.

"It's more the computer these days." Josh replied with a twinge of regret. "Basically it's taking a DNA sample to determine the species. Huh that's strange." Burnett craned her neck to peer at the screen over his shoulder. The words "No exact match found" flashed in large text a few times and then a cascade of text and diagrams started scrawling up the screen.

"What's it doing?" She asked bewildered by the sheer volume of information flashing past.

"It's trying to determine the closest match by running further tests on the leaf. At the moment it's using a laser to take an epidermal peel from the abaxial surface so that it can study the plants stomatal morphology." Burnett turned and looked blankly at him but before he even noticed a picture of the actual plant cells appeared on the screen as a beep went off signalling the program had finished. He hastily brought up the results, eager to prove his suspicions.

"85% probability plant cells are from a Williamsonia Sewardiana. There are no cells on record to compare against." Josh gasped and drew back.

"What's wrong?" Burnett asked concerned.

"These results can't be right." Josh answered recovering and restarting the program with a new leaf. "I didn't really believe it would actually confirm my theory that it wasn't a Cycad."

"I don't understand."

"According to this the plant is a Bennettitales which first appeared in the Triassick period but then became extinct towards the end of the Cretaceous period. So you see the results must be wrong otherwise how else do you explain its presence here." The same information flashed up the screen.

"It has to be broken." Josh said, giving the computer a tap, "or else somehow a previously thought extinct plant has managed to survive underground behind a door of mysterious origin." He had waited all his life to make a discovery of this enormity but he didn't feel like he had thought he would. There was no happy excitement but instead just a cold chill that pulsed through his body. A long drawn out silence followed at last broken by Burnett.

"It looks so similar to all the other plants you said were Cycads though, apart from the flower-like cones."

"That is the main difference. The trouble is palaeontologists only have or rather had fossils to examine of the Bennettitales, so nothing is absolutely certain about them and that is why the computer didn't have plant cells on record to compare against." The silence resumed as they tried to digest the information and harder still fit it into context.

"I suppose finding an extinct plant is no stranger than finding a cave full of plants." Burnett reflected.

"It is an amazing discovery." Josh answered, still in awe.

"We were so convinced it was the aliens down here but how could it be. I mean why would they have a prehistoric jungle deep underground containing plants that died out millions of years ago."

"I hadn't even begun to consider that aspect of all this." Josh admitted. "It's just a miracle that they are here." Burnett shook her head.

"This whole place is weird. Nothing makes sense down here."

"Don't worry. There's always an explanation for everything. Maybe we'll find things aren't as bad as we thought they were. I mean there's no sign of aliens yet."

"Except the one Kolinsky saw."

"If he saw one."

"Well I feel like there's something watching us, however crazy that sounds." Burnett glanced round at the forest but all was still."

"It's not crazy. It's just this place is a little spooky. That's all." Josh looked back down to the plant, examining it further. "Finding this species is an amazing discovery but also a chilling one." Burnett was still looking at the forest, feeling sure something was staring at them out of the gloom. The discovery of the plant only heightened her fears. Something was seriously wrong with this place.

Martinez suddenly looked startled. He moved quickly over to Henderson "Sir." He whispered. Henderson was sorting out some stuff in his backpack.

"Yes?" He half turned.

"It's Meriel Ellis."

"Well?"

"She's missing, I was talking to her earlier but I haven't seen her since we entered the forest."

"Are you sure?" Henderson's full attention was turned on him now.

"Yes. She's gone!"

"Great" Henderson mumbled "what else could possibly go wrong?"

## Chapter 13

O'callaghan sullenly watched the group disappear from sight before throwing down his pack and joining Atwell who had already settled himself on a large chunk of rock jutting up from the ground. His strange surroundings were much quieter now and O'Callaghan began to wish he had gone with the others, whatever the danger, rather than being stuck alone with a man who rarely strung more than three words together. He watched as Atwell silently removed a squashed pack of gum from one of the several pockets in his trousers.

"Want some?" Atwell held it out to him. O'Callaghan declined, feeling his stomach grumble in protest. He rummaged through his own pack, searching for his only fresh food before he would have to endure perhaps weeks of the dried, hard survival rations. O'Callaghan pulled a face at the thought. It wasn't so much that the rations tasted bad but more the fact that you needed a set of iron jaws to munch your way through them and they also looked far from edible. He brushed past packs of the things, making a grab for the small plastic box containing sandwiches. His stomach rumbled in anticipation. The lid was stiff and he had to give it a hard yank. He was unprepared when it suddenly opened and the contents were thrown out onto the matted undergrowth covering the floor.

"Oh great." O'Callaghan muttered mildly frustrated as he noticed Atwell pause chewing to smile and give a dry chuckle. As he bent to retrieve the scattered contents he caught a whiff of a strong sweet smell, its fragrance captivating and he eagerly searched round for the source.

"You're not going to eat that are you?" Atwell asked, nodding to the forgotten sandwich O'Callaghan held.

"Can't you smell it?" O'Callaghan returned moving away slightly to nearer the edge of the forest where the peculiar smell continuously lingered in the air. Atwell frowned, wrinkling up his nose as he inhaled deeply

"What is it?" Atwell asked joining his companion who was staring at clumps of cylindrical red fruit tucked up under long green leaves on one of the plants. The smooth slightly dimpled exterior looked highly edible and tempting. O'Callaghan broke one from the bunch and snapped it in half to reveal a mass of pink flesh oozing juice. The smell had grown even stronger and was almost intoxicating in its intensity.

"It has to be these causing that smell." O'Callaghan commented. Atwell reached up to take one, pausing as a flying insect of some description buzzed lazily past him before diving onto the red fruit.

"Now that has to be alien." He said drawing

O'Callaghan's attention to the insect. Its red stick like body was flecked with oranges and blacks and its long barbed tail stuck up at an odd angle that curved back over the top of it.

"I wouldn't bet on it. Some of the insects on the surface had been getting pretty weird over the last few years. The environmentalists kept saying it was due to all of us poisoning the Earth."

"They couldn't have been this weird surely. It's like everything has gone crazy since those aliens arrived." O'Callaghan shrugged, staring at his companion for a moment. These were obviously exceptional circumstances for Atwell to have said so much. O'Callaghan returned his attention to the enticing fruit feeling unable to resist its lures and especially the sweet aroma, any longer.

"What are you doing?" Atwell snapped grabbing O'Callaghan's arm before he could take a bite. "For all we know those things are poisonous."

"I suppose." He reluctantly admitted still staring intently at the fruit he held as the insect landed on it.

"I know you'll eat anything but that is going to extremes." Atwell grinned, his eyes motioning to his companion's large frame. O'Callaghan was about to make some derogatory reply when he noticed Attwell's face seemed to go hazy, in fact all his vision seemed to become blurred, like he was looking through a heat haze. There was also a sudden chill in the air and he shivered involuntarily.

"Do you feel that?" he asked. Attwell looked

disorientated and it was obvious from the expression on his face he felt the abrupt change in temperature.

"What is it?"

"I don't know." Attwell reached for his pack of equipment but his hand missed, despite his blurred vision telling him it was in contact. He groped about, his hand apparently moving away from his pack yet he now felt it make contact with it. It was like the displacement effect water created, where the object appeared in a different position to where it actually was. But that didn't make sense, how could that be created since they weren't looking into water? Unless somehow the air about them had been changed. Attwell discarded that thought straight away as madness, as he felt for the hand held computer and pulled it free from his bag. Still their vision was impaired as he tried to get readings about the atmosphere, the numbers appearing on the screen almost impossible to read. It seemed that the numbers recording the density, and volumes of different gases in the atmosphere were fluctuating wildly or maybe somehow the sensors weren't recording properly.

"We ought to get out of here." O'Callaghan was sounding stressed now.

"Just hold on, I've got to radio the others before we do anything"

"Did you see that?"

"What?"

"Something moving there, in the foliage." The forest about them seemed as deserted as ever to Attwell.

"You're seeing things." He pulled the radio out. There had to be some reasonable explanation as to what was happening.

"Henderson come in." There was no response. The light on the radio was out, indicating that it wasn't working. He shook it violently cursing at it before giving up and throwing it to the ground. "Where's your radio?"

"Here." Attwell took the radio and checked the light was on, thankful that it was.

"Henderson come in" only static replied.

"God whatever it is, is affecting the radio transmissions." O'Callaghan breathed.

"You might be right, stay here while I try and find somewhere it will work."

"Are you mad, going in there." Attwell ignored him as he strode of, tripping over a root that looked miles away. He shut his eyes and tried to feel his way towards the trees, away from all the insane things happening about him. Static was still blaring out of the radio. When he opened his eyes the heat haze effect was still there and now worse still, a strange gentle whirring noise had begun. It grew louder and he felt a strange pressure in his ears as though he were changing altitude quickly. The noise stopped, as did the static on the radio.

"Henderson come in." Still no response. He had stumbled further into the forest and all seemed darker about him, his vision nothing more than a blur of shadows, one moving at speed before him and then disappearing from sight. "Is that you O'Callaghan? Where are you?" Silence. "O'Callaghan." He heard a scream. It seemed distant but at the same time he felt sure it came from the entrance to the tunnel, from where he had left O'Callaghan.

## Chapter 14

"We'll have to split into groups to find her and head back in the vague direction of the tunnel." Henderson said. "She must have wandered off the path. When and if you do see any signs of aliens, remember the main priority is staying hidden and radioing to the rest of us." He paused. "I want three groups. Everyone sorted?" Josh looked round to see Burnett and Kolinsky standing next to him. Two other groups had formed, the first made up of Henderson, Evans and Jenkins while Martinez, Ricks, Lester and Styne made up the other group."

"All right spread out and be careful. We'll meet back here in half an hour."

The other two groups headed off, one down the path, while the other group disappeared into the forest on the left of it, finding it impossible to see anything through the foliage. It seemed unlikely they would find her with such a large area to cover.

"I guess that leaves us with the forest on the right of the path." Kolinsky said, after the other groups had gone.

"Looks like it." Josh returned. Kolinsky barged

into the matted foliage, slowing down when he realised they were dropping back slightly. He didn't want to get too far ahead, just in case there was something out there.

"All she had to do was follow the rest of us. I don't know how she managed to get herself lost. Now she's causing all this trouble." Kolinsky muttered back to them.

"What? You mean it's very inconvenient for you." Burnett said.

"She could be in any kind of danger." Maybe he did care after all, Burnett wondered but that idea was soon ruined. "Besides which now we have to walk back through this wretched jungle and I didn't even want to come down here in the first place."

"I'd hardly call this forest wretched." Josh said offended "It's full of fascinating plants. I mean look at the trees. They're magnificent specimens."

"So what? They're trees."

"That one there has a trunk on it that's nearly 3 meters in diameter."

"Is that normal?" Burnett asked interested.

"Well it's not unheard of for Beech's to get that big."

"I guess it's really old."

"Yes, probably been around for about 250 - 300 years.

"Really? That long?"

"Who cares how old some stupid tree is." Kolinsky interrupted.

"Don't you see?" Burnett turned her large eyes on him questioningly. "If the trees have been around for that long then it could be that this whole place has been here all that time as well."

"It couldn't have been. We would have found it before now."

"Maybe." Josh said. "But it was only luck we stumbled on that door when we did. I mean think how vast an area there is underground. It was amazing that we found this place."

"The more we find out about this cave, the stranger it all gets." Burnett said thoughtfully.

"What I can't get my head around is the plants down here." Josh shook his head. "Do you realise on the surface forests are becoming so scarce there are protection orders on most of them and it's getting more and more difficult to find large trees that are the size of some of these specimens down here. What's more, when I wanted to do fieldwork in the Amazon the amount of red tape I had to go through was horrendous."

"Red tape!" Kolinsky questioned, half interested.

"Just like the poachers wiped out the elephants almost, there's people trying to illegally cut down the rarer species of trees. They will go to any lengths and so the government introduced a screening process for anyone wanting to enter a protected area. It doesn't stop many of them though, which is why the jungles are patrolled night and day by park rangers, carrying guns. If you didn't have a legitimate pass they were more likely to shoot first and ask questions later."

"Sounds dangerous." Burnett said concerned. Josh shrugged.

"It was worth it, although having seen this place I think I would have chosen to come down here instead."

"You're even crazier than I thought." Kolinsky muttered, stopping abruptly. "Hey what's that?" They looked where Kolinsky was pointing. Thick roots from the trees were sticking up through the ground in a matted mess, across the path. Rock formed the floor on the other side, on which a small black box was lying.

"A computer!" Kolinsky said as he approached it. "Ellis must be close by." He started looking round for other signs. "What's that smell?" Josh caught a whiff of the very faint odour.

"This isn't right." Josh had picked up the computer and was examining it. "It's not one of ours it's the wrong make and model, none of us were carrying one like this were we?" He held it over to show Burnett.

"No, this one is really high spec compared with ours, though it looks like it's taken a beating. Someone must have dropped it or something to cause all that damage to the casing."

"It has to be hers. Where else would it have come from? It's human technology, isn't it?" Kolinsky said, pausing his search for a second. "That smells getting stronger."

"I wonder if it still works. Maybe we could find out how it got here." Josh said taking back the computer.

"There must be other people down here!" Burnett was peering over Josh's shoulder at the new discovery. "The big question is what happened to them."

"What were they doing and how did they get down here." Josh added.

"Ellis has to be around here." Kolinsky was still pushing through various bushes, searching for her. "Once we find her ..." He stopped short. "I recognise that smell ..." He parted another bush and peered beyond. "Oh my god!" Burnett and Josh followed his gaze.

"Everything's getting worse by the second." Burnett's voice trailed off.

"Henderson. I think you'd better take a look at this." Josh said into the radio.

## Chapter 15

The ground in front of the tunnel entrance was empty when Atwell returned. There was no sign of O'Callaghan except for the flattened undergrowth where he had left him and some kind of congealed dark liquid, oozing over it before coming to rest in a small pool. More droplets of this strange distorted looking liquid lay scattered around, with a faint trail leading into the tunnel and more into the jungle. Both backpacks lay ripped open, their contents scattered across the floor as though some kind of a struggle had taken place. He moved closer to examine the liquid the haziness still making identifying it difficult and now that strange whirring noise had started again, making him feel dizzy. With sudden horror he drew back away from the red substance not wanting to believe it but knowing with certainty it was blood.

Panic overtook him at being alone, with no way to communicate to the others. He wanted to turn and run after the others but he couldn't leave without first finding out what happened to O'Callaghan. After all maybe he was in need of help. He was torn as to what to do when, without warning clarity returned to his vision, the noise stopped and he was left wondering if it had all been in his imagination now everything was back to normal. The blood was still there though and he could see it much clearer than before. Tentatively he moved to the tunnel entrance, able to see droplets receding into the distance, despite the dimness of it compared to the main cavern. The tunnel was empty and the forest about him was as still as ever.

There was a sound behind him, the rustling of leaves. He forced himself to turn round. A branch was gently shaking before coming to rest but otherwise there was no sign of anything else.

"O'Callaghan is that you?" he half whispered and half shouted, not sure why he had any hope it was, after all that blood. He heard a word spoken, strangely distorted and difficult to understand, something between "yeah" and "help".

"What's wrong? Where are you?" Attwell rushed forward and pulled the branches aside, nothing was immediately obvious. A path twisted further into the forest, down which a figure lay crumpled up against the trunk of a tree. The canopy blocked out a lot of the light, creating a gloom that his eyes took a while to adjust to. He was sure it was O'Callaghan propped up against the tree, yet somehow the shape didn't look right. As he walked closer he noticed what seemed like great gaping cuts all over "O'Callaghan, from which blood was oozing. His clothes had been ripped to shreds, while his limbs seemed to lie at insane angles.

"O'Callaghan?" There was no response but then how could there have been with those injuries. "What happened here?" Attwell mumbled more to himself, moving closer to the body, wanting to make sure it really was in the state it appeared to be in.

Bright, stunning white light engulfed his vision, blinding him painfully. There was no sound and no movement of air, yet it had turned cold once more.

"O'Callaghan. For god sake talk to me." Attwell was surprised to hear his own voice sounding shaky and he trembled involuntarily from the coldness and fear. Something was happening to the air, as though it were thinning and breathing became more difficult. He felt a movement dangerously close to him and he froze. His stomach churned, as he felt for his gun, wishing he could see whatever it was. His vision had improved slightly and squinting he could now make out a bright light emerging upwards out of the dark undergrowth to his left. He couldn't believe it but the body had gone.

Without warning the trees parted and something came rushing out towards him, followed by another of the same dark blurred shapes. There was a staggering pain that ripped through his chest, making him gasp and stumble bewildered by it all. More dark shapes grabbed at him, followed by unbelievable pain that seemed to be screaming at him from all over his body. He let out a small wail of hopelessness as he was dragged into the forest, unable to do anything.

## Chapter 16

"What is it that's so important?" Henderson asked as he approached Josh and the other two. They had moved away from the new find, but the smell was just as strong and disgusting as ever.

"It's through here." Kolinsky moved forward to show the way, less affected by it than the others.

"What is?" Kolinsky pushed the branches out of the way to reveal a large ragged hole, perhaps five feet deep, at the bottom of which lay a body. Decay had already set in and now the flesh hung loosely, making the face unrecognisable. Surrounding it was a matted tangle of roots.

"It's not possible for it to be Ellis surely."

"No. It's a man. There's part of a military uniform on the remains, though most of the clothing has been burned." Josh said as he and Burnett joined them. "An army team must have been sent down here at some point, maybe there are even some of them still down here."

"What killed him?" Henderson looked across at Kolinsky, wrinkling up his nose at the smell.

"I'd have to do an autopsy to ascertain that but we lost most of the medical equipment so I'd only be able to do a preliminary autopsy."

"You must have some idea." Henderson pressed. Kolinsky sighed and approached the remains. He peered down into the hole, noting how the bones seemed to lie at peculiar angles. Under closer scrutiny he became aware that the dried flesh had been severed in places and in actual fact the body lay in pieces positioned tightly together.

"I need to get closer." Kolinsky said looking warily at the loose soil round the edges. Josh lowered himself into the hole, testing the firmness of the ground as he went.

"It's definitely in pieces so it would be easier if you come down here rather than me trying to pass it all up." Kolinsky frowned, gingerly sitting down on the edge. He tried to let himself down gently but his hand slipped and he fell, sliding down into the corpse and dislodging a leg bone from its resting position. He quickly pulled himself up, embarrassed as he focussed his attention on the calf bone.

"Where it's cut there appears to be lacerations or rather burns to the end of the bone. I've only ever seen similar damage to this once before. It was caused by lasers. I need to have a proper look at it before I can tell you more though."

Kolinsky grabbed hold of a clump of plant roots protruding from the wall of the hole and hoisted himself up onto the earth above with a lot more grace than he had employed in his trip down. Josh followed.

"I don't see what made the laser cuts?" he stared back down at the remains.

"Maybe we should do a study of this area while we're at it and try to piece together what happened here." Henderson mumbled to himself before pulling out his radio.

"All parties. Any sign of Ellis?" He scowled at the negative replies. "O'Callaghan, Attwell have you seen Ellis?" This time there was no reply. He tried again. Still no answer. "This isn't good" he mumbled as he tried yet again. "I don't believe this. Now we've lost them." He spoke back into the radio. "I want everyone to meet at my location now."

Soon people were emerging out of the forest, complaining of the smell as they drew nearer, unaware of the body concealed behind the trees. Everyone was there except for Ellis, O'Callaghan and Attwell. Three people that had seemingly vanished into thin air.

"Listen up." Henderson said loudly, trying to get their attention from the smell. "I have no option but to tell base to shut the door.

"You can't do that." Lester blurted out. "There's no reason."

"None at all, except that three people have disappeared."

"Just give them a chance to respond."

"I have." Henderson's face looked grim. "I can't wait any longer. The base could be in serious danger and it's not worth jeopardising all those lives." He once again lifted the radio. "Base. It's explorer party."

"Base here"

"Thank goodness for that." Josh heard someone say as Henderson continued.

"We can't get in contact with the two guards we left at this end of the tunnel and we've lost Meriel Ellis. I have to advise you to shut that door straight away."

"You do realise that once the door is closed you may not be able to get in contact with us. It might block the radio transmissions. You'll be trapped in there."

"We know. Just get that door shut now. We can't risk all those people back at base."

"No don't shut it." Lester shouted out, trying to grab the radio and then pulling at his own radio.

"Shut him up." Styne grabbed him.

"We're closing it now. Good luck."

"Are you still there base?"

"They're clo …"

"Base?" No reply.

"Now we're trapped. You shouldn't have done that."

"Shut up Lester. We had no choice." Styne snapped. "Besides which most of that tunnel had already collapsed and we probably couldn't have got back if we tried."

"Everyone just settle down." Henderson's voice was confident despite all that was happening. "We'll find another way out. Right now I think we should set up a camp in the clearing I saw just through there. That way we'll have some time to examine our find."

"What find?" Martinez asked coolly. Henderson hesitated, trying to decide whether to tell them all.

"I think it's only fair that you should all know we've found a body, just the other side of these trees."

"Ellis?" Martinez pushed aside the foliage before they could stop him, immediately turning away at the sight.

"It's not Ellis. It's a man's body." Burnett said, gently pulling him back.

"So it's O'Callaghan or Attwell."

"It was difficult to tell what it was, it was so mangled." Kolinsky said. Burnett glared at him as Josh intervened. "The body was entangled in the roots of a plant in a ditch. It appears to have laser cuts in places."

"Cut through the body, like a knife through hot butter." Kolinsky glanced at Burnett, expecting a rebuff.

"The bodies dressed in military clothing, so it can't be them." Henderson sighed deeply. "We'll find out more about it soon. That's why we need to set up the camp near here so Dr Kolinsky can examine the remains. The sooner the camp is set up the sooner we'll know more." Henderson paused. "I also want Martinez, Ricks and Lester to go back to the door to look for O'Callaghan and Attwell."

"I'm not going back there." Lester started, feeling safety in numbers.

"I'm not asking you to."

"Well that's ok then." Lester cut him short.

"I'm telling you to."

"But ..." Lester stopped, feeling weak under Henderson's unwavering stern gaze.

"Fine." Lester glared at the other two. "Well let's get going then."

"Can we have a word?" The rest of the team had already started carrying out their tasks, as Josh spoke to Henderson.

"What's up?"

"As well as the body we also found this." Josh produced the damaged computer. "It's not one of ours and so we reckon it must have belonged to that man."

"If we could access the files on it, they could explain what that man was doing down here." Burnett added excitedly. "I think that I could get some of the information off it but the trouble is that all the files are encrypted and some of the data may have been lost all together due to the damage it's suffered."

"What so this actually works! In this state!" Henderson took the computer from Josh and turned it over in his hands. "Well try and work quickly we need to get that information as soon as possible." He handed the computer to Burnett. "Forbes. You'd better help Dr Kolinsky with the autopsy." He turned to watch members of the group setting up hi tech equipment round the perimeter of the camp. "The more we know about this place, the more chance we have of dealing with whatever might lay out there in wait."

## Chapter 17

"It's knocking off time." Woodridge motioned to the two guards approaching to relieve them from duty. "How about a pint?"

"Can't tonight." Moore answered.

"Oh I forgot the big date."

"Yep, taking her to the swankiest place in town."

"You mean the only place." Moore half laughed as they said goodnight to their replacements. The lights in the tunnel had dimmed in an attempt to simulate night time but the result was more of a blue tinged, eerie light that made everything take on a ghastly appearance. The technicians were meant to be fixing it soon but it was just another thing on already too long a list.

"It might be the only restaurant but you have to admit the food isn't too bad and they do have a wide selection." Moore said as they made their way back towards the main settlement.

"You obviously never tried any decent places before. You ought to get out more."

"Kind of difficult at the moment."

"Yeah, maybe someday soon." Both men fell into a sombre silence, until they reached the main cavern.

"See you same time tomorrow Pete."

"Sure thing, have fun." They parted ways, Moore heading towards the stream and the fields in the centre, his home being situated on the far side past them. The rock beneath his feet had been smoothed and cut in places to form crude pathways, emulating the paved sidewalks that had once been prevalent in the now destroyed cities. The polished, metallic exteriors of all the accommodation reflected menacing distortions of his surroundings, while the buildings themselves threw out dark shadows. He could hear muffled laughter and shouts from the only bar and restaurant, as always packed with people. The fields were deserted, a rogue piece of equipment lay at the edge of the tall wheat, bearing testament to the trouble someone would be in for not putting it away. As he moved away from the restaurant, and the heart of their settlement, the streets became deserted once again and silence returned.

The wide metal bridge lay ahead of him, giving access over the stream. He stopped. There was a strange series of clicks like metal hitting stone coming from behind him, or at least he had thought so but now there was only silence. Moore rubbed his ears, sure he was hearing things but it did no good, there was definitely a whistling sound that had started. It was growing louder and changing tone as though some tune was the intended purpose but it was a long way out of key.

"Who's there?" he peered round the nearest building. Nothing. A large shadow fell across him, he turned tracing the shrinking darkness to a point where the form of a human stood.

"Jesus Quigly, you scared me." Moore let out a sigh of relief. "Making all those noises, what were you trying to do?"

"I was whistling" Quigly retaliated with mock offence.

"And the clicking noises."

"Wasn't me."

"Pull the other one."

"Honest."

"Must have been some other prankster."

"Or maybe you were hearing things." The clicking came again, only louder.

"Tell me you heard that please." Moore looked round for the culprit.

"It's just a noise. What's got you so jumpy." Quigly pulled out some chewing gum.

"Something is not right here. I just know it."

"Yeah I should be in my apartment on the surface watching the game."

"Is that all you think about." Quigly grinned, drawn back out of his pleasant thoughts.

"Pretty much. I don't get hot dates like some people."

"Does everyone know about that?" Moore asked taken aback.

"Should do by now." Quigly laughed. "Woodridge has got some mouth on him."

"Nothing seems to stay private for long down here."

"Well there's not much that happens so we have to make the most of what we can." Quigly laughed harder, slapping him on the back before turning to leave.

"Wait." Moore suddenly shouted. "There's something round the corner of that building."

"You'd better not be having me on." Moore had already moved down the street to where the movement had been, he heard Quigly clumsily follow. Gingerly he peered round, drawing back suddenly at the sight.

"What is it?" Quigly was finally becoming concerned. "Rats?"

"You don't want to know." The clicking sound came again and Moore looked back just in time to see it scuttling away at speed.

"We've got to stop it." Quigly said, joining him. He drew his stun gun and fired. Blue electrical energy flashed out. There was little more than a pop followed by a sizzling of electric and small wisps of smoke.

"Whatever it is I think you got it." Moore said approaching it.

## Chapter 18

"How come I'm the one that has to go back through this jungle?" Lester complained, fighting with a branch that entangled his arm. The forest seemed even more overgrown than before.

"We're here as well, aren't we? And we've got you to contend with as well as the forest." Martinez said dryly.

"I didn't ask for your company either." Lester returned.

"Oh stop it you two." Ricks sighed. "Look we're nearly there." They pushed through the last barrier of trees to arrive at the tunnel entrance. "Where are they?"

At first the clearing appeared empty but then they saw the torn knapsacks and the scattered contents, surrounded in some dark red liquid that covered the ground. There was a sharp intake of breath as Ricks drew back in alarm, realising what the liquid was. Blood. "What happened here?" she whispered as they all moved in closer, Lester and Martinez shocked into silence. "There's so much blood."

"It can't be. This can't be happening" Lester added.

"What's that?" Ricks gaze moved to a strange lump at the edge of the pool, from which trails of blood led of in different directions, the main bulk leading into the forest. Martinez picked up a stick and prodded it, surprised to find it soft. Carefully he manoeuvred the stick so as to turn the thing over.

"I know what I think it is but it can't be." He shook his head and then pulled out his computer and plugged in some wires connected to a pad. "Only one way to find out." Martinez leaned forward and placed the pad on the lump, drawing back his hand quickly as he felt it give beneath the slight pressure. He flicked a switch and the screen flashed on.

"You don't really think it is?" Ricks said startled as Martinez continued tapping keys.

"We'll now in a second, I'm just taking a reading now." A blue bar slowly progressed across the screen indicating the completion of the task. Finally it made its way to the other side. The bar disappeared and large words materialised.

*Substance tested is human matter.*
*DNA has been tested and identified as Fredrick O'Callaghan's.*
*More information is available on Fredrick O'Callaghan.*

Silently Martinez held the screen across for Lester and Ricks to look at. "I don't even want to think about what it actually is, mangled skin or flesh or …"

Martinez's voice faltered at the thought of what lay before them.

"With all this blood and now this, O'Callaghan must be dead." Ricks said still shocked. "We'll have to follow that trail though just in case he is alive." Martinez had reluctantly pulled the pad off the remains. He waited, as chemicals automatically secreted from some unseen place to sterilise it, before he dropped it onto blood lying closer to the forest. He tapped the keys on the computer and the blue bar began making its way across the screen again.

"We're going to have to radio this in first." He said as he waited.

"This is crazy. We ought to just go back to the others." Lester turned away from it all, wishing they could get out of this place and back to the safety of the shelter. Martinez ignored him, his attention absorbed with the words that had flashed up on the screen.

*Substance tested is human blood.*
*Two DNA are present in sample and have been tested and identified.*
*First DNA is identified as Kieron Attwell.*
*Second DNA is identified as Fredrick O'Callaghan.*
*More information is available on both Kieron Attwell and Fredrick O'Callaghan.*

"See they're both dead." Lester said peering over Martinez's shoulder. "We should just go back to the others."

"They might be alive." Ricks said hopefully. "We need to find out what happened to them anyway." She added stubbornly.

"I agree." Martinez looked at the trail. "If you just give me a sec I'll radio this in and then we'll see where that blood leads." He quickly stuffed the computer away and grabbed the radio.

"Henderson, it's Martinez here."

"Go ahead."

"We're back at the door. We've found blood all over the floor that is from both of them. There's also a trail of blood leading off into the forest so we're going to see where that goes." There was a brief pause.

"Understood. Just be careful. Something had to have attacked them."

"We'll be ok. See you soon." Martinez smiled as he saw Ricks's worried face. "We'll be fine." He said to her as he put the radio away. "Let's go then."

"I don't like this at all."

"Lester you don't like anything. Now just get moving."

## Chapter 19

"I think we're in trouble Styne." Henderson lowered the radio, despair showing on his face and his voice unusually quiet. They were sitting apart from the others.

"If aliens are out there, they won't be able to get through our perimeter defences."

"But we can't stay here forever. We haven't got enough supplies to last for that long."

"I'm sure we'll find a way out once we know more about those finds. It will give us an advantage if we know what's going on."

"But we don't." Styne dropped his eyes to the floor, speaking very softly.

"Either we give up now or at least go down fighting."

"I'm sorry. You're right. It's just everything has gone wrong from the start."

"We're hardly under constant fire. We've been through much worse than this." Henderson looked up, reminded of Styne's false eye.

"Perhaps you have but to be honest I've never seen much action. I spent most of my military life training new recruits. The few missions I ever went on were all civilian rescue missions in peacetime."

"Henderson." Kolinsky interrupted as he and Josh approached. "I've done as extensive an autopsy as I can."

"Well?"

"There was a lot of laser cuts all over the body and they're what killed him. But despite all the damage, there was enough to work out an approximate time of death."

"And?"

"I can't be certain but judging from the amount of decay, I'd say he had been there about three months."

"So an army team was down here three months ago."

"I don't know about that. I'm just telling you what I found from the body."

"Maybe Burnett has found something out from the computer?" Josh suggested.

Burnett was sitting at one of the portable tables, with her head bent over the computer, busily typing away at it.

"How's it going?" Henderson said as the three men peered at the screen over her shoulder.

"I don't know how it happened but half this information has been destroyed and I can't get it back."

"But what about the rest of the data."

"Well it's all encrypted but I think I've managed to unscramble it. I was just about to try bringing up one of the files." Burnett hit a key and then sat back in the chair. A second passed and then writing appeared.

*2nd May*

*I have just found out details of the mission I volunteered to go on. Apparently a mining company were recently looking for new materials underground when they found a huge void. They sent some of their personnel down to it, who reported back finding a huge cave, which the company sent them to explore. Two days later they lost communication with them and no one ever came back. Before their disappearance they sent some strange reports back of aliens and monsters. The mining company decided to call in the military to investigate what had happened to their staff and so that's where we'll be going, to a huge cave beneath ground. The whole team reckon it's one big joke. After all they had to be crazy, talking about aliens and monsters. I could never believe in them until I see one with my own two eyes and that's not very likely, since there are none.*

"Can you bring up the next file."

"I'm already on it." Burnett said as she typed away at the keys.

"This is impossible to believe." Kolinsky said as a new entry flashed up on the screen.

*3rd May*
*Day 1*
*We finally entered the cave after a long ride down the access tunnel that the mining company put in. Our underground military base had adapted it so that the tunnel connects directly to the base, which isn't far from*

*here, thank god. This place is so strange, it makes me feel better knowing the base is close by. I have to admit that this place is creepy, just like the mining personnel had said but there are no signs of aliens or monsters and I know there won't be. I don't know how we are going to find those people in such a large place but I guess we just keep looking.*

"Quick bring up the next entry." Henderson snapped.

"I can't the rest of the information has been lost like I told you."

"But there must be a way you can get it."

"I don't know how to. All the data's been corrupted and I can't retrieve it."

"Who cares about the rest of the data?" Kolinsky whispered, a broad smile spreading across his face. "There's a way out."

## Chapter 20

All the lights had been turned on in one of the research labs in order to illuminate the table in the centre in a stark white. A small group of people surrounded it on all sides, staring intently at Quigly and Moore's find. The object before them was made up of a mixture of bits of metal, glowing wires and rods and various other odd components. They formed a beetle shaped item about the size of an average dog, with an oblong yet organic body to which were attached ten legs down either side.

"I'm telling you, you should have seen it move." Moore was still raving about its sudden turn of speed as it had launched itself forward, alternating its legs in sequence.

"And you say you found this where again?" Hawkins questioned Moore.

"Just past the bridge in the main cave."

"How on earth did it get there?" he absently asked no one in particular.

"What is it, some kind of robot?" Moore asked not really expecting a reply.

"That's what my guess would be, possibly alien in origin too, judging from the materials used." A lean, grey haired man by the name of Jeff Dawson answered, continuing his inspection of it. "Jenkins was the real electronics expert, whereas I've got my work cut out just trying to fix the damage you two did, let alone working out its functionality. I think you managed to completely fry parts of it with the electrical shock from that stun gun; luckily the rest of it must have some kind of shielding. I'll have to try and replace all the damaged parts with what I think are equivalent components, by testing the way the current would flow through them, although ours are rather large and crude in comparison. It's going to take some time."

"Do we really want it working is more the question." Quigly said.

"I won't connect up all the systems, just one at a time to try and establish what each one does. Surely this is an opportunistic chance to examine a possible alien robot in detail."

"Unless of course it's some kind of spy or sabotage device and then activating it could prove fatal."

"I've already isolated what I believe are the communication chips and cut the power off to them."

"But you're not certain." Quigly looked to Hawkins for a decision but he remained silent, deep in thought.

"It's a calculated risk." He at last said. "Carry on but let me know before you activate any system after you've repaired them."

"Great, I'll get back to you on that one." They were about to leave when Dawson called them back.

"One more thing." He said dabbling at the robot as he spoke. "Even in this state it seems to constantly be emitting a signal of a particular frequency. Nothing more than an unvarying beep."

"What frequency?" Moore asked.

"Have you got your computer." Moore passed it over. "Here you go." Dawson said handing it back after typing in the information.

"Thanks."

"I just realised," Quigly spoke up, "if you think about it logically then either that robot had always been in this base or it somehow managed to get in here. Well I can only think of one place that wasn't sealed up tight."

"The door we found." Hawkins said, feeling a chill creep over him.

## Chapter 21

Martinez cringed as he heard the loud crunches of the undergrowth beneath their feet. He turned back to the other two and gestured for them to be quieter. The sight of the blood trail was making him nervous, especially now, as they followed it into the darkness of the forest. It was hard to believe that so much blood could come from just two men. They had to be dead.

"Can you see anything?" Ricks whispered from behind. Martinez looked ahead to see where the trail led. Not much further on it seemed to stop dead, with no signs of Attwell or O'Callaghan. The trees and shrubs at the end of the trail had been pushed back, some branches having snapped. Martinez pushed into the space created and began examining the ground as his two companions joined him. The blood did stop here and there were no signs of any more in the surrounding area.

"Where did they go?" Martinez spun round bewildered.

"Hey. Look at this." Ricks was bent over some strange indentations all over the floor.

"Who cares? They're not here so we may as well go back to the others."

"What caused them?" Martinez said, ignoring Lester. Ricks put her hand next to one of the large shallow holes, amazed to see her hand tiny in comparison. All the indentations were some strange shape and none of them were the same. There wasn't even a clear pattern to the position of them.

"Something must have made these footprints, marks or whatever they are." Martinez stood back to get a clearer look, hoping to see a pattern. "There's a huge indentation of the earth in this whole area! Something very large must have been here and the way the earth's been furrowed over there suggests something was dragged across here."

"O'Callaghan or Attwell?" Ricks suggested tentatively.

"It was dragged into the forest." Martinez continued with his own train of thought. "Where all the trees have been broken and pushed back, creating a crude path.

"We have to follow it." Ricks said keenly.

"Now wait a minute. We can't find them so let's just head back. We've done our job and searched for them. We don't have to do this." Lester frowned as he watched them disappearing down the path, ignoring him.

"What did all this damage?" Ricks pushed another broken branch out of her way. "It must have been large, or dragging something large."

"It's the aliens." Lester said bluntly, as he reluctantly followed after them.

"Don't start on about that." Martinez warned.

"Well it wasn't my idea to go looking for them down here."

"We're not. O'Callaghan and Attwell might be down here. Don't you want to know what happened to them."

"No not at the risk of my own life."

"Now which way?" Ricks interrupted. They were confronted by very dense undergrowth, with only the vaguest of signs that several paths headed into it. "You can only just see the occasional damage to the plants. It's going to be difficult following any of the trails. I don't know how anything got through it." She suddenly jumped with fright.

"What's wrong?" Martinez followed her gaze to see what she was staring intently at.

"That fern leaf moved."

"There's nothing moving out there, it's completely still."

"I saw it move. I know I did." There was a sudden thump a short distance from them, followed by creaking as though a tree were under an enormous strain. A pounding on the earthy ground began, resonating in their ears as the air turned frighteningly cold and still.

"This place is getting creepy." Ricks whispered, jumping as the sound of twigs cracking reached them. They all stood still terrified, for the first time sure that something was out there lurking in the shadows, about to attack at any second.

## Chapter 22

They were still gathered round the computer.

"You sure you can't get any more information out of this thing?" Henderson prodded the damaged computer, the screen flashing as if in protest.

"Like I said somehow all the other information on it has been corrupted.

"We need to know more about what's going on."

"At least we know there's a way out." Styne said.

"But we don't know where it is or how to get to it." Henderson looked wildly about. "And we don't know what it is out there attacking or perhaps killing the team off one by one."

"Perhaps we should all get some rest, it has been a long day."

"I suppose you're right but we need to keep watch." An insane look past over Henderson's face. The stress of it all was getting to him Josh thought, surprised at Styne's unemotional voice. Styne seemed to get calmer and more detached from any emotion, the worse the situation got.

"It's ok. Nothing could get past the perimeter without us knowing about it. As soon as that equipment detects anything it triggers an alarm and if it is identified as a threat to us, the automatic laser defences will be turned on. Anything attacking this camp would be killed."

"Fine we'd better all get some rest. Good work." Henderson said taking a last look at the tripods set up around the edge of the camp. A computer and other equipment was seated on top of each of the stands, slowly swivelling left and right, scanning the forest the whole time.

The rest of the team had already settled down for the night, exhausted after such an eventful day. Josh looked at his watch. 0003 Hours. He checked it again, tapping it but still the same time showed. It was three o'clock in the morning and the lights were as bright as ever, giving the illusion that it was daytime. As Henderson and Styne re-joined the rest of the camp Burnett lay down the computer.

"I can't help feeling I'm missing something."

"Don't worry about it now. Once you get some rest you may find a way to retrieve some more files."

"Don't bank on it."

"How's anyone supposed to sleep with all this light?" Kolinsky complained, as the three of them headed for the centre of the camp. All the others lay in sleeping bags round a heat source set up in the middle. They couldn't risk a real fire in case the smoke gave away their presence and so instead had to settle for a small fusion generator. Above it, a pot of coffee and some ration food was suspended. Wisps of smoke wafted up off the brown slush accompanied by smells of roast chicken. The food actually didn't taste bad providing you could avoid looking at it. Josh headed over and dished up some, offering a bowl each to Burnett and Kolinsky.

"I'm not eating that rubbish." Kolinsky turned up his nose. "Have you any idea what they actually put in it." He watched as Burnett and Josh began to devour theirs. "You can't have else you wouldn't touch it with a barge pole." He poured himself a mug of coffee.

"Kolinsky, I would eat anything at this moment I'm so hungry." Burnett managed in between mouthfuls. Kolinsky grumbled something inaudible as he moved off and began unpacking a sleeping bag.

"So what do you think happened to that army team?" Burnett whispered to Josh as they watched Kolinsky struggling in his task.

"There are indications this place has something to do with the aliens but then we find a dead man from a military unit down here." Josh reasoned. "Perhaps the military built this place out of new materials and then were attacked by the aliens."

"But he died three months ago, a month before the aliens arrived at our planet." Josh shrugged.

"I can't really get my head around any of this."

"Now that's something I can agree with." Kolinsky said snuggling into his sleeping bag.

"My past life was so much simpler. I can't believe so much has changed in such a short time. I bet if you had told most people even ten months ago that aliens would arrive on Earth they would have thought you were crazy."

"I haven't actually seen one yet though." Burnett said thoughtfully.

"I don't think anyone has." Josh absently stirred at a lump in the brown sludge. "I'm sure we'll find answers to all this soon, one way or another." They ate in silence, listening to Kolinsky toss and turn, before retiring for the night.

The beeping noise was growing louder and louder, as well as becoming more high pitched. Josh woke up, trying to make sense of the sound, not sure if he was dreaming. Around him the rest of the group had also been woken by the noise that had turned into a high pitched wailing. Styne was already at one of the perimeter defences as they all gathered round to look at the screen he was watching. The equipment on top of the tripod remained facing the same direction, occasionally turning slightly as it tracked some unseen target.

"Sir there's something large moving round out there but the computer hasn't been able to identify what it is." He glanced round at Henderson, waiting to see what to do. Josh shivered feeling goose bumps appearing on his arms. He felt like he was standing in a freezer, the air had turned so cold.

"You must be able to see what it is." Henderson pushed past the others. Nothing more than a large black object was shown on the screen, constantly changing shape and moving. The background was a blue, representing the foliage. "How's this thing work. It must have gone wrong."

"It's working fine sir. There's a thermal camera, sonar and various other sensors built into the equipment. It then takes readings from all of them and combines the results to build up a detailed picture of what's really out there."

"But it's just a black blob. It must be able to get more detail than that."

"The sensors are working; it's just having difficulty picking up information from that thing. The sonar keeps hitting nothing but trees. The thermal camera is picking up the trees and everything else, but only occasional heat signatures from that thing. There are only the background smells, sounds and radiation. We're lucky to see this much of whatever it is out there. In fact I don't know how the computers are managing to pick it up at all, when you look at what each sensor is reading. It must be the movement sensor detecting it." The black shape on the screen seemed to get larger indicating it was getting closer. The foliage in front of them shook violently as something or things rattled through it, still out of sight.

"We can't take a chance. If it's not one of the team members, fire on it."

"It's definitely not a person I know that much." Styne said as he tapped some keys on the machine. Words appeared on the screen for a moment.

*Automatic laser defence system operational*

"Kolinsky start packing up the gear." Henderson ordered.

The movement of the shrubs had stopped and silence had returned but still the same chill was in the air. There was no sign of the dark image on the screen, it was as though it had vanished. Without warning the lasers began firing wildly, the red beams darting out into the forest, singing any plants in their path. The black object materialised on the screen, disappeared and was then there again. The noise of the laser defences and the movement of the thing through the trees overwhelmed their senses. All hell had broken loose.

Flashes of light were now visible above the treetops, sparking and flaring angrily. The screen went a bright white.

"The sensor readings are off the scale." Styne yelled above it all. More sparks exploded upwards, full of energy. They could feel the static in the air, as if they were in a middle of a thunder storm and lightning would strike at any minute. The static in the air was rapidly increasing as was the coldness. They unconsciously began moving back quickly into the centre of the camp. There was a sudden loud crackling followed by a deafening boom and then they realised some kind of lightning bolt had hit the tripod and defence system on top. It exploded outwards with tremendous force, as another bolt of light hit the tripod a short distance from it. The lights in the cave looked as normal and the air was as still as ever. There was no thunder storm, something was attacking them.

"We've got to get out of here now. Grab what you can." Henderson shouted, trying to make himself heard above the roaring of fresh bolts of lightning and the sparks that still crackled upwards.

"The aliens are attacking." Someone screamed, frantic with fear.

## Chapter 23

In a darkened room hidden away deep inside the underground base seven individuals were seated around a large table at the head of which was seated Hawkins. In total they made up the government, allocated for the base but with so much hostile feeling about they had chosen to keep their existence a secret or at least for the present.

A rather large stout man took a sip from his glass of water, pulling a face that suggested he was rather disappointed that the contents wasn't anything stronger. As he spoke his voice boomed across the room.

"And you want us to believe that this er …"

"Quigly" Hawkins interposed.

"Yes, this Quigly actually volunteered."

"Without hesitation."

"And he's aware of the risks."

"I did impress upon him the danger."

"And he still wants to volunteer."

"I don't think we should try and dissuade him. After all we're getting rather short handed on volunteers and I doubt whether any of the others would go if I ordered them." There was a timid knock on the door.

"Come in." Hawkins shouted. A man hesitantly appeared in the doorway.

"Jake Quigly's here to see you."

"Well show him in."

"Yes sir." The man disappeared with startling speed and a thickset man entered.

"Hello, come in." Hawkins smiled welcomingly as he stood up and ushered Quigly to a seat. The man glanced round suspiciously at all the smiling faces, yet he seemed confident verging on the point of arrogance.

"What is this?" Quigly demanded. Hawkins looked at the others for support, wary of telling him the truth.

"I couldn't solely be in charge of running this base, we needed a democracy to make sure everything is fair and so these people were selected to …"

"Be a government." Quigly cut in angrily.

"I have the final decision but they advise me."

"Yes on how to get half the population killed. No wait it was more like three quarters."

"The truth is we have no idea how many which brings me to why you're here." Quigly's frown was replaced by curiosity that he was unable to hide, as he sat silently. Hawkins sighed. "It was decided by the world government that in the event of an attack that led to the world retreating underground, one person from each shelter would go up to the surface on the seventieth day from when it began. It would be this person's task, that is to say your task, to find out what is happening in this area. We've got the necessary equipment so that you can hopefully hook up to any remaining geostationary satellites focussed on this area and download all the pictures from it and information from it. You then need to send the information direct to the main base shelter, where they have super computers that will process all the incoming data from all the people and send back a global picture of what's going on. You will then wait to receive further instructions from the government, once they've had a chance to examine the data." Hawkins paused to give him a chance to take it all in.

"Go up there!" Quigly repeated shocked, yet excited as he thought of the sky's vastness.

"The trouble is once you've received further instructions you have to come back to the shelter to give us all the information, but if the airlock computer finds that you have been contaminated with anything potentially dangerous, you will not be allowed back in. You will have to transmit the data into the airlock computer and then head back up to the surface. If you fail to do this, the airlock will automatically incinerate anything in it after 15 minutes, in other words you."

"I understand." Quigly nodded.

"Any questions." Quigly sat for a moment trying to take it all in, to forget visions of his past life that had sprung to the surface of his memory.

"Nope, can't wait." Quigly said at last.

"Well let's get you suited up then." Hawkins grinned.

Five minutes later they were standing in a tunnel, in front of a large metal door. Quigly was already suited up and loaded down with equipment and now it only remained for him to enter into the air lock. This exit had been kept a secret from the rest of the community, since it was feared that people might try to escape to the surface and end up jeopardising their own lives and all those in the shelter.

"Should I tell them about that door we found?" Quigly had been one of the security personnel that had been guarding the door up until it was shut.

"No. There's nothing we can do about it. We can't find out what's going on without opening it but that is too dangerous." Quigly nodded. "Just upload the data package on the computer, all the information to be sent is in there."

"See you later."

"You do understand the risks?" Hawkins was beginning to get concerned about his blasé attitude but he was their only option.

"Don't worry." The metal door swung open as he pushed the final key code.

"This is really serious and important what you're doing. For god's sake don't mess it up."

"I have it under control." The metal door swung shut. Quigly moved further into the large chamber, his suit squeaking with every movement. With any luck, the suit would protect him from some contaminants and then he would just be sprayed down in the airlock, with special chemicals. He pulled down the visor on his helmet, locking it tightly shut. He carried with him a tank of oxygen that would last about 30 hours. After that it was either be back at the shelter or breath the atmosphere and any poisons that may have been released into it. The second door opened and the tunnel to the surface lay stretched out before him.

Through a small glass window, set into both metal doors, Hawkins watched him disappear into the distance, hoping when he saw him next he would bring good news.

## Chapter 24

Martinez and the others had waited a few moments but nothing had happened. The air was once more its normal temperature, though they still felt cold with terror.

"What was that?" Risks finally broke the silence.

"It must be them, the aliens." Lester's voice was shaky, filled with panic.

"It could just be an artificial wind." Martinez reasoned calmly, scowling at Lester. "We won't find out standing here though."

"We can't go in there, not now." Lester drew back.

"We have to find out." Ricks agreed following Martinez down one of the trails into the more densely packed undergrowth. Lester sullenly joined them as they beat aside thick foliage in an attempt to open it up enough to squeeze through.

"You two must have a death wish or something." He at last called forward.

"I thought you liked living life on the edge from what I've heard." Martinez replied mysteriously.

"What do you mean by that?" Lester asked threateningly.

"Nothing. I wouldn't dare offend a hardened

167

criminal like yourself." He slyly winked at Ricks as he watched Lester's face redden.

"If you must know it was embezzlement."

"Really! Not murder?"

"I'm an accountant. All I did was transfer some money that didn't exactly belong to me to an account in my name."

"How much?" Ricks asked

"Just 20 or so."

"Grand!"

"No millions." Martinez paused in his task and let out a low whistle. "Unfortunately they confiscated it though."

"The whole lot?" Lester remained silent, his lips curling up at the edges slightly.

"So how come you're not in prison?"

"I am." Lester held up his wrist, with a red dot glowing under the skin. "They inserted a microcomputer." He explained. "They track my every movement to make sure I'm not breaking any of their precious rules."

"I guess they didn't allow for a situation like this."

"I certainly didn't." Lester complained, his eyes lighting up with an idea. "I tell you what, get me out of this alive and maybe we could come to some sort of an arrangement."

"The embezzled money?" Martinez questioned his face hardening as Lester shrugged. "I've been a cop for ten years and not once have I taken a bribe so I'm not about to start now." Lester's face paled dramatically and he fell silent as Ricks burst out laughing. "When we get out of this you and I are going to have a little chat with the first law enforcement agency we come across."

"You've lost it." Lester retorted. "I don't think anyone would care if I did still have stolen money."

"I don't see how you could when all the banks have been destroyed." Ricks added.

"There might be ways." Lester said, examining her face closely for signs she wanted to take up his offer.

"In case you haven't noticed money doesn't count for much these days, even waters a more valuable commodity." They fell silent, as they worked furiously away at the foliage, their efforts failing miserably and even after some time they had made little progress into the jungle.

"This is crazy. I'm heading back to the others." Lester said at last, storming off back the way they had come as fast as he could, down the narrow path they had made.

"You can't go back without finding the other two." Ricks said lamely, not really caring what he did. Her concentration was absorbed with her surroundings. Whatever was out there couldn't be as bad as all the things she was imagining.

"What do you want to do?" Martinez was still by her side. "Go looking for it or wimp out like him?" He glanced over his shoulder but Lester had already disappeared out of sight.

"Aliens or no aliens, I want to face them head on.

Get this thing over and done with." The foliage was as still as the rest of the forest.

Lester stopped, realising that the other two hadn't followed him and he was now alone. He hesitated, wanting to be with other people, especially now as the forest became more dark and eerie, but at least there were no signs of anything out there. As if in defiance, what he thought sounded like a rustle came from behind him. He spun round, his gun raised and his hand clenched on the trigger causing a laser beam to fire at the surrounding vegetation. He stopped; leaving singed and burnt plants all around him.

He swapped the mode of his gun to explosive bullets, remembering he only had a limited supply of them but sure they would have more effect on whatever was out there. "Who's out there?" Every muscle in him trembled as only silence answered him. Everything was still.

Another rustle, much louder and nearer to him now, the plants shaking as though something large was rattling its way through. Lester pulled the trigger, his hand clenching in fear. The bullets darted out into the greenery, exploding into balls of flame as they hit the shrubs. He stopped firing, not wanting to waste ammo. The noise of the gunfire resounded round the cave, deafening him, eventually fading as he stood staring at the spot, now at rest.

"What the hell do you think you're doing? If the foliage weren't so thick we'd be dead."

"Rick? Martinez? Lester said in shock. They

emerged from where he had been firing, looking angry.

"What were you shooting at?"

"I thought I heard something."

"So did everything within a 5 mile radius." Ricks joined in sarcastically

"It must have been you two."

"We only came back when we heard the firing. You probably just imagined it; after all you're crazy enough to start shooting at us.

"I ... thought ..."

"Never mind what you thought." Martinez said, grabbing Lester's gun away from him. "Anything out there will know we're here now. We need to get moving." Lester was still shaken and went with them without protest. They headed back into the matted undergrowth, to continue looking for the two missing men, though they held little hope of finding them alive.

A few hours later and after a lot of hacking at vegetation, they finally emerged into a clearing, with one of the cave walls forming one side of it. Exhausted from their efforts they sunk down on the boulders that lay strewn along the wall, sweat dripping off them as they searched through their packs for drinks.

"Where now?" Ricks asked, not really caring.

"I don't know." Martinez managed in between taking great gulps from the bottle of cool water he had found.

Burnett mumbled "I'm so tired" and she threw her

empty bottle down. They couldn't resist leaning back against the wall for a minute, too tired to hardly care whether there was anything out there or not. Before they realised it sleep soon overcame them.

## Chapter 25

Josh grabbed one of the guns and someone's forgotten knapsack laying on the ground as he joined the others already tearing into the forest. They weren't about to stand and fight anything that could take out the automated turrets so easily. In a short time they had broken cover of the trees and now bounded over the rock-covered ground alongside the river they had previously found. The raging torrent of water drowned out all other sounds and he wasn't even sure if they were being chased anymore but the rest of the team were still racing on ahead.

As they neared the waterfall they found it harder to scramble over the progressively larger rocks that led up to the cliff face. The mist covered everything, making it slippery and they were in danger of falling into the foaming white waters some six feet below them. Exhausted, Josh looked down at the swirling mass, noticing that the artificial sunlight glinting off the calmer water was dimming and with dread he realised that night was approaching. Whatever had attacked them would now have an advantage under the cover of darkness.

Above him, Henderson was screaming something,

enthusiastically pointing towards the sheet of water he now stood next to. Josh pulled himself up the last few rocks as Henderson dived into the thick mist, behind the waterfall and was gone from sight. The rest followed, crossing over the surging beast on a slippery, narrow rock ledge that they had found behind it.

Ahead Burnett lost her footing, her face a mask of horror as she stumbled trying to regain a hold on the treacherous rock. He grabbed her arm just in time and hauled her up, the exertion draining away his last reserves of energy. Burnett clung to the rock terrified to move. He gestured her forward but she simply shook her head. Josh looked back, relieved to see that there was still no sign of anything behind them but darkness was closing in fast now. He gestured again, this time giving her a sharp push, all the time keeping hold of her arm in case. He tried shouting at her but his cries were lost next to the force of water hurtling past. Tentatively Burnett moved one foot, then the other, her confidence growing with each step. Styne was frantically waving them over on the other side, waiting to grab her. Carefully Josh made his way across the ledge behind her, feeling his clothes squelching with every step and the wet backpack weighing him down, making it more difficult. He breathed a sigh of relief, as he stepped onto the large rocks the other side to join the rest of the team, all staring intently at the forest from where they had just come.

There was barely any light left in the cave as he turned to see what they were looking at. A strange black thing was looming out of the forest, heading towards them; its shape continually changing as it moved. With the darkness and the mist it was impossible to get a clear view of it but one thing they could tell was that it was closing in on them fairly quickly.

Henderson shouted another command, lost in the noise of the waterfall, before taking off. In seconds they had all made it down the rocks and into the forest after him, not daring to look back to see where it was. The ground was muddy and they frequently slipped on it as they followed a rough path leading upwards before flattening out. The noise of water was less now and once again the thumps and rustles could be heard as it continued its pursuit.

Evans suddenly stopped dead, ahead of Josh and he ploughed into the back of him, knocking him over. As he helped Evans up he noticed the others were also standing in the clearing they had emerged into, staring at the alien ship before them.

"It has to be an alien ship." Jenkins said, as he walked towards the blue metal, that formed the exterior of the giant ship. The metal rose high above them and stretched into the distance on both sides, lost from view in the darkness. Vines twisted their way up over the metal and now covered a substantial portion of it, making it difficult to see amongst the rest of the forest. Despite the ships massive size and the vines, it resembled the giant disc that plagued the skies of earth and had destroyed countless cities.

They switched their lights on. An almost hairline gap in the blue material, close to them, was visible in a circular shape, the size of the original tunnel they had entered. The vines round it had all been broken back and were only just starting to re-grow over it. This metal circle had to be a door and they were all sure of it.

More rustles from behind, forced them into action.

"Quick get that door open, I'll try to hold it off." Henderson shouted, facing the forest with his gun raised.

"But what about the aliens?" Jenkins hesitated.

"Let's hope they're out. Now get that door open."

Some vines were still stuck solid to the door and without waiting they yanked on them hoping they wouldn't just come off. A groan of metal echoed as the door opened to a crack at first and then swung outwards, to reveal pitch darkness beyond.

"It's open." Styne said as he pushed the team members inside, while he waited for Henderson. The trees swayed as something pushed them, but there was no sign of it as Henderson ran for the door. They both grabbed it and pulled, as they crashed into the darkness, the door slamming shut behind them.

They lay in the pitch black room, not daring to breathe as they listened to the thing banging and pounding on the door, trying to get at them.

## Chapter 26

Quigly pushed open the flimsy metal door, turning away from the blinding sunlight, which was much more powerful than any of the artificial lighting underground. He smiled as he looked up at the clear blue sky, with no trace of a cloud in sight. It was a perfect summers day as he had often seen before, making the past two months seem like a distant dream. He was back home, in the city he had grown up in, only it was no longer there.

He nearly choked at the shock of seeing the devastated ruins all about him, unable to believe that they once formed the magnificent city that he fondly remembered. Everything was buried in a thick layer of rubble and debris and apart from a maze of single walls jutting up in places, it was impossible to tell where anything was. For all he knew he could have been anywhere, it all looked the same now.

He felt the rubble moving and crunching beneath his feet as he carefully walked over it, the noise a welcome release from the oppressive silence. Thousands of people had been trapped up here during the attack but there was no sign of them now and as hard as it was for him to except, he knew they all lay buried in the wreckage.

Quigly stopped a short way from the door, trying to continually remind himself that he had a job to do. He looked at the screen of the computer he carried.

*No poisons detected in the air.*
*Radiation levels are within acceptable parameters.*

Very good news and with any luck he would be allowed back in the shelter.

He now furiously typed away on the keyboard, to set up the satellite link as quickly as possible so that he could go back to the others. Despite the glorious sunshine, the sight of his surroundings were more depressing than he ever thought possible.

*Geostationary satellite found and link established.*

The words vanished and a picture appeared on the screen, giving a bird's eye view of the whole city and area around it, now nothing but a pile of rubble. Nothing had survived. He knew things would be bad but he had expected more of the buildings to still be standing intact, instead of this waste ground he was now confronted with.

With a few more key presses he had transmitted all the information, including that about the shelter, via the satellite to other satellites. A stream of words ran up the screen.

*Chicago completely destroyed.*
*Four thousand in ChicagoAlpha Shelter.*
*Five thousand in ChicagoBeta Shelter.*

More details flashed past before he could read them.

*New York completely destroyed.*

There seemed an endless list of cities destroyed but at least details on the surviving shelters followed. There was still a glimmer of hope while there were so many shelters and because of them, once they had destroyed the aliens they would be able to slowly rebuild everything to the way it was. Where they were, they had all the resources to do it. The only problem was if Noah's ark, as everyone called it, had been destroyed. That would mean there would be a severe shortage of animals, although there very nearly was no chance of Noah's ark surviving at all. Quigly thought back.

At one time the government had funded Noah's ark, allowing them to house several of every species in the world, along with their DNA, in an underground shelter that could be closed off in a nuclear or other war. Then the financial support had stopped, when some government official had decided that a war was very unlikely and so it wasn't worth all the costs involved. Not about to see their shelter lost, the people who ran it, turned the place into a zoo, which created so much publicity that in the end the government had to continue funding it.

He wondered how many other Noah's arks there were round the world and how many of them had survived even before the aliens had attacked. Words appeared on the screen.

*Information from all shelters has been transmitted to main base shelter and has been processed. Report is being sent now. Please wait for further instructions from the government which will be sent shortly.*

The blue line zipped across the screen as the report was downloaded.

*Report 1, Day 70*

*All populated areas on the Earth's surface have been destroyed. There are a large number of shelters reported, that are fully operational and are each currently sheltering near or at their full capacity of people. For security reasons the actual figures cannot be given at this time. One shelter, situated where Connellsville used to be, claims that the alien ship has landed nearby and smaller vehicles have been deployed from it. These alien craft are fanning out, in what appears to be a detailed search of the area. Unfortunately they have already attacked one shelter that they came across and it is unclear at this time, if anyone survived. The last report received, states that the alien ship is still on the ground at this time, with the circular door in the side of it still open. The alien vehicles have moved on and began systematically searching the surrounding areas and it is believed they will continue until they have explored the whole world or found what they are looking for.*

Quigly's mouth opened slightly as he repeated the word Connellsville.

"But that's not far from where we are." He breathed. "Those vehicles could be here any second." He brought up the latest satellite picture of his location, relieved that no alien craft were detected in it but by the sounds of it, it was only a matter of time before they reached him. He typed a command impatiently.

*Further instructions are not available at this time.*

"Come on, come on." Quigly glanced round checking he was still alone, his eyes eventually coming to rest on the metal door, the only sign that the shelter was there. He quickly walked over, slammed it shut and then piled some rubble on top to hide it. He didn't want the guilt of all those deaths on his conscience. Still no instructions had come, as Quigly sat back down next to the computer. It was going to be a long wait with the threat of the aliens coming, constantly hanging over him.

## Chapter 27

The whole team stood breathless in the alien ship, the pounding relentlessly continued on the door but at least whatever it was, didn't seem to be able to get in.

"We're trapped in here with the aliens." At the sound of Jenkins trembling voice, lights suddenly flashed on from somewhere. They were in a small room lined with the same grey coloured walls, floor and ceiling, as were in the tunnel. The room was bare and only a single round door led from it, which was at present shut.

"We can't go back out the way we came" the pounding was proof of Henderson's words "so we'll have to explore this place for another exit."

"But the aliens?" Jenkins face was horror-stricken.

"We have no other choice. We've got guns and we'll just have to fight our way through if we meet any." Jenkins wasn't looking any happier. "Anyway, with the power those aliens have we should be dead by now and so maybe they're not here but all on the surface with the others."

"Did you see the vines?"

"Are you mad Forbes? Who cares about them at a time like this?" Jenkins almost screamed.

"No listen. Vines take time to grow up and cover a ship this size to that extent. So this ship has been here a long time and the door hadn't been opened until fairly recently, judging by the health of the vines still on it."

"Great so aliens weren't here until recently."

"Or maybe they haven't been here for a long while and it was that army team that found this ship and cut the vines to open the door."

"It's all guess work." Henderson said feeling his way round the edge of the inner door. "We've got to do what we came down here for and check this place out. See what information we can find out about the aliens."

"Why bother? We can't get back to the shelter." Jenkins said, throwing down his knapsack.

A click came from the inner door Henderson had been inspecting and then it swung open to darkness for a second before more strong lights came on.

"What is it? Some kind of flight deck?" A huge white floor lay before them, on which stood what appeared to be a multitude of smaller ships, shaped differently to the large one. Most of them were long thin cylindrical shaped craft, with strangely shaped wings on the side, not so dissimilar from the human aeroplanes. They were made out of the same blue material and in all weren't much larger than a human laying down. Perhaps some hundred of these bizarre ships were scattered over the deck, the tops of them peeled back, as if ready for the pilots to jump into them at any time. Other strange machinery stood awkwardly on two legs that looked as if they would crumple at any second. Against the walls of this gigantic space, stood locker shaped silver coloured boxes, their rectangular doors shut.

Josh opened the door of the locker next to him surprised to find different curious equipment, none of it looking vaguely familiar. It seemed impossible that the aliens would design cupboards almost identical to their own. He opened another locker to see more strange objects piled high in it.

"Look a radio." Kolinsky was standing next to him, holding one of the pieces of alien equipment that did have a remarkable resemblance to their own communicating devices. "As if." Kolinsky continued about to toss it back into the cupboard.

"No wait." Josh managed to grab it off him before it was lost amongst the rest of the stuff. "Who knows it may be an alien communication device. After all somehow we have managed to both create other similar looking technology." Carefully he placed it in his pocket, hoping to find time to play with it later. He had the idea that if they could work out the aliens language they could then listen in to what they were saying, which would perhaps give them the advantage when they came to fight them.

"Look another door on the wall on the other side. We can get out of here." Jenkins was about to head off to it.

"Can you hear that?" Burnett asked heading over to the outer wall of the ship. The banging was more pronounced the closer she got. Cautiously she put her ear up against the wall to listen, her hands gently resting on the cool metal forming the skin of the ship. Suddenly the wall became opaque, revealing arms of light and energy rearing out of the darkness and slamming against the wall, inches from her face. Burnett stumbled backwards, looking round to the others for support. Lester had stopped in his tracks on his way to the other door. Burnett faced the wall, surprised to find the creature had gone.

"It's ok." Josh said approaching, we seem to be safe in here."

"For how long?" Kolinsky added pessimistically.

"We're going up there." Henderson pointed at the silver roof, and the two circular holes cut into it, leading to the deck above, both of them about 4 feet in diameter. Directly below one of them was a circular platform, the same size, resting on the ground, while a similar platform looked to be sealing the other hole.

"I'll go first, sir" Styne was too late since Henderson had already stepped onto the platform. It immediately shot upwards until it was flush with the hole. It paused for a moment before returning back to its starting position, this time without Henderson.

"Christ!" They heard his voice and then his head appeared, looking down at them. "Seems safe up here."

Shortly they had all joined him on another white deck even larger than the first. Instead of the alien craft, this deck was covered in a mass of weird and wonderful machinery, so closely packed together that it formed a maze, with pipes going all ways. In the walls around the edges were areas of opaqueness, permitting them a view out in line with the canopy of the outside jungle.

"This is impressive." Jenkins said, for the first time sounding relaxed as he wandered off round the room. "God knows what that is." He was looking at a horizontal cylinder of yellow light that ran round the perimeter of the deck, before joining up again, so as to create a circle that encompassed everything in the room. The cylinder was no bigger than a foot in diameter and it was held stationary in mid-air between the floor and the ceiling. Inside the yellow cylinder of light glistened some white material, looking translucent at times. "And that." Jenkins now examined more of the machinery, everything fascinating him.

"Jenkins you must have some idea what all this is?" Henderson spied another hole in the roof as he spoke and now hastened over to it.

"I think, though I'm not sure, that some of this machinery generates the power to run this place and the rest is the engines, though that's a rather over simplified term."

"Let's see what's up there." Henderson had stepped onto the new circular platform that he had found and the others followed his example.

They found themselves in a narrow hallway, with a maze of corridors leading in all directions. Blue, round metal doors stood shut at the ends of the passageways and more were set into the walls every so often. Another circular platform was nearby, with a hole in the ceiling above it, into the next deck.

"The doors seem to be locked." Jenkins said, testing one. "Guess it's upwards and onwards. Next deck should be smaller seeing as the diameter of the ship is smaller towards the top." He moved onto the next platform, steadying himself as it shot up to the next level.

"This is amazing!" They could hear his voice shouting down to them as they waited for the lift to return so that they could join him. "I swear this is one powerful piece of machinery. I'm sure it's a real super computer, albeit alien. Ours are dwarfed in comparison."

They were in a room, round the edges of which were strange light panels, displaying hundreds of different unrecognisable symbols. 3D holographic projections danced in mid-air in certain places, towards the centre of the room, showing planets with lines and symbols over the top, like some giant complex space map. Odd noises and whines sounded from time to time as though relaying information.

"It's Earth." Jenkins approached one of the projections, slowly walking round it. This projection was different to the others since no symbols or markings lay over the top of it.

"The continents are all in the wrong place. That picture shows just a few big land masses, which is nothing like our planet." Kolinsky said with contempt.

"I can assure you it is Earth." Jenkins then took out his own computer and began to type away.

"See" he held it up so that Kolinsky could see the screen, which displayed a picture of a planet, almost identical to the projection. "Earth."

"But …"

"It's Earth about 120 million years ago. Back then all the continents would have been in different positions."

"But why would they have a picture of Earth from that long ago?" Burnett had stopped examining one of the panels and was now scrutinising the 3D holographic image.

"Perhaps they've been watching Earth since then." Jenkins suggested.

"No. It doesn't seem possible." Burnett said, reaching out her hand towards the projection, unable to resist touching it. As her fingers slowly swept through it, any part of the image that they came in contact with distorted, wafting strangely round them, as though it were sensing. Without warning the whole projection disappeared and she drew back quickly, unsure what she had done.

Now a new image materialised of the Milky Way galaxy, covered in the strange markings and symbols, which soon vanished and then the projection continually changed as they were zoomed in towards the sun. Soon they had zoomed right the way in until a picture of the old Earth was once again shown. New symbols flashed up, as though readings were being taken of various parts of the Earth's surface, before again fading. The image zoomed out to give them a view of the Earth as it rotated slowly round the sun, stopping half way on its rotation. The landmasses appeared again, with a picture of a volcano displayed over the top along with numerous alien symbols and a line pointing to a position on the land. A jet of rock hurled up into the air as the volcano violently erupted. The image cut off and the Earths passage round the sun continued, stopping again before it reached the starting point. A new volcano was shown erupting; its location a long way away from the first one. Again the Earth rotated further, stopping to show the eruption of yet another volcano, in an apparently never-ending sequence of images.

"There was a lot of volcanic activity during the Cretaceous period which it seems to be mapping out." Josh remarked.

"What caused it to show the images?" Burnett was still standing away from the 3D projection unsure if anything else would occur.

"I think" Jenkins said waving his hand through the image "that the recording is triggered by sensors that detect certain movements in the image." As he spoke the image stopped and the recording was restarted. "I'm pretty sure we've found the main command centre of the whole ship."

"Why did they take a recording of the volcanoes erupting all those years ago?" Burnett said cautiously getting closer to the projection.

"Now that I don't know." Jenkins was hastily moving round the room triggering the other 3D projections, fascinated by everything.

"The aliens certainly are interested in this period of the Earth's history, judging by the species of plants outside." Josh said, examining one of the panels on the wall.

"What I want to know is why this ship seems to be deserted." Henderson looked back down the hole, as if checking to make sure they were still alone. "It's as if this place has been deserted for years."

"Apart from whatever it is outside." Josh added moving to the ships outside wall, his movement triggering concealed sensors, causing parts of the ship's exterior to become transparent. They were so high above the ground that they felt they could almost reach out and touch the roof while the tops of the trees looked like mossy grass below them. There was no sign of the creature in the darkness but Josh instinctively knew it was out there somewhere.

## Chapter 28

"Where is he?" Martinez asked, rudely nudging Ricks awake. While they had slept an artificial night had crept over everything, leaving them in pitch-blackness, save for the lights on their headbands.

"What?" Ricks answered, half asleep.

"Lester's gone. There's no sign of him." Ricks fully woke up with a jolt.

"The fool must have gone off by himself."

"He's not that brave."

"Maybe not but he's certainly that stupid."

"Great now we've got to find him as well." Martinez snarled.

Lester had woken early to find his two companions sound asleep and darkness closing in fast. He knew when they woke they would be on the same mad campaign to find Attwell and O'Callaghan but all he wanted was to get back to the others. He had to leave, to go back by himself or get dragged along on a suicide mission.

Carefully he picked up his gun from where it lay next to Martinez and then choosing a direction of least resistance and towards where he thought the main group were, left. He hadn't gone far when night descended fully, cloaking him in complete darkness. The light on his headband did little to cut through it, leaving him to stumble along over the roots and stones.

He had travelled some distance before he could hear the sound of the waterfall and river in the distance. He was sure he wasn't far from them now. The air was becoming chilly, making him wonder if the aliens had been trying to emulate the conditions on the surface at night time. Under any other circumstances, this place would really be remarkable to him.

The path was opening out more now, though there was still a lot of undergrowth about him. An enormous tree ahead of him seemed to sway slightly. They had been right he really was starting to see things. A low groan followed by cracking, as the same tree lurched over to one side precariously balancing for an instance before toppling over, crashing headlong through the foliage, its roots ripping upwards.

"My god!" Lester murmured, regaining enough presence of mind to ready his gun but too astonished to do anything further.

The other smaller shrubs and bushes between himself and the tree were now being uprooted out of the way with the same terrifying ease. Something was coming towards him, he was certain of it. In the darkness he was unable to make out any form, yet light seemed to be emanating from something approaching at speed. He fired wildly. He had no idea if he was even coming close to hitting it.

The light seemed to be forming into elongated shapes, changing as they advanced before disappearing entirely. He stopped firing, completely shaken. He had to get out of there.

The strange twisting length of lights momentarily appeared next to him barely allowing him enough time to see them before they flashed across his vision. There was a sudden surge of pain through his face and he stumbled backwards grabbing at it, feeling burning. It was as if the light had caught him across his face, leaving a band of burnt flesh and skin. He fell onto his back as more pain cut across his legs. Blinded and crippled he struggled desperately to get up, away from the unseen danger. He didn't have a chance to move as he felt more things hit him, until the intensity of the pain soon became too much and with a final push at the ground, slipped into a lasting darkness.

The silence was broken by more gunfire in the distance.

"It has to be Lester." Martinez said as he raced off towards it.

"What's he firing at now?"

"If it were light enough I'd say his own shadow."

"Maybe he really is in trouble."

"Lester, where are you?" There was no reply to Martinez's shouts. "Lester don't be a pain."

They had made good time and were close to where

they had heard the shots, but everything was quiet now.

"What happened here?" The devastation done to the forest was obvious, as though a herd of elephants had ploughed their way through it. Charred wood covered the ground and wafts of smoke rose up from several clumps of green leaves, fire still spitting from them as they burned up. By some miracle these small fires hadn't managed to catch the rest of the vegetation alight but then most of the area around them was now cleared, the uprooted plants tossed backwards into the edges of the forest. Fresh marks covered the ground, the furrows cutting deep into the earth indicating the heavy weight of the object that made them.

"Lester?" Martinez tried on the radio. Static responded.

"Something's happening, can't you feel it?" Ricks said shaking slightly. She was right, Martinez could feel it too, a build up of energy in the air. A whirring noise started, gradually building to a crescendo.

"We've got to get back to the others." Ricks screamed. She was halted by the appearances of blue lightning completely surrounding them, streaks of it loudly, crackling horizontally through the bushes to form a barrier. More of these sparking, sizzling strands appeared, looking just like electricity crossing between two points through air but there was no sign of anything causing it. The brightness of it turned night to a strange bluish coloured day.

The circle of electricity was closing in and now

they could see movement of something lurking just beyond.

"How do we get out of here?" Martinez looked round desperate, the glare from it hurting his eyes. It suddenly all stopped. Martinez grabbed Ricks and before she knew it they were crashing through the forest as fast as they could, in a bid for freedom. They heard more crackles and felt a wash of charged air slam into their backs but the blue lightning hadn't reached them.

They broke free of the trees, running across the open expanse towards the river. Martinez risked a backwards glance, relieved to see that nothing had followed them out of the forest, though he wasn't about to wait and see what, if anything would emerge. He gave Ricks, who had stopped at the edge of the river, a shove, jumping in after her without even breaking out of a run. The water foamed about them, a sign of the strong current now trying to drag them under. Sharp rocks stuck out everywhere, causing the water to churn madly round them, creating whirlpool effects that would suck any unsuspecting creature under. Their clothes weighed them down as they fought against the ferocity of it all. Every so often the current became too strong, sweeping them into rocks and almost knocking them unconscious. Water forced its way into their mouths, causing them to gasp, frantic for air, but only finding more water. They kicked out hard, slowly crossing the expanse, not knowing how to keep going. In seconds Ricks had been swept towards a whirlpool, she struggled more frantically than ever, feeling forces sucking her downwards. No matter how hard she kicked it was useless against the current and she disappeared under, slamming against a rock on the way down. The force of water released her and she struggled back upwards, horrified to find she had been pulled underneath an out hanging rock. She moved round it, needing air, forcing her way up to the surface as quickly as she could. The current took hold of her once more, not wanting to let go of its prize, dragging her back down. She fought it till she could no more. The strength of water was just too much, pulling her further down to a watery grave.

His head just above water still, Martinez struggled onwards against the current, barely sure where he was let alone Ricks. A surge of water, flung him towards another rock, making him cringe as his shoulder hit it painfully. He had barely recovered as he was swept further across the river, straight into another rock, his head hitting it with such force that he passed out.

## Chapter 29

Two hours had passed. The scorching sun beat savagely down on Quigly, as he sat huddled over the computer feeling sick with the heat. All around was the deserted rubble wasteland, devoid of anything close by that could give even just a little shade. His one relief was the cool oxygen that was slowly pumped into his helmet, though the air in the rest of the suit was stale and humid. Normally he would switch on the built in air conditioning unit but he wanted to keep all the power for the computer, to help speed up any large processing jobs it had to do. With any luck, when the further instructions finally did arrive, the computer would get all the information a lot quicker and then he could get back down into the shelter, away from this god forsaken place.

He jumped, startled, as the computer began beeping. The noise could mean one of two things, either the instructions were being transmitted or an alien presence had been detected in the near vicinity. The horizon was clear of anything, as was the satellite picture, so it had to be the former. He sighed heavily as he saw the blue bar appear on the screen, with large letters above it.

*DOWNLOADING*

This was the best news he'd had since he had been up here. Now he could get back to the others and to noise, something he missed the most. At last the download was finished. He quickly shut the computer down and grabbed his things together, checking to make sure he hadn't left anything behind. After moving the rubble of the door and opening it, he entered. He couldn't think of a way to conceal it now. He brought his arm back down and let the metal fall shut above, sealing him in darkness. Quigly headed down the tunnel, guided by the light that still remained on in the airlock, shining dimly out of the small square window. As he entered into the chamber the light became much brighter and he could now see a guards face looking in on him from the shelter. He slammed the door shut, the computer on the wall activating as he did so. In seconds chemical liquid began spurting out from the walls, completely covering the whole room, leaving nothing untouched. The spray stopped. A computerised voice echoed round the walls. "Please remain where you are. Scanning airlock now.

The guards face at the window was brushed aside, as Hawkins appeared, staring in at him, looking nervous.

"Scan complete." The voice continued, pausing before giving the results. "No dangerous substances detected." The door hissed open and Hawkins rushed in, immediately grabbing the computer from him.

"Have you got all the information?"

"Yes" Quigly replied, popping up the visor, relieved to be able to pull off the stuffy suit.

"And the instructions?"

"Should have. I haven't checked them." Hawkins had walked off and Quigly nearly tripped over as he scrambled the rest of the way out of the suit, at the same time as trying to keep up with him.

"Well let's hope it's good news."

"I think you'll be disappointed." Quigly said, as he followed him into the secure room in the town hall, where the seven other people that made up the new government for the shelter, were already seated around a long table.

"We have the information." Hawkins said, placing the computer on the table and linking it up to the large screen on the wall. The report appeared on the screen and there were gasps as they read it.

"But that ship's not far from here." Hawkins addressed Quigly. "Did you see any of these vehicles?

"No. I kept updating the satellite pictures and just before I left there were still no signs of any of the alien craft. We must have been lucky and they haven't got this far yet."

"But they will do soon." Hawkins mumbled as he brought up the new instructions on the same large screen.

*23rd August*
*Central World Government Orders*

*It seems obvious that the aliens will not stop their relentless attack until every human is dead and therefore we see no option but to launch an attack on the main spaceship. We have tried communicating with the aliens in the hopes that we could get a team on board, to attack from inside but unfortunately we can get no response from them, even when we claimed to have the device, which of course we don't. Since the bluff failed, we will have to launch an attack and try to force our way inside. We are ordering that as many people and vehicles as possible from each shelter meet at the co-ordinates given for their shelter and begin the attack at 0900 hours on the 24th August. In this way we hope we will have people approaching from all directions, giving us a greater chance at beating them. One person from each shelter, should remain posted on the surface until the attack time, so that they can receive any revised orders, depending on any new developments.*

*If all the shelters join in this attack, we will destroy the aliens and take back the Earth. Failure of any shelter to comply with these orders will result in court martial for all members of the government in that shelter.*

*Finally Good Luck.*

"They can't court martial us, we're not military." One of the government advisors was complaining.

"Probably all be dead before they get the chance." The large advisor boomed pessimistically. "They're just trying to scare us into sending people to fight, or rather on this suicide mission."

"It doesn't seem a very sensible course of action to me." The large advisor stood up and paced the room before re-seating himself, the oak chair creaking in protest under his weight. "We already sent everything we had at them, which need I remind you didn't work and now they want us to send people on foot."

"We do have transport and some attack vehicles." Hawkins interceded.

"Yes but even so it's hardly going to succeed when missiles failed.

"What do you propose then?" Another government official asked.

"We don't have much choice in the matter." Hawkins fretted. "We can't go against a world government decision."

"And I suppose you'd be the first one out the window if they told you to jump." The large advisor chuckled as Hawkins opened his mouth to say something but then thought better of it and promptly shut it.

"It sounds to me like the aliens will attack our base if we don't do something," Quigly spoke up, "but this plan is ludicrous."

"It doesn't matter what you think." Hawkins tone was cutting. "We have to follow these orders. I only informed you all as a courtesy but you must understand you have no say in this particular matter."

"Madness" the large official snorted as Hawkins

turned to Quigly, whose face fell, as he realised what he was about to be asked.

"I assume you'll be prepared to remain on the surface." The thought of the barren surface returned to Quigly. "Good. I'll take that as a yes." Hawkins said before Quigly had a chance to speak.

"But …"

"Quigly, you'd better get going before you miss anything." Hawkins said dismissing him with a wave of his hand.

"You could at least give me the chance to get something to eat." Hawkins stared back impatiently.

"Very well if you must but be quick about it." He turned back to the disgruntled advisors talking animatedly with them as he planned the attack party.

Wearily Quigly headed back to the airlock, stopping at a tunnel staff room on the way and making use of their food dispenser. Everywhere he went there was a general background noise and he relished all of it, knowing that soon he would be alone, waiting, with the threat of alien craft approaching at any time and the hot sun burning him. This time he would use air conditioning and any new information would just have to be downloaded a little slower. Though the power packs recharged all the time, he just hoped they would be able to recharge quickly enough.

In a short time he was once again on the surface hunched over the computer, waiting.

## Chapter 30

"This is hopeless." Jenkins said dejectedly moving away from one of the panels. "I can't seem to get anything to work, except those holographic projections. It's as if all the main computer systems have somehow been shut down and only some basic functions still work."

"Maybe you're not using the system correctly. After all we don't know how the aliens designed this thing." Burnett suggested.

"No. I can't get any response at all with most of it, yet I know I can get the projections to work, although they seem a bit limited. I would have thought they would be able to display all the information about the ship and everything."

"Perhaps you haven't moved your hand through the image in the correct pattern to access the other information."

"No, it may sound crazy and it's just a gut feeling but I think that the main computers been damaged and not even the aliens would be able to make it work."

"If we can't do anything here shouldn't we go and investigate the rest of this place?" Evans was standing by the hole, where the platform now sat waiting to descend to the deck below.

"What do you think Jenkins?" Henderson motioned to the panels.

"Nothing I can do here. Perhaps we can find something of more use."

"Fine then." Evans had already stepped onto the lift and had disappeared from sight.

The doors still remained locked on the deck below, with the only exit, the next platform to the deck below, containing all the machinery.

"Maybe we need to start some of this machinery working before the computer becomes fully operational." Burnett said as they gathered in the middle of it all.

"I have to admit that I'm not sure where to begin." Jenkins replied, gently touching the cool blue metal as if in the hopes it would give him inspiration. "Besides which starting some of these machines may do all kinds of weird stuff."

Jenkins paused and silence resumed.

"Do you hear that?" Evans was listening intently.

"What?" Henderson shut his eyes to focus on the noise but he couldn't hear anything.

"The continuous dull pounding, from that thing trying to get in has stopped. So" he hesitated "either its given up or its succeeded."

"It stopped ages ago." Henderson's returned. "It might have gone, I think we'd better make a move though. We'll search round the perimeter and see if we can find a door so that we don't have to go back out the way we came, in case it's waiting for us."

"Over here sir." Styne had already ducked under the yellow cylinder of light and was now a short way from them.

"What's this do?" Evans stopped at the beam, raising his hand up into it. As his flesh touched the light there was a sudden blinding flash and he felt himself thrown backwards, his head slamming down onto the floor and pain shooting up his back where he had landed hard. There was also something he couldn't make out at first but then it sank in, the realisation of terrible pain, overwhelming his sense as he looked down at the source, his now ruined left hand. Kolinsky rushed forwards.

"Do something." Henderson ordered. Kolinsky looked back worried.

"I can't we lost all the equipment. He's got severe burns to his hand and some of the flesh has been burned away but all I can do is wrap it up in a wet cloth for now." Evans groaned as Kolinsky applied the makeshift bandage.

"Here you go." Jenkins offered a bottle of pills. "They're just box standard painkillers but they might help a little." Kolinsky took them questioningly. "I always carry some for an old knee injury." Jenkins explained.

"There, that's the best I can do." Kolinsky helped Evans up.

"I'll be okay. We'd better get going." Despite his brave words they could see him cringing with pain.

"There's a door." Styne was feeling round the

edge of the shut circle of metal as they joined him, ducking under the light. "Got it." A click resounded as it popped open and squeakily swung outwards to reveal another chamber, similar to the one they had entered the ship through. Another shut door was opposite leading to what they assumed was the outside and the dark foreboding forest. The remains of another body, ripped savagely, lay on the floor, its tattered military garments still hanging loosely on it. Various items of equipment lay scattered on the ground around the corpse, including a computer, guns and breathing equipment.

Josh immediately grabbed the computer, ignoring the sight of the body.

"You can get the data of this can't you?" He said, handing it to Burnett. She jumped as Styne banged the door shut behind the whole group.

"Should be safe in here for a while." Styne was now examining the other exit. "I don't think it can get through very easily and we can escape out this door."

"About the computer?" Josh encouraged. With the whole group now facing her, Burnett looked down at it nervously.

"It's working and it looks like they have used the same encryption algorithm. It must be a standard military one. I can just ..." her voice trailed off as she began pushing buttons. "Done. Fairly simple to do and by the looks of it the files are still intact." A list of file names sped up the screen. "Hundreds of them but these ones seem to be the most important, since they were most recently used."

"Well bring them up so that we can see what's in them." Henderson ordered impatiently.

"This appears to be a journal or diary of a man called Alan Davis. The file was already open when we found the computer." Writing appeared on the screen, slowly scrolling up at the speed of the man's voice that had now begun talking.

*"2nd May*
*When they asked for volunteers today I didn't hesitate, after all action is what I signed up for. The job seems to be easy though. Apparently in their quest to find new minerals and supplies of materials, a large company found an enormous cave underground. They sent a large team of people down to investigate, but none of them came back. Before they disappeared they had sent back reports of monsters and spaceships. Sounds to me like they just went crazy and I can't understand why anyone is taking them seriously, still it beats being at the base. I guess we'll find out what's really down there tomorrow.*

*3rd May*
*We set off down in the tunnel to reach the cave and couldn't believe it when we came across all those plants, a complete jungle. We immediately headed in the direction of the reported space ship. During the trek one of my group went missing and there's no sign of them anywhere. How could he just disappear? I must be losing my mind,*

*since I'm starting to doubt whether those survivors really were crazy.*

*4th May*
*We continued in the same direction until we at last reached the space ship that we had been told about. A women disappeared but this time we saw it all. God it was awful. That thing dragged her away and we couldn't stop it. We don't even know what it is. All I know is that we are trapped in here with that thing waiting out there for us. It will be a miracle if any of us make it out alive.*

*5th May*
*The only two scientists left in my team are working on deciphering the strange symbols we found on panels and holographic projections in what appears to be the control room. They are both experts in translating old and rare texts but neither of them have ever seen such writing before. Even so they think that they will be able to translate at least some of it within a couple of days, since the writing contains many pictures and the computer programmes they use nowadays help a lot. So I suppose we are stuck down here until then.*

*6th May*
*I know that thing is still waiting for us out there, sometimes pounding on the door, knowing we will have to emerge some time. Lord knows where it came from or what it is. We know one thing though, that it's not an alien or whatever built this ship, otherwise it would be*

*able to get in, since there is no way we can lock or barricade the doors. One thing is for sure, we'll make a fight of it. As soon as that text is translated we are heading back to the base and it won't stop us.*

*7th May*
*It's a relief that they have at last translated most of the symbols and so we can get out of this hell hole, though we've got to take that cumbersome black box with us. I have written my report and each member of the group has a copy. That way there is a chance that at least one copy will get back to the base. They are just opening the door now and then we'll make a run for it, while that things not out there."*

There was a shuddering clang of metal and then another voice now broke in.

"Where did it come from? How did it get the door open like that?"

"Get moving, go, everyone." A shuffle of feet could be heard as they ran over the floor.

"Oh my god. It's here."

"You two get the box and go. The rest of you keep it busy." The noise of feet ripping their way through the undergrowth and then several dull thuds, followed by a dragging sound. Bullets being fired, explosion and then high pitched screaming, full of terror.

"No, No." The original voice shouted. Sounds followed indicating a violent struggle. Bangs, crashed and then Davis's voice, with a strange choking gurgling to it as though he was having trouble talking through the blood. "The door. Fight it." Bang. Perhaps the door had closed. Now there was a wet thud. "What do I do?" the word "do" was lost through the gurgling noise, eventually fading and then silence.

"He must have died then." Evans said downheartedly still gripping the wrist of his bandaged hand

"Just state the obvious Evans, why don't you." Kolinsky snarled.

"What about the others?" Evans continued ignoring him.

"Maybe the report will tell us more." Josh looked at Burnett "can you get it?"

"It's no good. They've used a different encryption algorithm. It will take me a while to get into it."

"We shouldn't stay here. We need to start looking for that exit." Henderson nodded to the computer. "You'll have to decipher that later on. For now we've got to get moving. At least we know there's a door out there to a military base and we need to tell them about this ship. It could help us defeat the aliens." He produced his radio.

"Lester, Martinez, Ricks come in." There was no answer.

"We can't risk going back for them." Styne said gently.

"We don't have much choice, with that thing between us and them, it's too dangerous." Henderson agreed. "We need to get back to that base and tell them what we've found down here." He carefully put the radio away. "Open that door to the outside if you can." He motioned to Jenkins.

"Wait." Styne put a hand up to stop him opening the door to the forest. "What if it's out there sir?" Henderson pushed past roughly.

"It's a chance we'll have to take."

## Chapter 31

A few seconds passed before Martinez regained consciousness. He grabbed out at anything, relieved when his hand caught hold of a root. He had been lucky that the currents had worked in his favour, sweeping him across the river to the bank on the other side, where he now held fast. Laboriously he pulled himself up the vein, hand over hand and onto the muddy bank the other side. He lay for a moment panting hard, trying to catch his breath. He felt like he had broken every bone in his body, after the beating he had taken. Even his days playing American football hadn't been as bad as this and he had taken some hard knocks in his time. It had been worth it though with the roar of the crowds pushing him on at every stage to bigger victories. Now he found himself alone, playing for the ultimate stakes.

With effort he succeeded in hauling himself up enough to look back at the still churning water and the bank on the other side. Although the light on his headband had broken, artificial day was beginning to dawn, giving enough illumination for him to realise Ricks was nowhere in sight.

"Where are you?" The water drowned his voice out.

Lying on his front, Martinez peered down at the rushing water, scanning along the banks either side, disappointed to see no trace of her. The rocks protruding from the centre of the river looked clear of any debris or bodies. He shouted again, feeling his throat strain with the effort and his chest ache where bruises were starting to appear. Ricks had to be still in the foaming waters below but there was no sign of a body and he would at least expect to see that.

Carefully he leaned over further, searching for any dark objects below the surface, certain if he found one it was already too late but unwilling to give up. That thing would be coming soon. He was about to give up when he saw it, a distortion under the water's surface. He reached down, pulling back sharply as the object was abruptly released by the currents and sprang to the surface. More fast flowing currents worked on it, dragging the limp form swiftly downstream. He had seen enough to know it was Ricks. He had to concentrate on himself now, on finding a way out of the jungle and the cave and away from that thing.

Over on the other bank a dark shape appeared, emitting a yellow radiance from its edges, its shape distorting as it headed towards him.

Martinez didn't look back as he scrambled to his feet and was once again crashing headlong through more forest, his feet slipping on the muddy ground. He was now pushing his way uphill, making the going even tougher. He had not gone far before he had to stop, his hands on his hips as he bent over, trying to recover his breathing. He had to get further away and pushed himself onwards.

He was running out of energy and his breathing was becoming erratic. His foot caught on a rock, sending him flying straight through a bush and onto his hands and knees. The adrenaline that had pushed him onwards could no longer fight the tiredness he felt and he remained collapsed on the ground. He clutched at his chest hoping the pain that cursed through it every time he breathed, would go away.

Martinez felt the Earth shudder and instinctively rolled into the shrubs on one side, waiting for it. So far all was still and quiet, save for his ragged breathing that he vainly tried to subdue. He stared back scared at the faint shadow he saw, dancing over the trees.

## Chapter 32

"Got it." Jenkins stood back as the door swung open to expose the forest outside, cloaked in darkness, save for a very slight amount of light, perhaps the indication of a coming artificial sunrise.

"We'll just have to start moving, looking for any signs of a door and Burnett" Henderson turned to her "I want you to decipher that encryption while we're walking if you can."

"Are you kidding?" Burnett looked aghast "I have enough trouble not tripping over roots as it is." Henderson continued to glare at her until at last she sighed in resignation. "Ok I'll do my best." She glanced down at the screen as the group filtered out of the door feeling less trapped now but still apprehensive at what lay in the surrounding forest.

"Perhaps we should have stayed in that ship while Burnett worked on that computer." Styne muttered to Henderson. "After all that report may contain the location of the door."

"And if that thing had come back we would have had to fight our way through it like that army team. Do you really think they're up to it." Henderson answered gesturing the rest of the team members.

"We could have used a different door."

"I get the impression that army team would have done that if they could. It probably tracked their movement through the ship so that it could block off their exits and they didn't even realise it."

"We could have split up in to two groups and taken a door each." Styne persisted not content until he had exhausted all alternative possibilities.

"And how do you know there is only one of whatever it is out there. It wasn't worth the risk." He paused. "We were jolly lucky that it was lured away by something."

"That's what concerns me." Henderson looked uncomfortable reluctant to voice Styne's anxiety.

"You mean Lester, Ricks and Martinez."

"I tried them just now on the radio but they weren't responding."

"We have to go back for them then."

"No." Styne glared at his surroundings. "It goes against the grain to leave people behind but it is vital we get to that base and tell them what we've found down here. It could have serious implications in our survival against the aliens above."

"I suppose you're right."

"Besides there is no tracker signal coming from any of the missing people. The computers could have got broken but the chances are they are dead."

They continued in silence fighting their way through the jungle.

"Look at them." Henderson at last said to Styne in

disgust, gesturing to the people struggling at the back of the group. Styne pulled a rare smile.

"They look about ready to collapse."

"We're going to have to let them rest again." Styne nodded in response. "How about here. There is no indication of anything around and at least we can make a run for it, since it's fairly open."

"Have to be." Styne agreed watching Kolinsky stumbling along at the very back.

They had moved some way into the forest and now the trees had been replaced by barren rock stretching out all around them for some distance. Hot muddy water bubbled up through fractures in the rock and every so often a sudden gush of steam vented out at speed.

"We'll rest here for a while." Henderson kept his voice low as he gave the command. "How's it going Burnett?"

"I think I've got it. It was only some slight variations on the other algorithm."

"Let's see it then." Henderson peered at the screen.

"Just a bit longer."

"Time isn't on our side I'm afraid."

"Just a sec, I've got to …" She continued working away, at last a report flashing up on the screen.

*7th May 2096*
*Report 1561492*
*By the time we found the space ship on the second day, three members of the team, Gary Roach, Jeff Felding*

*and Liz Mason had disappeared and our search for them proved fruitless. Before we could extend the search some kind of creature attacked us, dragging away Donor Simms. Our weapons seemed useless against it. We had no option but to shut ourselves in the alien ship we found, otherwise I think it would have killed us all. At this time I am unable to give a clear description of it, since it all happened so quickly and the creature remained partially hidden in the surrounding foliage.*

*Since we have been trapped in the ship, we've begun our investigation of it and found what appears to be a control room, filled with strange symbols and writings. The two scientists remaining studied these and from them have managed to piece together the history of the ship and the aliens, which is as follows.*

*The spaceship we found is an alien ship. About 120 million years ago the aliens that built it were having a war with another alien faction. We are unable to ascertain the reason they were fighting. The aliens who built this ship managed to disable and board and take over a ship belonging to their enemy, on which a new prototype technology was being developed. All information on it was coded, making it difficult for them to even find out the purpose of the device. They transferred the device in its entirety onto their own ship, along with all development information on it and then deleted any records remaining on the enemy ship before destroying it entirely. They then informed their leaders of the capture of the device but meanwhile had begun examining it while awaiting instructions. Accidentally they managed to trigger the device and somehow it transported their ship and them millions of light-years away from their own galaxy, though they were unsure how far.*

*They found themselves stranded back in our galaxy every time they triggered the device. The only hospitable planet was Earth and with no hope of escape back to their own galaxy and the threat of volcanoes erupting along with inhospitable wildlife, namely the dinosaurs, decided to take cover. They built an underground world, that is to say the cave we found and then began working on finding a way home. They had to strip part of their ship for parts, to survive down here, while they tried to learn more about the device.*

*The scientists had trouble working out the little that the aliens wrote after that but they did find that they were saying something about being attacked. I can only assume that they were stuck down here all this time, during which something killed all of them. We have found what appears to be the device, which is little more than a black box that we hope to return to the base for further examination.*

"This is unbelievable." Kolinsky muttered.

"It would make sense why there's an alien ship underground." Henderson reasoned.

"Do you realise that this device could be the one the aliens are looking for." Josh said in amazement.

"Don't be stupid." Kolinsky glared at him. "They wouldn't have spent 120 million years looking for this thing. They probably could have reinvented it hundreds of times over, so why go after it.

"Maybe all their top scientists had been killed off and they couldn't reinvent it." Evans answered.

"They must have realised how far they had to travel to retrieve the device and how long it would take. You'd think they would have given up after a couple of years."

"Who knows?" Josh joined. "Maybe they have long life expectancies and therefore several years wouldn't seem like much time to them or maybe they wanted to get away from the fighting. The point is this is all just supposition. We don't know." There was a pause of total silence in the vast cavern.

"I guess the whole army team was killed." Burnett said quietly. "Otherwise the government would have known about the device."

"huh." Kolinsky said, almost amazed by her. "The government wouldn't think twice about lying if they wanted it, regardless of how many people died." A look of disgust flashed across Burnett's face.

"Maybe if the government had taken it, it was for the best." Evans joined.

"How can you say that?" She glared at Evans, "all those lives lost because of it."

"Yes but who knows what this device does and what the aliens could have done with it."

"It's no good dwelling on what might have been. We've got to find that exit to the base and get away from that thing out there." Henderson looked round, a worried expression covering his face, as he began muttering to himself. "If it can wipe out a spaceship of aliens, it can take us easily."

## Chapter 33

Fragments of walls from the once colossal skyscrapers threw out long shadows over where Quigly now sat, shielding him from the burning glare of the early morning sun. Even so the warmth of the day still reached him and he had to struggle not to doze off. He knew the aliens could arrive any second but somehow he found it hard to believe anything could disturb the oppressive silence that lay over all his surroundings. He felt as if he was the only one left alive on the whole of the Earth when all he could see was wreckage stretching out into the distance. The feeling of loneliness was overwhelming, worse even than the thought of the approaching battle; at least he would be with other people then.

Again he checked the satellite link for signs of any life forms, chilling despair creeping over him as it returned the same negative answer as all the times before. How could the aliens have wiped out all life, surely there had to be one tiny animal alive out there. There had to be.

There was a sudden groan followed by a sharp bang behind him as the door was roughly thrown open. A stream of suited figures emerged, one heading towards him, whilst the others began assembling equipment.

"How's it looking?" he could tell from the grating voice it was Hawkins, even though he couldn't see his face through the darkened visor.

"It appears to be all clear and no new orders." Hawkins nodded satisfied and moved back to check on the other's progress.

There was now a small army of suited figures surrounding the door, hauling out more large pieces of machinery, most of which barely fitted through the opening. These strange looking metal monstrosities were soon bolted together to form small assault vehicles and planes with a much more familiar appearance to them. They couldn't carry much weaponry but they were certainly fast and manoeuvrable, although even in this area they were only slightly more than comparable to the agility of the alien craft. They were embarking on little more than a suicide mission. After all what chance did they have against such superior technology, not to mention the fact that every movement was difficult in the bulky suits they all wore.

Quigly watched silently as the last pieces of machinery were assembled into transport hovercrafts, with their large flat decks. As they all clambered onto the hovercraft decks he realised how little protection they offered to their passengers but they did at least save them from a long walk and they could easily move over any terrain including land, water and ice without any problems.

The hovercrafts sprang into life, as Quigly glanced at the computer he still carried.

"Wait." Quigly raised his hand. "There's someone coming." He zoomed in on the screen.

"Aliens?" Hawkins tried to peer over.

"No, one of our guys heading straight for us." They looked up at the horizon to see a small dust cloud approaching, that soon became apparent was a rider on an air bike. The hefty jets that propelled the vehicle forward and kept it above the ground blasted away any debris that the bike passed over. Its colour seemed to change keeping in tune with its surroundings and providing it with camouflage. At a slow speed it would have been impossible to see it at all.

"We're going to be late for the party if we don't get moving soon." Hawkins glanced at his watch his eyebrows knitted into a frown.

"I get the feeling this is important." Quigly pointed at the rider who just then hit a plate of metal that had come to rest angled slightly upwards. It sent the bike hurtling into the air and over the remnants of a brick wall to land so heavily on the other side that the underside scraped along the ground. "He's not bothering to go around anything, as if he's in a hurry."

The rider skidded to a halt before them and lifted the darkened visor over his helmet all in one flowing action. "Are you Hawkins?" he barked with an air of authority. He waited until he had received a curt nod of the head. "Shaun Willis." They shook hands, as a vexed frown rapidly spread over Hawkins features. "I have orders direct from the government here." Willis thrust a computer into Hawkins hands. "Couldn't risk it being intercepted over the satellite link." He explained before Hawkins even had a chance to ask the question. "They don't have much faith in the current encryption algorithms we're using, or at least not when it comes to the aliens.

I need to borrow a couple of your people. We haven't got much time so I'll explain to them on the way." Hawkins frantically scanned the screen trying to make sense of it all, though the government seal plastered at the top remained clear enough.

"Moore, Woodridge grab a couple of bikes. You're with Willis." Hawkins ordered, watching as the three men took off across the wreckage as fast as the bikes would take them.

Quigly looked at the picture on the screen; relieved to see the surrounding area was still clear. He felt the hovercraft lift as the cushion inflated and then they were moving at speed across the rubble-strewn landscape, air blasting against them. The vehicles weaved skilfully between the few fragments of remaining walls and buildings, occasionally moving off the continuous rubble onto clearer patches of road. In places ragged forms of cars lay discarded as a reminder of what had once been their grand civilisation.

Soon they were out of range of the geostationary

satellite Quigly was linked up with and it was several minutes before he could establish a link with a new one. At last a bird's eye view appeared on the screen, the large alien ship blatantly obvious with a multitude of dots scurrying round it like ants. He zoomed in, the black specks turning into the forms of smaller alien vehicles. He looked back out across the landscape; a mass of taller ruins lay ahead, providing concealment from what he knew lay on the other side, in the middle of what had once been a park. They could wait without too much risk of discovery but they would then have to move fast when it was time to attack, if there was any chance of getting to the ship before its door closed. Then again for all they knew it could already be shut, since there was no sign of it on the image on the screen. He zoomed out to the furthest view, their own vehicles appearing as spots speeding ever closer to the ship. More groups of the black spots appeared on the edges of the screen as the various human attack forces moved into position.

"Quigly … Quigly will you answer me?" he was suddenly aware Hawkins had been talking to him. He looked up to see Hawkins shuffle over and peer at the screen.

"The alien ship's just the other side of what's left of those buildings there." Quigly pointed to the ruins.

"Good we'll lay in wait behind them." Hawkins motioned to all the vehicles as he gave instructions. They all slowed at once and stealthily covered the remaining distance to come to rest behind the tall walls. Hawkins voice echoed round inside their helmets once more. "Don't forget that door is our primary target. We have to get inside whatever. Good luck."

An anxious silence stretched on forever as they waited, Hawkins staring at his watch. Quigly readied his gun, one eye still on the screen as he checked the enemy's movements.

The other teams were still getting into position with ten minutes remaining before the planned attack. One black spot, an enemy craft was edging in on their own position, the shattered walls still hiding it from view. Despite the air conditioning in his suit, Quigly felt beads of sweat running down his face as he held his breath. If the craft continued its current course it would soon come into view, destroying any possibility they had of a surprise attack. He checked his watch. Nine minutes to go. The alien craft wasn't slowing down or changing direction but steadily drawing nearer. He motioned to Hawkins to check the screen. Hawkins tensed as the realisation dawned of what was going on. They were in trouble. There was nowhere to hide and the noise of the engines starting would surely give them away. The alien craft had approached the corner of the wall and still seven minutes remained. The other teams were now all in place but there was no way to communicate with them.

The blue cylindrical material of the alien craft's nose emerged into sight a hundred yards or so in front of them. The sunlight glistened wildly off the reflective material, shattering it into an array of colours. No sound could be heard from it as it slowly moved more of its bulk into sight. Somehow it hadn't appeared to have spotted them yet but that was only a matter of time. Six minutes to go. The craft seemed absorbed in its task, the pattern of the other alien vehicles suggesting that they were formed in some sort of search pattern, perhaps trying to locate more shelters.

It was now in full sight, a bizarre looking contraption suspended above the ground in between which dazzling white energy sparked. Quigly could feel everyone round him stiffen, breathless with anticipation. Suddenly a tremendous explosion engulfed their senses, covering them in an air of confusion. For a brief moment everything about them was quiet and the alien craft still continued slowly in the same direction. Sharp cracks sizzled through the air. In the distance a ball of fire mushroomed upwards while plumes of smoke spread outwards.

"Someone must have been discovered." Hawkins shouted, trying to regain his wits. "Head for the door and don't stop for anything." Their own vehicles roared to life drawing the attention of the alien craft, which veered sharply to face them. They were all moving at speed now round the wall and up the incline towards the battle. The alien craft fired several shots of light that ripped through the air. The first two pulses blew out the remnants of the wall they had been hiding behind whilst the third caught one of the fighter planes, sending it spiralling out of control. The fighter flipped end over end as fire spurted out in all directions. The remains crashed into the alien vehicle creating a huge deadly fireball of metal that careered towards one of the hovercraft. It swerved just in time and the ball narrowly missed it, instead smashing into a twisted metal structure. The rest of their small team raced on, clearing another wall to arrive looking down on where the park had once been. The sight that confronted them made their hearts stop.

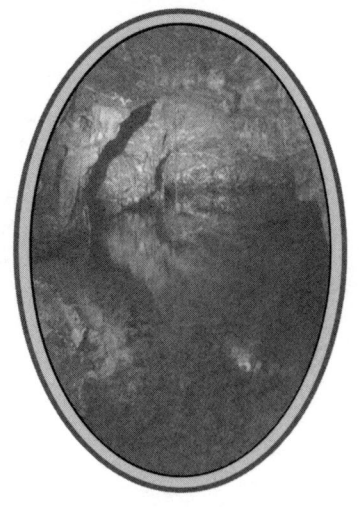

# Part Three

### Flight of Fear

## Chapter 34

Martinez could hear dull thumps, as though something heavy was trudging its way over the earth floor, getting ever closer to him. There was another crackle of static in the air. He felt his heart pounding hard and a new surge of adrenaline rushed through his body. Whatever it was, alien or otherwise, he felt sure its intentions weren't good and he wasn't about to wait and find out.

With effort Martinez scrambled to his sore feet and was once more dragging himself on, stumbling over roots and rocks in the dim light. Shocks of pain cursed up his legs every time his feet hit the now hard earth, as he ducked and weaved his way through the forest.

Suddenly Martinez emerged from the trees, frantically trying to stop as he realised there was no ground before him but instead a sheer drop to unknown depths. The grit on the floor gave way under his feet and he skidded along, only just managing to avoid going over the edge. He dizzily stared at the abyss that ran some distance to either side of him and perhaps eight feet wide, blocking his path and trapping him. Several seconds had passed before he heard the grit that had gone over the edge hit the bottom, indicating its frightening depth.

There was no way he could jump it, that he felt sure of. The foliage was too thick to push through on either side, destroying any hopes he had of going round. His only choice was forwards or backwards into whatever was pursuing him. He frantically searched round for a makeshift bridge, in desperation tugging on sapling trees to no avail. It was too late, that thing was emerging from the jungle just behind him. He turned to face his aggressor. There was a central dark form that he couldn't make out in the still faint light. Only the yellow glow of light that haloed it was plainly visible; a rough sphere of illumination and more strands that led off from it, moving erratically and existing as anything but straight. These strange lengths of light didn't seem to obey the laws of nature; instead they moved and bent, sometimes swishing through the air like tentacles, by their very nature pulsing with energy. He couldn't even begin to imagine what it was; it seemed too bizarre in appearance to even be alien. He tensed as he felt the air seem to become charged with a strange energy. The thing appeared to float across the floor towards him, the strands of light generating heavy thumps every time they came in contact with the ground. The shattering noise of its movement pounded through his brain as it just kept on coming.

"Somebody help me." Martinez screamed into his radio. It was all he could think to do in his desperation before remembering the gun he still carried. Seizing it he fired. The deafening shots rang out, as explosive bullets tore through the approaching thing, apparently having no effect other than an occasional small distortion of light. He swapped to laser. As before it made a big impact in the surrounding vegetation but none to the strange entity and he began unconsciously backing up, unaware that he was perilously close to the edge.

It was relentless in its advance and with his next backwards step he found nothing but air beneath his foot. The gun was discarded in panic as he tried to grab at anything, knowing with despair he was falling into that deep hole he had peered down. His fingernails felt like they had been wrenched from their sockets as he gripped onto a small rocky ledge, his feet scrambling about below, trying to find footholds. All the time the darkness lay underneath waiting to swallow him up.

Martinez became aware of a glowing light emerging over the edge, feeling its way down towards him, almost sensing his heavy breathing and struggling form; its movement causing a shower of pebbles to reign down around him. His breathing reduced to shallow gasps as he watched the light close in on his left wrist, increasing in opaqueness to almost a solid form. It reminded him of some kind of tentacle and he had a feeling that it wanted to drag him up to whatever it was attached to. There was nowhere to go except down. He didn't much like the chances of that option and instead hung on tightly, helpless, trying to find any purchase on the rock face.

He watched in horror as the arm, still emitting a faint yellow light made contact with his wrist and he was suddenly aware of excruciating pain surging up his arm, causing him to let go with that hand. Tentatively he looked up to see his heavily burned arm, the tentacle wrapped around it but the light now diminished to a faint glow and no longer burning. He felt it tug sharply on his arm sending fresh waves of pain through the damaged tissue. The thing gave another yank, this time succeeding in ripping his fingers of his other hand free from the rock and dislodging him. It began pulling him upwards with force. He was powerless against it.

Martinez fumbled for one of the explosive devices he carried on his belt, determined to be ready for whatever lay in wait above. He was almost at the top of the hole before he finally succeeded in prying it free and arming it ready. Not an easy task with only one hand free, which was shaking uncontrollably. The destructive capabilities of the explosive felt reassuring. Another arm of light assumed a more solid form as it reached out to entangle him round his waist, pinning his arm holding the explosive to his side. More burning pain consumed him where the remnants of the light touched. The static in the air was building as he was hauled clear of the hole and upwards. A mass of sizzling blue light greeted his vision in amongst which appeared a body of faint yellow that the arms holding him were attached to. He felt his hair take on a life of its own as the static electricity enveloped him.

There was no time left, He was being pulled in towards the frightening spectacle below. He released his grip on the explosive trying to aim it as much as he could, given the restrictive grasp the thing had him in. A surge of heat and fear hit him as the rock below him exploded, the ground crumbling away.

He was again falling aware that a body of yellow was following him into the gloomy depths of the pit; its arms ablaze in light, twisted painfully into him before finally releasing their grip. There was nothing to grab onto as he plummeted downwards scared of what would come at the end of the fall, scared of his imminent death.

Above the limbs of light were hauling the glowing mass back up to the top with ease as though gravity had little effect on it.

## Chapter 35

Moore felt the front end of his bike lifting threateningly, as though it were about to flip upwards at any minute. These bikes were normally stable but he was driving it flat out in an attempt to keep up with Willis.

"So what's going on?" He asked over the suits communication link.

"Hopefully the obliteration of all things alien on this planet." Willis answered, enjoying the puzzled tone in Moore's voice as he questioned him further.

"And how do you intend to do that, after all nothing's worked so far."

"That's the problem, we've tried all conventional weapons including nuclear missiles but somehow the aliens are managing to destroy them before they get close enough to do any damage. That doesn't mean that a nuclear bomb wouldn't work though."

"You can't be serious, you can't set off a nuclear device here." Moore said horrified, feeling sure Willis was mad. "We wouldn't be able to return to the surface for years."

"What other option is there? If we could detonate one close enough, the radiation might just be enough to kill them."

"You haven't got a bomb on that bike have you?"

"No, that's already been tried without success, somehow they just detect them no matter how well camouflaged they are. I had a hard enough time getting to your base, there's alien vehicles everywhere, which is why the government decided to just send me, since they thought I'd be able to hide easier by myself."

"So what is the plan then?" Woodridge asked as Moore sunk into sombre quietness.

"There's a nuclear power station not far from your base or the alien ship. It somehow survived the initial attack just about intact, although we're not sure how. They think it's probably because of all the extra shielding added as a safety measure when it was built, in case of any accidents. It's being heavily guarded by numerous alien vehicles but if we could get past them and managed to start a chain reaction in the Uranium rods we could create the same effect as a nuclear bomb, only somewhat larger in scale. If it doesn't kill them I don't know what will."

"But we'll be blown to bits, and so will all those people attacking the alien ship." Moore tried once more.

"That whole attack was just a diversion so we can get into the power station, the government doesn't actually believe it will succeed. Why do you think the orders were transmitted over the satellite link with a minimal amount of security."

"But all that other vital information about the shelters was also transmitted."

"I believe someone just uploaded the data package they were given and didn't even notice the added layers of encryption algorithms used on any of the sensitive information. If you linked all the computers in the world up, they'd still have a job to crack it, so it's highly unlikely the aliens could either."

"It doesn't change the fact all those people are going to die when this bomb goes off."

"You two are going to help me get in there and set it." Willis continued ignoring Moore. "The chain reaction will take a little time to get going once I start it. Hopefully you'll both be able to get to the alien ship and tell everyone to retreat to the shelters, over the suit's intercom, before it goes off."

"And what about you."

"I need to stay with it right up until the end to make sure nothing stops the process."

"You'll be killed."

"I'll go down in history as the man who saved the world. I'll never die, I'll always be remembered."

"Fat lot of good that will do you when you're dead."

"And if I don't sooner or later they'll take my family out. Someone has to do this."

"The whole plan is madness." Moore stated in disgust.

"There it is." Willis pointed to the lone building on the horizon, set apart from the rest of the city, its walls blackened and chipped but otherwise in good condition. Even the roof remained attached in most places. It had obviously had fencing round its perimeter at one time but now the posts were scattered all over the place along with tangled lengths of barbed wire.

"Ok now comes the fun part." Willis held his hand up, gesturing for them to stop as he brought his own bike to rest. They hid in the last remains of buildings before the power station. In front of the building sat several alien vehicles, like ancient guardians. "The attack should start in a few minutes and hopefully draw them away." Willis checked his watch as a plume of smoke billowed up in the distance. Two of the alien vehicles turned and headed in the direction of the disturbance, whilst the third and sole remaining one began to slowly patrol the perimeter.

"I was hoping they would all leave." Willis said disappointed.

"We'll not get past it." Moore stated darkly.

"There's no cover between here and that power station for us to hide in so we'll have to make a run for it."

"It's not going to work."

"It's got to. Ready." Before they could answer, Willis slammed the bike into top speed, sending it shuddering forwards. They followed, watching as the alien vehicle disappeared round the corner and was lost from sight. They reached the remains of the fence and not bothering to slow headed straight for the main door. It was too late the alien craft had come into view, its course immediately changing to their direction.

"We'll have to take it out." Willis yelled, swinging his bike towards it and firing both guns. The beams of red light pounded into their target, evaporating as they hit some sort of protective shield round it. Moore and Woodridge fired, their own weapons proving as useless. "Keep firing at it." Willis shouted.

A yellow light flashed out from the alien craft, directly towards Moore, who swung the bike and hit the brakes so hard it was sent over onto its side, skidding along the ground before at last coming to rest. His leg was trapped under it, as he lay dazed. Willis and Woodridge continued their assault feeling exalted when they noticed the unseen force field flicker. Moore pulled himself free as the alien craft made another dive for him, firing wildly. He threw himself to the ground as Willis's shot finally ripped a hole into the alien ship. Another shot sent it up in a ball of flame to become just another piece of wreckage to litter the ground.

"You ok?" Willis drew up alongside as Moore dusted himself off.

"I'll live. For how long I don't know."

"Come on we haven't got much time." Willis jumped off the bike and ran up to the doors, hurriedly typing in the code on the keypad before undergoing an eye scan. The doors opened. "Nearly home free." Willis smiled and entered. They trailed behind as he led them through a series of rooms to at last arrive at a door marked "Main Control Room". Inside it was entirely filled from wall to wall with banks of monitors, dials, switches and other electronic equipment.

"Now we're here what do we do?" Moore asked. Willis began rushing round checking equipment.

"We make a bomb." Willis flicked several switches. "Good the backup generator is working," he concluded, briefly examining the pictures that had flashed up on the TV monitors.

"I know but how?" Willis sighed, tapping a gauge in front of him.

"It would take too long to explain exactly what I'm doing but basically the first thing we have to do is start a reaction going." He pointed to the cameras, "they're showing pictures of the nuclear reactor. Inside that is Uranium and basically all we have to do is bombard it with neutrons to start the reaction."

"And then it blows up."

"No." Willis typed some commands into one of the consoles. "Seems to be working so far."

"So how do you get it to blow?"

"At the moment there's neutron absorbing rods of boron steel inserted into the Uranium-235, which limit the number of fissions produced and stops a chain reaction occurring. If I remove the rods of boron steel then the fission neutrons will cause further fission of the Uranium, resulting in a chain reaction. That's basically what an atomic bomb is, an increasing uncontrolled chain reaction."

"Say again." Woodridge looked blankly.

"All you need to know is that if I remove the rods

of boron steel after a short time we should have the same effect as an atomic bomb going off. There's going to be a lot of radiation for miles around."

"So have you done it?"

"No, it's all set up and ready to go but I need you two to get going back to the others to tell them to get back to the shelters before I start it, otherwise you won't have enough time."

"You sure you want to do this." Moore asked once more.

"Positive, now get going." There was an awkward silence for a moment, as Woodridge and Moore stood unsure what to say. "You'd better hurry up, I'm setting it to explode in 30 minutes from now." Willis clicked a timer on his watch.

"That's not enough t…" Woodridge raced for the door, seeing the expression on Willis's face and realising he wouldn't be able to change his mind.

"Good luck." Moore, hit his watches timer, as he left cursing himself that he hadn't known what else to say to a man who was about to die. Within seconds they were mounted and racing towards the raging battle in the distance. They skidded to a halt as a line of alien vehicles cut off their path.

"What do we do now?" Woodridge shouted. "We can never take them all." Moore remained silent, deep in thought as alien vehicles closed in on them. "What do we do?" Moore pulled out his computer, accessing a file before activating a continual transmission of the frequency the robot they had found underground had been sending out. "What are you doing?" Woodridge asked confused. The alien craft slowed before them, as if no longer sure what to do. Moore held up a hand for silence as Woodridge began to talk again. An alien vehicle swivelled 180 degrees heading back towards the main ongoing battle, its companions following its example, leaving the two men staring after them.

"How did you do that?" Woodridge asked in amazement.

"It was just a hunch I had. Our military always use a signal so they can distinguish who's friend and foe. It looks like we've just discovered their particular signal identifying friendly targets. I wouldn't like to test it too much though."

## Chapter 36

It had been a full five minutes since Josh and the others had heard Martinez's frightened voice over the radio, followed by noises of a struggle and the explosion. Now they stood stunned as the lights in the roof brightened and a strange red hue spread over the forest. Soon artificial daylight would return, bringing with it the false sense of safety.

They had no idea of Martinez's location and there was no response from him or the other two. In the chaos they had completely forgotten about the rescue team they had sent back.

"We'll have to go back for them." Burnett said her face full of determination and her eyes focused intently at the mass of foliage they had just trekked through.

"I think it's probably too late." Henderson muttered.

"What do you mean it's too late? You just heard him he needs help." Burnett snapped.

"But that thing has probably …"

"What thing?" Henderson looked at Burnett as though she had gone mad. "We don't even know what's out there. All we've actually seen is perhaps some dodgy sensor readings and some kind of light show. We need to go back and find the rest of them."

"But there is something out there, they found blood remember." Kolinsky stated.

"We don't know what caused that. We're running around terrified of something we thought we saw through all that mist at the waterfall, that's probably harmless." Burnett retaliated, refusing to back down.

"I'd say it is most likely to be alien in origin and we know they're bad news."

"Oh now you become a believer."

"Well something definitely made that electricity or lightning, caused those sensor readings and got an entire military team scared witless."

"We need to find out what though."

"I'd rather be ignorant and alive." Kolinsky returned.

"We're wasting time."

"Burnett's right we can't leave them behind." Josh agreed.

"This is not a democracy." Henderson stepped in front of Burnett, blocking the confined route back through the trees.

"I don't care I'm still going back." She tried to barge past unsuccessfully.

"We both are." Josh stepped forward just as the air suddenly turned chillingly cold. All the bushes around them took on a life of their own, swaying gently as though caught in a phantom breeze that they couldn't feel.

"I think we're about to find out what it is." Jenkins said stumbling backwards away from the bushes. "I don't get the impression it's friendly."

The redness of the fake sky was fading into bright light as flashes of blue lightning streaked horizontally around them. The trees behind shook violently and a tree uprooted. Some kind of heat haze effect began to cloud their vision as a form, shrouded in a yellow glow emerged onto the path. Arms of light were attached to this central mass, constantly fluctuating in shape. They flowed over the ground, scorching anything that lay in their path, its mass following suit. The arms and main body seemed to merge into a new shape for a fleeting second at the same time as more crackling light rippled through the trees. It changed again and now a new form continued bearing down on them, translucent yet with a strange glittering, reflective quality to it. The irregular shaped entity returned to its previous form, tentacles of light lashing out on all directions.

Its dynamic shape and movement was hypnotising and frightening, yet they couldn't take their eyes off it. An arm of light shot out at startling speed, becoming more solid as it ensnared Jenkins ankle. He screamed insanely as it burnt into his flesh, unaware of a second arm approaching.

"Shoot it." Henderson ordered but no words came out. He realised then how dry his mouth was, he had never been so scared before. Josh had already fired his gun, careful to avoid hitting Jenkins. The others followed his example, sending a volley of red beams and bullets into their target. A sudden blinding white light was emitted from their aggressor, engulfing everything and causing them to turn away. Josh had the impression the entity had changed form again. The light subsided enough for them to see the lack of effect their weapons had had. It seemed impervious to anything.

Jenkins was still being held and more arms were sweeping in on him but remaining as yellow light. They savagely cut into him. They must have used some solid form this time since, instead of burns, blood oozed from the gashes all over Jenkins body, pooling into patches on the ground. His incredibly high pitched screams drowned out the sound of more weaponry being fired at the entity, which momentarily paused, emitting a flash of white at the same time, before resuming its activities. Its tentacles whipped into Jenkins, pulling him towards its main bulk the form of which was still unclear behind the wall of light.

"What do we do? Nothing's working." Burnett yelled above the chaos. Jenkins torn and battered body reached the main mass where pulses of pure energy licked over him, burning and electrifying at the same time. The strands of light were still cutting into him as his screams became muffled before turning into gurgled cries. Briefly silence flared over everything.

The body disappeared in a wave of electricity and then brilliant white light burst forth accompanied by a barely audible deep base sound that shook the very ground and made their bones vibrate. A field of blue electrical energy slowly dissipated outwards as though a colossal amount of energy had been released from his body. The energy field passed over the bloodied ground, frying the remnants of his clothes and scattered leather boots on its unwavering course straight towards them.

"What is that creature?" Evans gasped.

"Creature?" Henderson repeated. There was no time to debate or even think about it further, they had to act quickly. "You lot go and find that door to the base and when you do, tell them to seal it off. We don't want this thing getting out." Henderson commanded, wiping away sweat from his face. His breathing had become ragged, more from nerves rather than tiredness.

"But ..." The creature and energy field would be on them any second.

"Go and don't go back for anyone." Henderson turned his attention back to the creature, mumbling under his breath too quietly for the rest to hear. "You'll be lucky if any of you make it out anyway."

They took to their heels as Styne drew up alongside Henderson, fiddling with an explosive.

"Get ready to run." He shouted before Henderson had a chance to protest. The energy field had slowed further in its rate of approach and looked as though it were weakening. Even the static energy in the air seemed less intense but the thing before them was still advancing, its form once more shifted, this time into a sleeker body with more strands attached to it. Though its core seemed to remain solid matter, the rest of its body now existed only as energy.

"Go. Quick." Styne lobbed the grenade and then dived out of the way to take cover from the blast that followed, pulling Henderson with him. He felt the heat from the explosion wash over them and shifted his position slightly to see the creature go up in a ball of flame. Smoke billowed up off it, soon engulfing them. Choking, both men stood up, feeling the stinging in their eyes increasing to the point where it was too painful to even try and keep them open. The sound of the electrical field had gone.

"Is it dead?" Henderson asked in between coughing, all the while rubbing at his eyes and trying to brush away the tears that kept springing out. A nauseating stench hung in the air, making them feel sick. Styne tried once more to squint through the smoke but the pain was too much and he had to close his eyes, cursing at his temporary blindness.

"What was that?" Henderson started next to him. Styne listened to the silence abruptly broken by a rustling close by.

"Don't move." He ordered.

"I wasn't."

"It can't be. It couldn't have survived!" A dull thudding resumed, getting louder by the second. "Nothing could have survived a direct hit like that." For the first time Styne actually sounded scared. "We'd better get out of here." Styne said, regaining his composure as he checked for the cool metal of the gun beneath his fingers. Somehow it still felt reassuring to have it with him despite its apparent ineffectiveness.

"Which way?" Henderson was groping about next to him, completely disorientated and blind. There was a hiss of static. Now they knew it was alive. They began making their way through the jungle, Styne almost dragging Henderson behind him as all the while they heard the creature persistently following them at its steady unwavering pace.

## Chapter 37

Below Quigly and the others lay the giant alien ship, light refracting off its surface into a rainbow of colour. The other human vehicles were already attacking, converging as fast as they could on the door, which still lay wide open. Alien craft darted in between them, pulses of sparkling beams rapidly emanating from their tips, spraying the area. Any object that happened into their path was obliterated in the ensuing explosion.

The human vehicles were laying down some cover fire but it was nowhere near as effective as the advanced alien technology. Waves of red laser beams littered the scene accompanied by explosions as various allied weapons detonated. Smoke from all the destruction was beginning to cover the battlefield along with fallen comrades.

Quigly's group began to pick up the pace as their own vehicles sped down the embankment, straight towards the gigantic main ship. They felt blasts of air and sound batter them from all sides as fighting ships swooped past, beams darting all ways and explosions threatening to throw them off balance. The ship lay fifty meters away, surrounded by grass that had once been green and lush but was now wilted, blackened and charred. The hovercraft came to an abrupt stop to let most of its passengers off.

Quigly jumped down with the others, their group quickly spreading out, in a planned attack that would hopefully give some of them a chance. The incoming fire was heavy and they had to duck and weave in an attempt to escape the onslaught.

As their hovercraft sped away, dazzling alien rays, caught it in the side, glancing off after first cutting deep gauge marks. The vehicle passed them, continuing its course to the door as more alien craft flew down, firing wildly. This time the beams hit the tiny fuel tank, causing it to burst into flames. A concentration of fire from their own vehicles sent the attackers on the run, and one of the alien ships plummeting earthward to join the hovercraft in a blaze of flames. On the whole though, things were going badly, with already a third of their vehicles destroyed or incapacitated.

"Get moving." Quigly heard Hawkins commands echo round inside his suit. The others were all running and he pursued with a strange detachment to everything. His senses were overloaded. Over the suit's communication system he could hear the others all yelling as they charged down towards the ship, their weapons blazing.

Ahead another hovercraft had moved in between them and the ship, looking like it would easily cover the remaining distance. From nowhere a blast hit it with such force it was propelled into the side of the main alien ship. The hovercraft disintegrated into a ball of flame as it hit some unseen shield or barrier around the exterior of the alien ship. A flash of blue roared past them, as it circled they could make out the form of the pointed alien craft, its nose still firing yellow beams. He realised then what had initially hit the hovercraft and was now mowing down the people on foot. More of their remaining vehicles attacked the alien craft, their fire at last sending it spiralling out of control.

Their own weapons were now in range, the laser beams vanishing as they hit the unseen force field round the massive ships exterior, leaving no trace of their presence. Another smaller alien craft had turned its attention on them, swiftly reducing their number with the strange sparkling but devastating beams. Perhaps a quarter of the human vehicles remained now, all trying to give cover fire to the ground troops but finding it tough against the far superior alien vehicles. Things were not going well.

Explosions rang in Quigly's ears as the ground all around them took a beating from all the different weapon fire being used. Smoke sprang up into the air. Screaming replaced the confident war cries, as groups of suited figures were blown up, debris flying outwards. Planes and vehicles, of alien and allied forces alike, exploded with frightening force around them. Shards of metal flew through the air like bullets, striking other unfortunate souls, sending them sprawling to the ground.

One of their surviving hovercraft took off, deserting them, hotly chased by an alien ship. Quigly gasped as he saw them head in the direction of the base, scared lest the crew of their vehicle should give away its position.

The door of the ship was still open. The aliens seemed to have no fear of them at all but nothing is invulnerable, Quigly thought as he made another sprint towards it before dropping to the ground again under a sea of weapon fire. Somehow they would take it out, it was only ten feet to the door.

They all made a last dash towards it, unable to stop as sparkling light flashed out from the ship, causing explosions all around them, that threw soil and rock high up into the sky, only to rain down on those that remained. The smoke and dust left was thick and hung heavily on the air, blinding them.

Quigly looked around desperately and then he caught sight of it. A strange shape moving through the screen of smoke, the same alien glinting blue surface, yet its form was different to the craft they had already encountered. It stood more upright, almost human looking. More blast and smoke closed in concealing whatever had been there.

"Retreat." Someone's shout came over the suit's communication system.

"Moore is that you." Quigly found himself saying, everything becoming so surreal to him that he wasn't sure of anything now.

"Retreat, hurry up." The voice repeated. Someone

slammed into him; he guessed from the direction that they were running away from the ship. He couldn't even see his hand in front of his face now. He felt a fresh blast against his back and he began running, with difficulty in the suit, frequently tripping over. He didn't know which direction he was headed in but it had to be away from the ship, since the smoke was beginning to thin. A yellow beam narrowly missed him, instead hitting the ground to his left and sending more dirt. He felt the impact of it on his arm. Around him very few of their vehicles remained, and the number of suited figures had also diminished drastically. The alien craft didn't let up though, in their relentless assault.

They hadn't stood a chance. He had known they wouldn't. He reached the rise of the hill.

"Everybody head for the shelters." He knew for sure this time that it was Moore's voice.

"We can't give away their positions." Another voice responded.

"Just trust me. We don't have time to debate this. You've got ten minutes to get there." Quigly stared at his surroundings, trying to get a bearing, at last seeing the old ruins they had first hidden behind. He ran down the other side towards them, leaving all the scenes of carnage behind, now hidden from view. His heart sank as he suddenly saw the distinctive blue alien vehicle, stationary on the ground up ahead.

## Chapter 38

"Come on, we've got to keep moving." Josh encouraged as he herded the others forward. Gently he pulled on Burnett's arm. She was staring back from where they had come and whatever nightmare they had left behind for the time being, along with the two men.

"We can't go."

"Come on." Josh urged pulling her arm more sharply and at last succeeding in getting her to move. "They'll be ok. They'll probably even get to the door before us." Burnett glanced behind, catching sight of the smoke rising up through the trees as she did so.

"How will we be able to live with ourselves knowing we left people to die."

"I'd be satisfied with just living." Kolinsky pronounced in annoyance at their slow pace. "Besides they told us not to go back and at this rate it'll be a miracle if any of us survive this." Josh frowned at Kolinsky who shrugged it off.

"He is right about one thing." Josh continued. "We won't make it if we go back. We've got to keep moving on until we come across that door."

"Over here." Evans, now some distance ahead, called back.

"Shut up will you. If you're not careful that thing will hear you and then come after us all." Kolinsky rebuked him.

"Who's making the noise."

"Will both of you just keep it down." Burnett snapped as she and Josh pushed through the ferns to join them.

"What do you make of that?" Evans was looking proudly at his discovery of a blue metal wall, the round door in it hanging ajar."

"Great more alien structures or maybe another ship, just what we need." Kolinsky growled "As if we haven't already got enough problems." He stole a glance back at the still forest and the distant smoke.

"It has to be part of the alien settlement they built down here." Evans continued ignoring Kolinsky.

"Who cares what it is. We need to keep moving." As Kolinsky and Evans continued bickering, Josh pulled out his radio.

"Henderson, Styne are you ok?" Static answered him. All their attention turned to him as he tried again. This time there was a sudden beep and the radio sprang to life.

"We're fine. Can't talk." Henderson's voice sounded breathless.

"We've got to get moving." Kolinsky fidgeted impatiently as Josh ran a hand through his hair, which had become more ruffled than usual, his mind running over everything that had occurred.

"Something's done some serious damage to this

place." Evans disappeared through a door as he continued his exploration. Kolinsky frowned. "I think there used to be a roof, judging from the structure of it and these walls clearly have been blown to pieces in places. We could easily climb over that section there with all the damage that's been done to it." Evans pointed.

"What are you on about." Kolinsky's frown grew. "We haven't got time for this."

"It's a good place to rest. Right?" Josh said with a look back at where the smoke still smouldered up off the trees. "We can get out quickly if we had to, yet are hidden from view."

"We can't stop."

"Well which direction do you reckon we should take then? That door could be anywhere."

"Besides it will give the others a chance to catch up with us." Burnett added

"It's not them catching up to us that I'm worried about." Kolinsky stormed into the building.

Evans was right about the wrecked condition of the place. Some of the walls were so badly smashed up that it was difficult to tell where the complex had been divided up into separate rooms. More bizarre equipment lined the few shelves that remained clinging to the walls, while debris littered the floor. Other doors led back out to the forest, some sealed tightly shut, perhaps by the vines that had sprouted up all around and covered most of the metal walls.

"I didn't realise until now how exhausted I feel."

Burnett flopped down onto a clear space of cold, hard floor in one of the maze of rooms, its walls still in a fairly good state of repair, providing more protection.

"How can you think about sitting down?" Kolinsky prowled the room, grumbling. "It has been hell since we first entered that tunnel. Millions of years old alien ships, an ancient jungle and no aliens anywhere unless of course that's what that creature is. It's certainly aggressive enough to be one."

"I'm not sure it even was a creature." Josh said as he warily sat down besides Burnett. "It looked more like light or energy of some kind."

"I saw some kind of central solid form to it, most of the time and I think even the rest of it briefly turned solid at one point." Burnett joined in. "It certainly has co-ordination and control over whatever it is made up of. Besides it just felt like it had the presence of an animal." Josh looked thoughtfully at Burnett's drained face, still covered in dried blood from her previous head wound. The green eyes were bright despite the tiredness he knew she must have been feeling.

"It knew exactly what it was doing when it killed Jenkins." Evans spoke up. "It must have a brain."

"The question is if it's not alien then how did it end up down here?" Josh closed his eyes as he leaned back against the cool wall. Burnett shook her head confused, her hair matted with blood banging against her face.

"More to the point can we outrun it and if not

how do we kill it." Silence resumed after Kolinsky's remark before Josh at last spoke.

"I don't see how that thing could have built this place or the alien ships we've seen, so it can't be the same aliens. Its limbs didn't appear to be able to transform into any form capable of holding small items and so it couldn't have possibly built the advanced technology we've encountered. It was human's ability to handle tools, due to their dexterous fingers and thumb that allowed us to evolve. We would never have accomplished as much as we have without our hands and I don't think any life form would be able to build technology without some kind of similar limbs."

"Its arms looked pretty dexterous to me." Evans thought back.

"No. Josh is right. I don't see how that thing could be the same aliens that built that space ship." Kolinsky said, surprising everyone by actually agreeing with Josh. "Mind you it's still alien to us. I don't have a clue how it got down here though or what it is." Kolinsky took of his glasses and began cleaning them, for the first time realising the grimy state they were in. "We ought to just find that base door and get out of here."

"What if that thing gets out and it really is indestructible. We need to find a way to kill it." Evans slammed the wall with his hand as if to emphasise his words.

"Everything that's alive can be killed, it goes

without saying." Kolinsky replaced his glasses to look at Josh thoughtfully.

"We just need to find a way." Burnett said.

"We need to move soon. Look how quickly it got to us from wherever Martinez was."

"Unless there are two of them." They all turned shocked at Evans's suggestion.

"Let's hope not."

"We've got quite a few explosives still." Burnett put forward, choosing to ignore the possibility.

"I don't hold much hope for them." Kolinsky snorted.

"If it's alive then I don't see how blowing it up can fail."

"So what do you think we should do Kolinsky." Evans asked irritably.

"Just no more running." Kolinsky at last slumped to the floor and stretched out his aching legs. "It's one thing I hate. I've never seen the point to it. I thought they were all fools, all those people that used to jog pointlessly round the park opposite from my office."

"Well next time we meet up with that creature you can stand there and tell it how pointless running is." Evans sarcastically remarked.

"Probably is." Kolinsky returned. "It's only delaying the inevitable, unless we can find that door, which I suppose is like trying to find a needle in a haystack."

"There has to be a way to kill it. We've just got to

work out what it is." Josh passed his hand through his hair again, a look of intense concentration on his face as Burnett watched his mind working, hoping he could find a solution.

## Chapter 39

There was no sign of movement as Quigly slowly approached the alien craft, which was leaning insanely to one side on the rubble, as though it had crash-landed. The blue metal looked dented in places and there was a gap round most of it, where it joined the top. Cautiously he moved closer, his curiosity overcoming any fears he had. The alien craft looked similar in design to their own fighters, except for its lack of any windows. He remembered back to reports he'd seen of a new prototype fighter where the pilot laid flat inside and saw all the images of the outside world, with relevant information overlaid, through special glasses. That ship too had been devoid of windows. Perhaps the alien plane was a similar design.

He reached out and touched the blue metal, surprised at the heat he felt, even through the suit, it surely couldn't be this hot inside. Maybe it was something to do with the way it was powered or then again it could just be a property of this curious material.

"Is it safe?" Moore's voice suddenly broke through into his helmet, as he looked round startled at the movement behind him, before realising it was Moore drawing up alongside him on an air bike."

"It seems deserted."

"Hop on, we've got to get back to the base. Woodridge and the others have already gone."

"Shouldn't we check this out, it seems a really good opportunity to see their technology." Moore sighed as he checked his watch. Nine minutes left.

"I guess a minute will be ok, we're not that far."

"Here, give me a hand with this." He indicated to the top of the craft. Moore backed off, nervously.

"Examining it is one thing but do you think we should be messing around with it?"

"This is important."

"What's it matter, the aliens will all be dead soon and then we can check it out."

"What do you mean?"

"We're going to Nuke them."

"This might get destroyed, just give me a hand would you." Reluctantly Moore helped him to pry open the gap at the top. "Nearly got it." The slit round the front and sides of the ship widened as the top swung upwards, pivoted on the back.

What is it? The cockpit?" Moore peered inside. "It's empty!"

"I guess so. Strange. It's nothing more than an oblong box. If a human were using this, then he'd have to lay down flat on his back to fit in, though it's certainly long and wide enough."

"Doesn't look very comfortable." Moore pushed

the grey slab of material, surprised to find it give beneath his hand, almost like some kind of gel, moulding round his fingers.

"Perhaps it somehow helps with G forces; after all they were pulling some impressively high speed, tight turns."

"How do you even know that G forces have an effect on the aliens?"

"You're right. The gel material could be for something else like comfort but the way it moved round your hand just made me think it was sensing and then reacting to your hand."

"You don't even know that this is a cockpit."

"The designs so like our planes." Quigly shook his head in bewilderment.

"What I want to know is where the occupants of this ship are."

"They must have deserted it when it crashed. Though I don't know where they got to, I haven't actually seen one alien yet."

Just then they heard a deep rumbling sound and became aware of an alien vehicle rapidly closing in on their position. Moore immediately scrambled into the cockpit and pulled the lid down, while Quigly dropped to the floor, as tightly against the ship as he could, pulling debris over him. Sharp metal and other debris dug into his chest but he dared not move as the alien craft roared overhead, hotly pursued by one of their own vehicles. As it passed beams blasted out, striking Moore's bike and completely destroying it. The alien ship effortlessly pulled up and over in a dramatically tight loop to end up behind the pursuing vehicle, turning the hunter into the hunted. The bright yellow beam flashed out again, immediately destroying their ally. It disintegrated into fragments and flame as the alien craft flew over it back towards the main ship.

"It's gone." Quigly stood up, finding it difficult to believe they had gone unnoticed. He raised his arms to lift the canopy, hearing a hiss as he did so. He looked down to see a gaping hole in the suit.

The lid opened and Moore emerged. "We've got to get back to the shelter in five minutes. He stopped. "The bike! What's happened to it?" He turned to Quigly. "We're dead, we'll never make it in time." Quigly didn't move. "Don't mess about." Moore looked at him closer, now seeing the torn suit. "How did that happen?"

"Doesn't matter." Quigly had recovered from the shock and now shrugged out of the suit, in some ways feeling relieved to be able to move freely again.

"What are you doing? It might give you some protection"

"I doubt it. It's pointless wearing it now." He started off at a run towards the shelter, with Moore following, knowing it was probably pointless but not willing to just sit and wait.

## Chapter 40

Now out of the thick smoke, Henderson's vision had cleared enough to see blurred images of Styne ahead of him, crashing through the dense foliage. They could hear the creature still chasing them as they broke free of the forest to come face to face with the cave wall, stretching into the distance on either side of them, with no trace of a way out.

"Now where?" Henderson gasped. They seemed to be trapped.

"There." Styne panted at last, pointing to a small hole no larger than two foot in diameter, barely big enough to crawl into. "You first." Styne pushed Henderson forward as he turned to see the creature no more than 30 foot from them.

Styne dropped to his hands and knees and began scrambling into the darkness after Henderson. He felt a sudden breeze of cold air behind him and something slammed against the soles of his shoes that he could only imagine was one of the creature's limbs. Pain cursed through his hands as they fumbled over the rough rock beneath him, quicker than before, in an effort to get out of the reach of the creatures arms.

Styne peered vainly into the gloom for Henderson.

"Where are you?" he whispered, as though frightened to speak louder and give away their presence. Another movement came from behind and he felt something make a grab at his leg. He turned, startled, trying to kick out at it, his heart unusually pounding with fear.

"It's only me, calm down. That thing can't reach this far. We must have crawled in over 20 foot." A torch light switched on, illuminating Henderson's face next to him, his eyes widening as they looked past him.

"What is it?" Styne followed his stare. They were in a small cave some four foot in height and not much more in width and depth. Rock surrounded them on all sides apart from the hole that they had entered through. They were entombed in rock, the only exit guarded by the creature, its limbs still thrashing about, trying to reach them.

"There's nowhere to go." Henderson muttered. "How could we have been so stupid to crawl into here?"

"We didn't have much choice."

"What are we going to do now?"

"We just have to wait it out. If it can't get us it will give up and go away eventually."

"It seems so determined. We could die of starvation before that thing gives up." Henderson aimed his torch at the rock. "Couldn't we try blasting through it?" The creature's arms illuminated the cave entrance as it thrashed and probed in as far as it could reach.

"If we try a crazy stunt like that we could end up bringing the whole roof down on our heads." Styne answered, calmly watching the tendril of threatening light. "All we can do is try to keep quiet so that it doesn't know we're still here." he reasoned.

"It might be able to sense us some other way, like heat energy." Styne didn't respond, instead choosing to sit down and lean back against the wall. He closed his eyes feeling a tiredness sweep over him."

"You can't go to sleep." Henderson fumed. "What about your wife and daughter back at the shelter. Don't you want to get back to them." Styne's body tensed as he opened his eyes and glared at Henderson, his false eye looking redder than ever.

"You know I would do anything to get back to them." Styne responded tightly.

"I didn't mean anything by it," Henderson stammered realising he had hit a raw nerve, "but can't you think of something we could do to get out of here."

"Rest up. We'll need all our energy when we finally get a chance to get out of this cave."

"You think that's really likely to happen?"

"It's about as likely as being in this situation in the first place." Henderson went quiet not sure how to take Styne's last comment. It sounded like he held little hope for their escape.

The light from the creature still emanated down the tunnel. Henderson groaned as he watched Styne's head droop, wondering how he could sleep under the circumstances. As always it was left to him to think of a course of action.

## Chapter 41

"It seems to be able to release huge amounts of energy. In fact I don't see how it is physically possible for a creature to generate that much." Josh silently paced back and forwards as he mused aloud. "It's a basic principle "energy and matter cannot be created or destroyed but only changed from one form to another" but that thing seemed to have unlimited amounts of energy from nowhere. I don't understand how it's producing it."

"How's this helping? We should start trying to find that door." Kolinsky interrupted.

"I'd rather find a way to kill it than wander aimlessly round this place with that thing in pursuit." Burnett said. "Let's just find some way of stopping it."

"It's almost as if it isn't a life form." Josh shook his head as if dismissing his own remark, utterly baffled.

"I don't see inanimate objects such as rocks running around killing people." Kolinsky glared at him.

"We'll just have to try explosives, a lot of explosives." Evans stated.

"Nothing we used made any impression." Josh said.

"If you want to get that close to it, go ahead." Kolinsky looked nervously towards the entrance to make sure it was still clear. "As far as I can see we're all dead short of using a nuclear bomb on it, which we obviously don't have."

"Wait a minute." Josh's eyes lit up with the beginnings of an idea. "How does a nuclear bomb work?"

"I would have thought you'd know that by now." Kolinsky said annoyed.

"Humour me."

"In layman's terms it blows up."

"Yes but it releases huge amounts of radiation, which carries on killing people years after the initial explosion. A strong enough dose of radiation can kill just about anything."

"Apart from cockroaches." Kolinsky added.

"It might work."

"If we had a nuclear bomb handy."

"Or a radioactive source"

"And where exactly are you going to get one from." Kolinsky frowned. "You're talking nonsense."

"I think I know where there's one." Evans said quietly.

"Oh yes, you'll just wave your magic wand I suppose." Kolinsky huffed.

"Where?" Josh asked.

"When I first started on the drilling machines at the shelter, all the operators were made to sign a secrecy document about the dump sites. They only told us, since we had to avoid drilling into any of them."

"Hold on a minute. Dump sites?"

"They are sites where years ago all the rubbish was buried and then the holes were sealed in. A company accidentally dug into one once and a lethal amount of radiation along with toxic gases was released. The government managed to cover the incident up and were trying to keep the knowledge of the sites hidden from the public to avoid a scare."

"What the hell was buried in them? I thought there were regulations in place on what could be dumped."

"I don't know. I got the impression after a few backhanders companies had managed to dump illegal waste. Whatever it was decayed over the years until it became lethal to dig into any of the dump sites. That's why Henderson was so worried when I hit that door, until he got there and found we were still alive and had checked all the readings. The trouble is if the radiation doesn't get you then the poisonous gases will."

"So how do we find them?"

"The operators were given maps with the co-ordinates of all known dump sites on them. There is one around here somewhere." He held up the computer. "If it's close enough to one of the cave walls we might be able to blast through into it."

"But that would kill us all, if these dump sites are as bad as you say they are." Kolinsky said horrified.

"Where's the location of that dump site?" Josh asked.

"Here. Yep it's right next door." Evans typed commands into his computer. "Kolinsky's right though it would be suicide."

"If we do find that door I can't leave here knowing it's still alive and might escape one day."

"So what are you saying?"

"You should all get going. The door must be nearby, this place can't be that big."

"What are you going to do?"

"I'll go and set some charges, if nothing else it might prove a distraction and give you a chance to get away. Don't worry I won't blow them until I hear you're all at the door and safe."

"I'm coming with you." Burnett announced.

"No, I'll be quicker by myself."

"And if anything goes wrong and the timers on the explosives don't work he's going to blow them himself. Aren't you?" Kolinsky prompted. "He knows he's dead if he does that."

"Don't be mad." Burnett appealed. "This creature's probably been down here for millions of years and it hasn't managed to escape in that time, so what makes you think it will now."

"Nothing, it's just a risk I'm not willing to take."

I've built up a rough idea of where we are based on information the computer automatically takes on the direction and distance we have travelled in. I then overlaid it with a map of all the dump sites and if my calculations are right there's one just beyond that far wall. The only problem is that I think it's at a higher elevation than we are and so you'll have to climb up to place the charges. That way you'll be blowing through a relatively small piece of rock rather than trying to take the whole lot out. Once it gives at one point the wall above it should also give and hopefully collapse down into this cave."

"What about the missing people?" Burnett asked.

"We have no option but to assume they didn't make it." Josh answered softly.

"You mean dead."

"Yes. Don't worry we're going to make it through this." Josh smiled, with a show of confidence, while inwardly he was shaking.

"There is still Henderson and Styne out there somewhere."

"You know I won't blow it until I know everyone is at the door."

"Don't do this." Burnett pleaded. Josh pulled himself to his feet, choosing to ignore her, and headed for their only two backpacks of equipment.

"There has to be something in here to drink." Evans pulled out a hip flask that had been hidden away in his jacket.

"Try this." Josh took a swig, the contents nearly taking his head off and inducing a fit of coughing."

"Got a bit of a kick to it." He commented as he passed it back. Evans laughed proudly.

"Special underground home brew." He explained. "Me and the other drilling boys have been working on it for the last two months. Of course we haven't quite perfected the recipe yet but the bonus is you don't notice that after a few glasses of this."

"I can imagine." Josh said refusing it along with Burnett, as Evans passed it round.

"I've already had the pleasure." Burnett smiled remembering the experience.

"How about you Kolinsky?"

"I never touch the stuff." He paused and then grabbed the flask. "Why not? Maybe I won't notice when that thing kills me." Kolinsky barely took a mouthful before the coughing started as he felt the liquid burning the roof of his mouth and throat. "Water" he gasped.

"I warned you." Josh laughed handing him a canister of water he'd found during his rummage.

"We ought to get going." Evans drank deeply from his flask, smacking his lips together at the end, oblivious to the strength of his precious home brew. Kolinsky pulled Josh to one side as Evans and Burnett sorted the equipment. "Whatever happens, try to get back to that door, even if you've blown the wall."

"What's the point if I get irradiated?"

"Trust me." Kolinsky said knowingly. "Take this for the toxic fumes." He handed Josh a breathing mask, that would cover his nose and mouth, two filters on either side produced fresh oxygen and recycled the air he was breathing. "It lasts for about half an hour."

"Thanks, I think." Josh raised his voice and spoke into the radio.

## Chapter 42

"Styne, Henderson?" Josh's voice came over the radio.

"Go ahead." Henderson replied.

We've come up with a plan to kill that creature but you two are going to have to get to that door as soon as possible." Henderson gulped, as he looked from Styne to their only equipment, the guns. "But we're trapped." He said quietly

"What?"

"Nothing." Styne grabbed the radio off of Henderson. "Just kill it, we'll be ok."

"We can't leave it alive it has to be destroyed. I'll give you a warning just before I blow it to make sure you've reached the door. See you there hopefully."

"Blow it?" Henderson looked in amazement at Styne, who shrugged as he watched the creature's limbs still flailing about in the tunnel entrance. "There is no way out Styne. You know that." He nodded silently in return.

"We were going to starve to death anyway. At least this way it might be quick."

"We can't just give up." Styne looked at Henderson, waiting for him to offer a suggestion, the time quickly ticking away.

"We … I … look its withdrawn." Henderson was right, there was no sign of the creature in the tunnel. "We've got to make a run for it." Henderson said, picking up his gun.

"It's waiting out there for us."

There was that feeling of static in the air again, slowly increasing. A crackling started before the electric sound of an energy bolt ripping through the air.

"What's it doing?" Henderson shouted as more crackling filled the air.

"This is good." Styne sat up looking excited. Another bolt tore through the air outside and the ground shook as the creature pounded down on it. There was a splitting sound as a fracture appeared in the rock next to them. More lightning bolts and tremors through the ground, causing it to grow until the rock ripped apart, creating an opening into a space beyond.

"It gave us a way out without even knowing it." Styne laughed, as he crawled through the fissure into a narrow tunnel beyond, running along parallel with the main cave wall.

"Go." Henderson shouted from behind, giving Styne a push. "It's opened up the tunnel so it can get through. It's right behind me. Hurry up." Styne quickly pulled himself forward, all the while hearing the rock tearing apart behind and the energy bolts hitting it.

"It nearly got me." Henderson's voice sounded small and scared.

"The tunnels narrowing ahead. I can't go any faster."

Behind Styne Henderson felt the creatures arm, entwine his boot, stopping him from moving. He kicked out, struggling frantically in the confined space the shoe at last coming loose. The arm was about to snatch at him again, as he hastily crawled after Styne, only just making it out of the creatures reach.

"Hurry up." He was finding it difficult breathing as his heart beat violently against his chest.

"It's too narrow. I'm going as fast as I can."

Another bolt of lightning and more rock crumbled behind them. There was a sudden surge of air as the creatures arm flew into the small cave, this time succeeding in catching hold of Henderson's ankle. He screamed, as it burnt into him. The creature was pulling him back as he twisted round and shot at it. The laser beam darted out hitting his ankle and the creature's arm. He was too shocked to scream, with the pain that his ruined foot caused him, but he was free of its grasp. Some instinct took over and he scrambled on, dragging himself forwards, ignoring everything but his desire to get away.

Styne was some distance in front of him now. He was nearly out of the creature's reach when, with despair he felt it seize his injured leg again, the throbbing he already felt disguising the pain of its hold. Styne had managed to turn awkwardly and reached out to grab his hand, as he was brutally hauled backwards, the rock scraping him as he bounced over it. It was all happening too quickly. He had no way to escape.

In seconds he was outside, more arms eagerly shredding him as he was hoisted above the main body of the creature. Its bulbous form below pulsated with energy and he had a strange sensation he was looking into something more. It was hypnotising. The arms roughly began lowering him down, as the creature changed shape and became translucent. The main bulk opened to reveal a core of pitch-black darkness, which he was being pulled into. The arms tore at him but his attention was solely focused on the strange depth of darkness below. It was like looking into another world. He panicked, struggling feebly but before he could do anything he was inside, its body shutting tightly around him, causing blinding pain throughout his body. It was the last sensation he felt.

Styne twisted round to see Henderson disappearing from sight. He was trying to decide whether to go back for him when the creature's arm shot in after him, not quite able to reach. He drove himself onwards, feeling the adrenaline rush through his body at the sight of light up in the distance. There was an opening, maybe back to the cave. The rock round him trembled and for a dreadful moment he thought it was going to collapse in on him. The creature was lashing out at him again and the static in the air was as strong as ever.

He thrived on fear normally but for the first time in his life he was so scared that he felt weak and sick. The light was the only thing that kept him going, like some beacon guiding the way to a small calm in the furious sea of fear that he was in, his only escape.

## Chapter 43

"It sounds like they're in trouble." Burnett said as Josh lowered the radio. "And if they're still trapped will you detonate it?"

"No, I will get them out somehow before I blow the wall."

"I can't believe you're still determined to do this."

"We can't risk that creature escaping this place. Think how many lives would be lost if it managed to get into any of the shelters."

"We'd better get going before it finds us." Evans said, shouldering his bag of equipment, holding the computer in front of him. "This way." he exited the alien building through another door that led back out into the tranquil forest.

"Wait a minute before we go out there." Kolinsky looked at Josh. "There must be some way we can protect ourselves against that creature."

"Yeah, run." Evans shouted back.

"Can't we talk about this on the way. The quicker we find that door the better." Burnett said impatiently, as she waited for Kolinsky to get out of the doorway.

"What if it finds us?" Kolinsky reluctantly emerged from the remnants of the alien building.

"I'm more concerned with finding that door." Burnett continued.

"It's that wall straight ahead." Evans handed Josh the computer containing information on the location of the wall and his own calculations on the predicted positioning the explosives needed to be set at.

"I just hope there are enough charges here." Josh gently patted the backpack in which he had stuffed the mask Kolinsky had insisted he take and all the charges he could find, three in total.

"Should be, although my calculations were a little rushed." Evans answered.

"Thanks I'll see you all later." Josh headed towards the wall. "We can still talk." His voice came over the radio.

"Can't get rid of him." Evans nervously laughed.

"Which way do we go?" Burnett asked, surveying her surroundings.

"I figure since we haven't come across it yet, we should keep heading in the same general direction we've been walking in." Evans reasoned. Silence resumed as they pushed their way on.

"If we could damage one of its senses." Kolinsky pondered as they followed after Evans who had marched on ahead.

"Like blinding it, do you mean?" Burnett asked

"Yes but I don't think that creature had eyes. It must sense movement or sound or perhaps thermal heat signatures or even something we haven't seen any animals on this planet sense before."

"So what do we do?"

"To be honest I don't know. Since the weaponry doesn't have any effect, we couldn't damage its senses even if we knew what they were."

"Perhaps certain parts of it are more vulnerable to our gunfire."

"This seems too easy." Evans said in front.

"Don't moan about that." Burnett responded

"I'm surprised it hasn't attacked by now. Perhaps it's planning an ambush."

"Maybe it hasn't realised we're here or it's after Styne and Henderson." The sound of a distant explosion reached them. "We've got to go back for them." Burnett said turning in the direction it had come from.

"We mustn't, remember" Evans called back.

"I'll try radioing them." Burnett looked in surprise at the large droplets of rain that fell onto the radio as she pulled it out. It was as though the heavens opened up and suddenly there was a heavy downpour. "The aliens have replicated the conditions on earth pretty well or at least what I think they would have been like." Burnett commented but the others were still looking around themselves as if expecting an attack any second.

## Chapter 44

Moore could hear Quigly's heavy breathing through his own suit. They had been running for four and a half minutes, and they were still some way off. Lone alien craft still roamed the area, looking for human survivors to pick off. Several times they had been forced to duck under wreckage to conceal themselves. In seconds the chain reaction in the power station would reach fruition sending out massive amounts of lethal beta and gamma radiation. Another alien plane approached. Both men crashed to the ground, wriggling their way under a jagged metal sheet. Moore could see Quigly shaking with exhaustion as they lay still. There was no point continuing, since there was only ten seconds left. They watched silently as the craft slowed overhead, before coming to a halt. It floated in mid-air motionless. His watch timer hit zero and he knew waves of deadly radiation would be heading towards them right now. He looked to the horizon, expecting to see some kind of explosion but none came.

The alien craft turned through 360 degrees, as though surveying the surrounding area, before flying back towards the mother ship. It looked completely unaffected. The radiation must have reached them by now.

"Shouldn't we be dead?" Quigly peered over at his watch.

"I don't know, maybe radiation takes a while to kill you or he's late." Moore admitted.

"Look." Quigly was pointing back, further under the sheet, where there appeared to be a crawl space heading downwards behind more mangled carnage. Quigly pushed in front of Moore, following the twisted path the confined tunnel took before at last widening enough for him to be able to stand up. There in front of him stood an airlock door, identical to the one at their shelter. Behind Moore gasped.

A face appeared behind the small glass window, set into the door, the look on it mirroring their own surprise. The face hesitated and then the door swung open.

"What are you doing here?" The man approached them, holding up a computer to scan images of their faces.

"Is this a shelter?" Moore scratched his head puzzled. "There's no indication of it on any maps." The man frowned, typed some commands into the computer and then looked up.

"Jake Quigly and Fredrick Moore I presume." He held up the computer screen so they could see their details on it. "You're some way from your own shelter."

"We need to get inside straight away." Moore

urged, remembering the power station. "It might have already gone off."

"Calm down, what are you talking about."

"The makeshift nuclear bomb." Moore forced his way past and into the airlock. "We're probably already exposed to lethal doses of radiation, you included." He prodded at the man.

"It's protocol to go one at a time." The man stood firm.

"Trust me we're all exposed if it's already triggered." Quigly entered as Moore pulled the rather baffled man inside.

"If we've been exposed to radiation, what then." Quigly reflected.

"We'll worry about that when it happens." Moore assured him. The door hissed shut and a computerised voice echoed round the walls.

"Please remain where you are. Scanning air lock for contaminants now." The time slowly rolled past as they watched the screen that showed all the readouts from the sensors and the procedures that had to be carried out with meticulous care. Finally the voice spoke up.

"Scan complete. No dangerous substances detected, you may now enter." The inner door opened as Moore stood in shock.

"It couldn't have worked." His two companions looked quizzically at him. "If no nuclear reaction occurred, the aliens wouldn't have been destroyed and they'll probably have tracked more than a few people back to their bases. They'll be completely wiped out."

"Maybe your watch went wrong, or the nuclear reaction was late for some reason." Quigly tried to reassure him. It could be happening as we speak.

"You need to talk to the general." The man with them motioned them inside.

"It doesn't matter now, we're all dead anyway." Moore groaned.

Quigly stopped at seeing their surroundings. Unlike their shelter, cut from rough rock, this base looked as modern and up to date as any building on the surface. Clean smooth walls, tiled floors and a maze of proper corridors leading to different sections. People were scurrying to and fro all about them.

"What is this place and why wasn't it on any of the maps as a shelter?" Quigly asked

"I'm not supposed to say but I guess it wouldn't matter if I told you, after all you'll have to stay here now."

"So?" Quigly prompted.

"It's a military base. Its location was purposely kept a secret for security reasons."

"Military base?"

"Well we actually specialise in scientific research."

Moore remained staring vacantly forward, as a woman approached.

Willis sat edgily behind the banks of controls in the nuclear power station. He wanted to enjoy the last few moments of his life but all he could do was worry about being discovered and he found himself staring intently at the only door into the room. He had made sure it was securely locked but he didn't doubt that the aliens could easily blast through if they suspected his presence there.

A beeper on his watch went off signalling it was time to remove the rods of Boron steel. Apart from overriding various safety protocols, which went berserk at his actions, the task consisted of little more than pushing a few buttons. Immediately the computer screens displayed details that the number of fissions produced was rising and he sat back satisfied, awaiting the inevitable.

Two more safety protocols tried to kick in but he managed to disable them before they initiated the process of reinserting the Boron rods. Everything in the power station had been geared up to avoid the very catastrophe he was trying to invoke and it was only the high security codes, direct from the government that allowed him to proceed.

The level of fissions were getting very high and warning systems started wailing throughout the building as a computer voice ordered evacuation of the facility. Willis tensed as the computers ignored his commands to shut off the warning systems. It seemed they would let him blow the station but not without telling everyone first.

There was no way the aliens would fail to hear all the commotion and it was almost certain they would find him any second but the fissions were already reaching the threshold and once past nothing could stop the imminent chain reaction that would follow. There was nothing to do but wait. It seemed to be taking forever to reach the threshold and until that happened the nuclear explosion wasn't a certainty.

Willis threw up, his nerves getting the better of him as he watched the number of fission neutrons level out just below the threshold.

"Insufficient fissions for chain reaction to occur." The computer droned, automatically shutting off the warning lights. He looked blankly at the screen. It was indicating all Boron rods had been withdrawn but that couldn't be the case, otherwise the fissions would have continued to rise. There had to be 100 or so rods that had failed to be removed and a false reading was being shown. It was the only explanation he could think of. He cursed at himself for not diverting the cooling water or entering the chamber and manually checking but there was still time. It would only take a few key presses to reduce the cooling water, which in turn would overheat the core.

The door to the room blew in, smashing into the window next to him and bouncing off. Willis backed into the corner away from the odd looking two legged alien monstrosity that entered. He would have given his life willingly to save the world but he didn't want to go like this, without taking the aliens all down with him. Willis didn't get the chance to hit any keys or for further thoughts to cross his mind as the alien vehicle marched towards him, its weapons blazing. He was cut down instantaneously, shot to pieces.

## Chapter 45

The forest seemed deserted as Styne pulled his legs free from the hole. Not far from him was an enormous area covered by some kind of long grass, most of which was about twice his height. He could hear noises still coming from the tunnel as the creature continued fighting its way through the rock after him. His only other option was to head into more jungle but he had seen enough of that to last a lifetime.

He was about to enter the tall grass when there was a deafening bang behind him and he turned to see the tunnel collapse in a cloud of dust. Styne smiled, imagining the creature trapped beneath tonnes of rock, crushed to death. The thought was shattered by the dark form that had appeared in the dust cloud, its long limbs reaching out towards him.

Styne turned and ran into the grass, causing it to sway as he pushed his way through. Every so often he looked back for signs of the creature. It was still behind him; he could see the waves in the grass as it pursued him. He emerged from the last barrier of grass into the forest, surprised that he could no longer see any of the grass shaking. It was as though the creature had disappeared.

He jumped as he felt something touch his arm. Warm liquid. A droplet of rain followed by more as a deluge began pouring down over everything, dropping from some hidden piping in the ceiling. Still the grass remained motionless as he set off into the forest, the canopy providing some shelter, though he felt comforted by the sound of the pounding rain.

"Styne, Henderson." The radio came to life. Styne hesitated before replying, cautiously keeping his voice low.

"Henderson's gone." He didn't like to say the word dead and Josh seemed to understand what he meant. "I'm looking for the door now."

"I'm nearly at the wall. I dare not wait too long."

"I don't expect you to." He returned the radio to his belt, quickening his step half-heartedly. He hadn't got a clue which way the door was and that creature could be lurking anywhere. He looked upwards at the sheer size of the roof, originally breathtaking but now he cursed at it and this whole place. Why was he even bothering, he should just give up.

He pictured his daughter's face, the anguish in it when he had told her he would be away from home for a while, working in a distant part of the underground base. It was a stupid pretence that no one believed for a second, including his own daughter. Somehow news of the door had leaked, without causing the panic Hawkins had predicted and by the time they had left everyone knew full well where they were going. That's why his daughter had been so scared and now it was beginning to look like her fears were justified.

He kicked a low lying shrub in anger and frustration, the leaves sweeping aside to reveal a small piece of torn material, drenched in blood. He stopped realising there was blood spots all over the floor and tiny pieces of clothing. It looked like a battle had taken place here.

There was a blood trail leading off down a crude path, the shrubs well pushed back. He had a gut feeling that the army team had been attacked here and by the look of it not too many of them had survived. Styne began following the blood trail down the path, finding that it soon turned off into the dense jungle.

The tracking became more difficult and he was unsure whether there still was a trail. A ripped backpack up ahead gave him fresh hope and he continued in the same direction. There was definitely no blood trail now but there was a clear path where, by the looks of it, something heavy had been dragged over the earth. Faint footprints appeared every so often in the muddier patches of earth. He felt certain they would lead to the door.

He breathed in sharply in horror as the forest stopped and he was confronted by the cave wall. The trail he had been following had also come to an abrupt end. "Now where." He growled as he strolled forward lost. "There has to be a door somewhere here." He felt the sudden urge to bang on the rock and scream let me out. He looked back to the wall, suppressing his urge, stunned as he noticed a jagged opening in the base of it. He flew towards it, unable to believe the sight of the grey metal door set a little way into it, unmistakably man made. He'd found it.

## Chapter 46

Burnett and the others had been walking for a while and the warm rain had been gradually getting worse, creating the effect they were in the middle of a tropical storm. Kolinsky cursed as he stumbled over another root, hating the feel of the wet trousers clinging to his legs. Water dripped continuously from his soaking hair and the rain made seeing through his glasses almost impossible. He was feeling as wet as the others looked.

"There's has to be some sign of it." He shouted forward to Evans.

"We've nearly reached the far wall, so all we can do is check along it." Evans pointed to the jagged rock face jutting up above the treetops only a little way away. "After all the door has to be in one wall of this massive cave."

A mass of climbing plants had taken root and spread their way over most of the wall, so that the it blended in with the rest of the jungle. From a distance you would never have known there was even a wall there. Kolinsky tried to wipe his glasses to look but it was an almost impossible task, since everything seemed to be wet and he only succeeding in smearing dirty water over them.

"There can't be many more places to look." Burnett said encouragingly.

"No only a few more miles of wall round the perimeter of this vast area." Kolinsky sneered sarcastically. "What I wouldn't do for a hot meal and a nice warm fire to sit by." Kolinsky said dreamily.

"Be careful what you wish for, you could end up with the whole forest on fire." Evans half chuckled at the frown that appeared on Kolinsky's face. "Might do if Josh gets the explosion wrong."

"Don't joke." Burnett snapped.

"Who's joking?"

"I don't like this, it has been too quiet." Burnett commented.

"Perhaps it doesn't like rain." Evans suggested as he pushed his way through the last of the foliage.

"If only but somehow I don't think that will have much effect on it." Burnett said brushing aside wet hair from her eyes.

"Well don't complain. As long as it's not here I don't care where it is." Kolinsky stated.

"I suppose we may as well head right along this wall and see what we can find." Evans headed off.

"Have you found that door yet?" Josh's voice came over the radio.

"No sign of it." Burnett responded.

"I'm at the wall now."

"Josh, Burnett are you there?" Styne's voice spluttered over the radio. "Anyone?"

"We're here." Josh answered.

"Good. Listen I've found the door or rather a door. I'm guessing it leads to the military base but I don't know for sure."

"Where is it?" Kolinsky shouted.

"I'm going to leave my gun firing a laser beam on a low setting at the roof. You should be able to see the red beam above the tree line."

"In that case I'm going to set the charges now and join you all shortly." Josh said.

"Do you need help?"

"No you lot just get to that base."

"I've set the gun up, can you see it?" Burnett and the others looked round, at last spying it a short way off in the direction they'd been heading in.

"Affirmative." Evans answered.

"I …" Styne's voice trailed away, as static began to consume the radio, accompanied by a crackling. "… go … thing …"

"Styne are you all right?" Burnett screamed as Kolinsky tapped her on the arm, staring intently at something. "Styne talk to me." Kolinsky yanked her arm, drawing her attention.

"It's here." Evans drew back.

"The static is not coming from Styne's end but from ours." Kolinksy explained. "That thing is here, somewhere."

"We've got to get moving." Burnett said taking charge.

Blue light surged from the trees at the same time as a strand of light lashed out, catching Evans across his body, cutting right the way through. A look of horror crossed his face. More strands of light, swung at him as the rest of the creature emerged from the jungle. In seconds, his body had been cut to shreds, blood spurting and spraying all ways as his remains fell to the ground.

Kolinsky and Burnett stood paralysed not able to take their eyes off what was left of Evan's face, shrouded in a death mask, the wide eyes still staring at them pleadingly. The creature had turned its attention towards them. Kolinsky came to and shoved Burnett hard.

"Start running." Burnett stumbled, as a wave of blue electrical energy was unleashed behind them. There was a sizzling of vegetation and cracks as trees toppled underneath the destructive force the creature had thrown at them.

Burnett didn't look back as she ran along parallel to the wall, keeping the red laser beam in focus all the time. Behind she could hear Kolinsky panting heavily, his breathing soon deteriorating into wheezing. She could feel the increases in static electricity and knew it was gaining on them but at the same time they had nearly reached the red light.

An arm flashed passed Kolinsky's leg, grazing it, the pain causing his leg to buckle. He screamed, driving himself forward to where Burnett was stood frantically waving at him. He felt a breeze of air as the creature lunged at him again, just as he reached Burnett. She grabbed him, pulling him inside a rocky crevice, into which was set the door. She slammed it hard into the tendrils of light trying to reach through. The door momentarily halted ajar as a force pushed at it from the other side. Behind her stood Styne. He and Kolinsky threw their weight against the door and she felt it shudder as if deciding which way to go. Burnett dug in with her feet, feeling all her muscles cry out in pain as she strained as hard as she could. Something had to give. It slammed shut and she drove the heavy steal bolt across, immediately slumping to the floor from the effort.

As Styne had begun to speak Josh's radio had also erupted into static before going completely dead and now no one was responding to him. A red beam had appeared above the treetops, positioned along the wall perpendicular to the one he was now stood at the bottom of. He paused unsure whether to continue with his plan or go after the others to make sure they were alright. The radio was still dead. He slammed his hand against the wall in the frustration of indecision, trying to think things through.

The chances were that they were all dead or they had escaped through the door. Either way it wouldn't matter to them if he blew out the wall. He would finish what he'd come here to do; he had to kill that creature.

With his mind made up, Josh began examining the information Evans had transferred to his computer. Not only was the position of the wall carefully plotted but he had also done a rough calculation on the number of explosives required and their positioning. The data was displayed in a diagram, on the screen, that showed the wall with three explosive packs drawn on it about 20 feet up and positioned 5 feet apart. According to Evans calculations the explosives would have to be detonated simultaneously.

Josh once more checked the co-ordinates before starting the climb. The rock wall was cut roughly, providing a multitude of hand and foot holds and the vines that entwined their way up it made the climb even easier. Only the heavy rain and his soaked clothes hindered his climb as he scaled the rock face. Josh paused momentarily as a shudder from the forest reached him. Chilly air from below crept after him as the forest flashed white.

Josh reached the spot and placed the first charge, wedging it into a crevice hard with an improvised clip. He risked a look down, only to see a dark, yet glittering object emerging from the denser part of the jungle. He scrambled sideways, rushing to reach the next location Evans had advised on. His foot slipped on the wet rock, his fingers taking the strain of his weight as he tried to regain a foothold.

Above the driving rain he could make out a humming that grew in intensity, at last developing into a whirring as air whipped around him, trying to pluck him from the wall. He placed the second charge and moved on to the third and final one. The wind was growing in force sucking in any fine, loose material and sending it up into a spinning vortex. Twigs and leaves narrowly missed hitting him as he edged across to the last location.

Josh placed the charge as a wailing started from below where the creature now sat, waiting for him. He couldn't go down without it catching him, so he carried on sideways, away from where he had placed the explosives. The creature below was following his every move. The wind grew in force, until he didn't know how to hold on and a final surge of air, sent him falling to the ground. He landed heavily on top of a tall plant that broke his fall but its sharp leaves left scratches all over his body and tears in his clothes. He lay for an instant dazed. The creature was approaching; he felt it in the pit of his stomach and the static in the air. He was as good as dead.

Josh fumbled in his trouser pocket for the detonator switch, his every movement causing pain. His fingers at last encircled it and without hesitating he hit the switch. A beeping began, he knew it was only a second or so but it felt like hours as the creature loomed over him, its arms about to strike. He didn't even bother getting up but lay still. A branch caught up in the turmoil of wind was suddenly released with a vengeance, smashing into the creature. It hesitated in its attack on Josh as behind the explosions erupted.

Josh pulled the mask Kolinsky had given him out and put it on. The echoes of the charges going off resounded round the cave as Josh looked back to see the wall blown outwards in a cloud of dust. If Evans calculations had been right a dangerous mix of poisonous gases and radiation would be rushing into the cave.

The creature's halo of light intensified as all its arms lashed out at Josh. He froze. Suddenly the light of the creature flickered as though extinguished, its attack stopped as it became translucent. It seemed to be struggling to maintain any form, as though it was being erased. Josh took the opportunity to haul himself up and head for the wall. Behind him the creature vanished completely for a few seconds. It seemed to be dying or rather fading away. Repeatedly it vanished, each time for longer periods until at last it did not reappear.

Josh pushed past the last ferns to reach the wall and the gun that lay wedged between two rocks, its beam still firing upwards. The remains of blood soaked garments along with heavy indentations littered the ground, all indications of a previous fight. Inset into the wall he saw the door, hanging loose, its hinges broken and the heavy bolt that had been used to secure it bent back on itself.

Without a look back at his strange surroundings he entered the tunnel beyond the doorway, glad to be free from the place and away from that creature.

## Chapter 47

Beyond the door sat a motorised cart, on a track, that was still in working order and with relief Josh sat back in the seat as it trundled its way slowly up the slope. At the end of the long passageway lay a vacant air lock, the door still intact. Through the tiny window Josh could see that the chamber beyond lay in darkness. He pushed open the door and entered, automatically activating lights as he did so. He knew he was already a dead man walking but he was determined to let them know the creature was gone and the cave was now a death trap.

The outer door shut as the computer began its procedures to test for contaminants.

"You're alive." Burnett's delighted face appeared, staring in from beyond the inner door. It was quickly brushed aside to be replaced by Kolinsky.

"My god, your face, it's red." Josh raised a hand to his face, for the first time realising how tender and sore it was, as he removed the breathing mask.

"Radiation burns right?" Kolinsky nodded. "I guess I was exposed to a very strong dose of radiation but I knew that was going to be the case." Just then the computer cut in, having finished scanning the chamber.

"Higher than normal levels of alpha, beta and gamma radiation. Numerous toxic gases also present in the atmosphere."

"I only came to tell you it worked. I saw the creature disappear before my eyes but I wouldn't come in this cave for a few years."

"Access is denied." The computer droned.

"Listen you're not dead yet." Kolinsky started.

"As good as."

"Please vacate the airlock at once." The computer cut in.

"I might have a cure. See the syringe by the door?" Kolinsky gestured.

"If you do not vacate the airlock, incineration will begin in 20 seconds." The computer voice happily announced.

"Can't you shut that damn thing off?" Kolinsky yelled back at someone beyond the door. The countdown continued. "He'll be dead by the time you've stopped it." It stopped on 5 seconds. Kolinsky pushed his face up against the glass once more. "Now as I was saying if you inject yourself with the contents of that syringe it should give me another hour or two to finish my work."

"I'd rather know what's in it first." Josh stared warily at it.

"I haven't got time to explain, you need to do it straight away if you're going to." Josh hesitated. "What's the worst that can happen, a slightly more painful death."

"That's what worries me." Josh held up the syringe and stared at the clear liquid it contained. It looked harmless enough.

"Trust me, please." Kolinsky appealed. Josh injected the contents into his arm as water began spraying down from the ceiling. "It's to get rid of the contaminants from the chamber before they open the inner door." Kolinsky explained, seeing Josh's puzzled look.

"So what have I just injected into myself."

"Nanobots."

"Pardon!" Josh remembered back to Kolinsky's failed experiments.

"This place is actually a military research facility so they already had a few nanobots, the trouble is, as I've said before, they're expensive to produce and so there were not enough of them to repair the damage quick enough."

"Great so I'm still dead."

"Not if I can help it. I'm trying to iron out the last problems with my research. If it works I'll be able to make enough to repair all the damage done to your tissue by the radiation, quickly and easily." The water had stopped and the inner door opened, to reveal Burnett, Kolinsky, Styne and another man stood the other side.

"I thought you were having major problems with that research."

"I had a brainwave but I need to get back now, if I'm to get it done in time."

"See you soon hopefully." Josh suddenly felt weak and would have collapsed if it were not for Burnett and Styne supporting him.

"I'm ok." Josh pulled himself away; nodding in the direction Kolinsky had taken. "Looks like he's moved in."

"We've only just got here ourselves. Kolinsky demanded the nanobots straight away and then forced them to take him to whatever facilities they had to begin work. I think he was delighted when he found out we were in a research facility and they had proper labs."

"This place, the people here, do they know what happened to us back there and what we found?"

"I'm General Daniels." The man who had been standing back quietly now pushed in to shake Josh's hand."

"We told him the rough details but we haven't had the opportunity to speak properly yet." Styne said with menace tingeing his voice. "But don't forget they already knew about that place, they sent a military team down there."

"We …" The General was cut off by Burnett's quietly spoken voice her face dawning with realisation.

"They made it out." She looked the General squarely in the face. "At least one person from that team made it out didn't they and with the device."

"We've only sent the one team and no one since." The General mumbled into his beard.

"There were signs of a struggle outside that door

and tracks leading all the way up to it as if something heavy were being dragged and there was soil on the floor inside as well." Styne carried on Burnett's theory. The General was looking guilty despite his denials. "I don't believe this." Styne paced in frustration. "The government had that device all along and you didn't give it to them. Do you realise how many millions, even billions of people died because of that decision."

"You wouldn't have done that, would you?" Josh moved forward, forcing the General to back up his eyes widening.

"No" he began, faltering slightly.

"That creature didn't seem interested in anything but killing people." Josh's brows knitted. "It wouldn't have touched the device and we didn't see any sign of it. You must have it."

Styne grabbed the Generals lapels before he could move and thrust him up against the wall. Guards that had been standing back in the shadows rushed forward, guns raised but he was oblivious to them.

"You did have that device didn't you?"

"They probably would have killed us all anyway." The General managed to stutter, his face reddening "and who knows what that device does." Styne looked as if he were about to shake the man to death in his uncharacteristic rage.

"Don't." Josh intervened, conscious of the guns pointed at them. "It's not worth it." The weakness returned tenfold and Josh collapsed onto Burnett.

"We need to let you get some rest." She said.

"Not yet. First I want to see this device. To see what all those people, what I might even die for."

"It's just a black box, nothing to look at." The General reasoned.

"Take us to it now." Styne gave him a shake, making the guards become edgy. "And don't even try to pretend it's not here." He released his grip, the guards responded by lowering their weapons.

"I don't see what good it will do you but if you really want to see it it's this way." The General led them down modern decorated corridors, with tiled floors, concrete walls and strip lighting that flooded every inch of it. There was nothing to give away the fact they were deep underground. "We have had our top scientists working on the device but so far it seems to have no functionality to it. It's just a black box with marks etched on the outside. We're starting to wonder if we even have the actual device the aliens were referring to.

"Perhaps it has some religious or cultural significance to them." Burnett suggested.

"If that's the case there was no reason not to hand it over." Styne growled.

In silence they traversed several more branches of corridors before arriving at a door marked with a large sign reading "High Security Personnel Only". The General keyed in a code on the security padlock and underwent an eye scan before the door opened to admit them. Inside was a concrete room filled with several desks, various electrical equipment and banks of computers. Uniformed people busily shuffled round, carrying out their assigned tasks and processing information. As they moved further into the room they finally saw the device sat on a table in the centre.

"I told you nothing but a box." Josh weakly stepped closer, ignoring the General, his head spinning as the radiation took its toll.

"So this is what all the bloodshed was for." His voice was thick with contempt.

"We should destroy it." Styne strode forward, pushing past the scientist who had turned to observe them.

"No." Two guards, accompanied by the General cut him off. "We need it, if only to bargain with the aliens."

"You haven't used it so far." Styne stared the General down, "and while I think about it I bet you know more about that creature than you're letting on. Does it have something to do with all this?"

"We don't know anything more about it than what you've told us. There was one survivor who brought the device back but he was out of his mind. Whatever happened to him down their sent him over the edge and the only things we could get out of him were wild ravings about his childhood and life before the cave. He even tried to top himself twice."

"As if we can believe anything you tell us."

"It sounds plausible to me." Burnett shivered at her own memories of the past days. "That creature and the experiences he must have gone through were enough to drive most people mad with fear, it's just the trauma of it all. The worst part is knowing you left people behind to die."

"They were already dead, they had to be." Josh reassured her, feeling blood throbbing in his face and body.

"Are you ok?" Burnett's voice sounded distant.

"I'm going to have to sit down for a while." He barely finished the sentence before collapsing to the floor unconscious.

Some time later when Josh opened his eyes he was vaguely aware of feeling the comfort of a warm bed, in fact everything felt burning hot apart from his brow. Someone was dabbing a cool cloth on it. He groaned feeling discomfort all over but not able to formulate a sentence or even the words to convey it. He tossed and turned not knowing what to do with himself. He was going through hell and there was no end in sight. He knew the pain would pass one way or the other but at the same time it nagged at him, never letting up. He wanted it to stop, not sure how to get through much more of it and not caring what was going on around him. Everything was blocked out in his semi-conscious state of pain and anguish. With relief he slipped into unconsciousness again.

"Is it ready yet?" Burnett asked Kolinsky as he entered the room, briefly moving from Josh's bedside.

"Done."

"And they will work?"

"I haven't had time to test them but assuming they do work, I've made enough of them to cure him." Kolinsky injected the contents of the vial into Josh's arm. He lay twisting and turning even in his sleep. Sweat glistened on his red skin as the violent fight continued inside him.

"And if they don't." Kolinsky pulled off his glasses and rubbed his tired eyes, only managing a brief shake of the head as an answer. Burnett already knew though. She only had to look at him to see he was close to death.

"We'll just have to wait and see." Kolinsky at last said.

## Chapter 48

The bright artificial sunlight was still flooding the forest contained within the underground cavern. Some time had passed since Josh and the others had escaped from it and the creature had disappeared. The forest now lay completely still as if it sat in a vacuum where sound could not travel. Yet some strange residual energy did remain where the creature had last been seen. An energy that was invisible and impossible to detect. It lay on the edge of what scientific theory suggested was possible and pushed the physics of our known universe to its limits. However it did exist within a fixed volume of air.

At last some of the energy tentatively shifted position to exist in the same space as a solid rock. The position of the volume moved again, part of it now overlapping a cluster of trees. It seemed to be able to pass through anything it desired. Its movement was becoming more fluid and confident as it experimented with its new found existence.

## Chapter 49

Josh slowly opened his eyes, feeling more groggy than he had before but that terrible discomfort that had agonised him was now gone, leaving him in a flood of relief. Slowly his head began to clear and his eyes focused on his surroundings. He was lying on a bed that was much more comfortable than the one he had at the shelter. The room itself was decorated with rich carpets and wallpaper. Wooden furniture stood elegantly around it and a vase of fresh flowers had been placed on an ornate hardwood table next to a plush sofa. It was more like a hotel room and he started to believe the last months had been a dream but then he noticed Burnett in a chair by his side.

"How are you?" Josh tried to sit up but his tired and sore body let him down. "You need to rest for a while."

"What happened?"

"Kolinsky managed to make some more nanobots and they actually worked." Burnett smiled as she spoke. "He said you might feel a bit drained. It's all the repairs that they've done to you."

"How long have I been out for?" Josh pulled himself up into a sitting position, this time successfully.

"About nine hours." At that point Kolinsky burst through the door.

"Ah good, he's awake." He marched over and checked all Josh's vital signs on his computer.

"So how did you get hold of your research? I thought you lost most of it when you lost your internet account and what you had managed to re-do is back at the shelter."

"Internet account! I wouldn't keep anything vital on that and certainly nothing pertaining to my lifetime research. It could get hacked far too easily. I only had extra notes on it that would have been helpful and saved time rather than being crucial to my work."

"But you said you lost all your research."

"No the ongoing experiments I was carrying out. As it turned out I managed to fix the problem first time. It's remarkable what a stressful situation can do."

"But your research is still all back at the shelter isn't it?" Kolinsky smiled slyly.

"I had a microchip embedded in my arm. It's a round disc less than an inch in diameter but can hold up to a gigabyte of information. I can download or upload onto it at any time."

"You've got to be kidding me."

"I wasn't about to let anything happen to my work."

"For once I'm glad you are so paranoid about it."

"Everything's looking ok." Kolinsky concluded. "I don't think you're up to it yet but the General wants to see all of us as soon as possible. Apparently it's quite urgent. I think they're having trouble on the surface or something from what I've heard from the scientists down here."

"I'll come now, if you give me a chance to get dressed."

"We'll wait for you outside." As they left Josh grabbed the clean clothes, similar to his own, that had been placed on a chair. He still couldn't get over his luxurious surroundings but at the same time he had a nagging feeling there was something missing. As he finished dressing he suddenly realised what it was. Windows. Hardly surprising since the only view would have been solid rock.

The other two were standing impatiently waiting for him, as he slowly walked to meet them.

"I don't suppose there's any food round here?" Josh asked as he caught a whiff of some culinary delight.

"The canteen is right around the corner on the way. We can head there first." Burnett helped him along as Kolinsky swung the door to it open. Inside the large room was laid out with rows of long tables and chairs. At the far side was the serving counters where steam still rose up off the hot food and delicious smells wafted across from. As they seated Josh and brought him a plate of food Styne entered.

"I thought I'd find you all here. How you doing?" he pulled up a chair. Josh examined the contents of his plate, amazed at the fresh vegetables that had been served up. He nodded, gratefully tucking into the food with a vengeance. It felt like he hadn't eaten for a week.

"You know I can't believe all that really happened down there." Burnett reflected.

"It did, no thanks to the government." Styne said. "Not only that but now apparently there's bigger problems with the aliens on the surface only no one will tell me exactly what's going on. The General wants to see all of us."

"We know." Burnett frowned. "At least let Josh finish his food."

"Of course." Styne threw himself back in his chair.

"At least we're away from that place and safe now." Kolinsky contributed.

"Not if what I'm hearing is true. There's some sort of trouble on the way."

The General entered and headed for them. "I was told you were all here. I hope you're feeling better." He asked Josh, who had finished clearing his plate.

"Getting better all the time. So what's up?"

"I think we should talk privately." The General suspiciously looked round at the other people seated at tables. "If you would like to come with me."

"It had better not be too far. Josh is still weak." Kolinsky demanded.

"Actually I'm feeling stronger already." He stood without difficulty.

The General exited to the corridor and entered the room a little way down it. A single large table stood in the middle with chairs around it in which sat two occupants. They felt their feet sink into the thick carpet that covered the floor, whilst refreshment machines stood by the walls. Josh's attention was drawn back to the two men. The short stout man with fair hair he recognised as Quigly, whilst the other tall, bulky man, with a beard and curly dark hair remained anonymous to him.

"This is Jake Quigly and Fredrick Moore. Apparently you were all at the same shelter originally." The General motioned for them all to take a seat, keeping the one at the head of the table for himself. "Quigly and Moore are up to date with your adventures underground."

"You make it sound like we were having fun." Kolinsky complained.

"More to the point did you tell them about the device you had all the time." Styne said tightly, glaring at the General.

"For the hundredth time we don't even know if it is the device the aliens were referring to but yes I have told them about the box we found. We have more pressing matters to talk about though."

"More bad news." Kolinsky rolled his eyes and slumped back in the chair, a look of disbelief spread across his face.

"If you'd like to explain." The General gestured to Quigly and Moore.

"We were ordered to launch a full scale attack on the main alien ship." Quigly began. "Each base for miles around, including ours, sent as many people as they could spare. Turned out to be nothing more than a slaughter."

"It was only ever intended as a diversionary tactic though." Moore continued. "Myself and two other men were meant to be creating a nuclear explosion to wipe all the aliens out in one go, only something must have gone wrong since, as far as we can tell, it never went off. Now the aliens are systematically searching and destroying all the bases so it's only a matter of time before they find us, unless we can think of some way out of this mess."

"There was one other interesting thing." Quigly took over. "On our way back we stumbled across an alien craft that, by the looks of it, had only just crashed but there was no sign of any aliens. We didn't get much time to study it though."

"So it would seem you four are the only ones who have seen a large alien ship up close." The General continued. "If we know more about the aliens then it may help us, perhaps they have some weakness we could exploit. You must be able to tell us something."

"Why don't you just give them the device?" Styne volunteered.

"There are no guarantees they won't kill us anyway and besides we haven't been able to find a way to tell them that we will agree to hand it over. They have cut off all communication with us."

"Maybe they don't trust you." The General scowled, biting back a sharp response, instead he continued in a restrained voice.

"Try to think back and describe everything in detail."

Josh thought back to their first encounter with the ship underground and its immense size. He could see the flight deck, crammed with alien vehicles, the strange lifts, the corridors lined with doors and the main control centre. Nothing seemed of any importance now.

"… deck full of vehicles." Burnett was saying.

"Describe it in detail." The General snapped. Burnett shrugged at the half forgotten memory.

"There were rows of alien vehicles of different types. Some were like our planes are, others were compact tiny things, too small for a man to fit in." She paused. "It's no good I don't know how to describe half of it."

"Besides the vehicles what else was in the room?" The General prompted.

"There were two lifts, lockers and strange flooring …"

"I almost forgot." Josh shot up from his seat, swaying slightly as his sudden movement made his head swim.

"What?" The General asked impatiently.

"I took something from one of the lockers. I left it in the pocket of my clothes back in my room."

"The guards should have checked you all though, for security reasons."

"Guess they didn't do a very good job." Styne said as they all followed Josh back to his room.

"Good, they're still here." Josh grabbed the old clothes off the back of the chair where someone had left them. Fumbling around in the pockets he at last produced a small black rectangular object, with no straight lines to it but instead gentle curves blended together to produce an organic looking exterior.

"This is it." He twisted it round, wondering how to tell if it really was some communication device as he suspected. The others all surrounded him, puzzled at the lack of any sign of an interface on it. There wasn't any apparent way of working it at all.

"It may be alien junk that they've just discarded and those lockers were equivalent to dustbins." Kolinsky said disdainfully. Josh paid no attention, absorbed in his search for some type of trigger to activate it.

"Maybe it needs power to drive it." Burnett suggested. Josh looked up.

"Any ideas." He placed it on the polished wooden surface of the table and stood back as he considered what to do.

"Or maybe …" Burnett approached and began moving her hand through the air above the device.

"What are you doing?" The General scowled as realisation dawned on Josh.

"The alien computers we found all used some kind of motion sensors and then certain patterns triggered certain responses."

"Speed may be a factor too." Josh stepped closer.

"I hadn't thought of that." Burnett began moving her hand faster.

"I'm not sure we should be trying to trigger it." The General intervened.

"Like you said it's only a matter of time if we don't do something." Josh said briefly looking up.

"This is pointless. If you're right there could be millions of combinations." Kolinsky rebuked them.

"It's more likely to be a simple movement if it is a communication device though, since they would probably want to activate it frequently and quickly. They wouldn't want to mess about and they wouldn't need the security of a complex movement." Burnett persisted, trying more erratic and then flowing movements. Nothing happened. One more sweeping gesture and suddenly a blue light appeared over the box. The light expanded and increased in shades until a picture of the interior of an alien ship materialised before them. Quickly she repeated the gesture and the light disappeared before anyone had properly seen the image.

"Well you've managed to trigger something." The General said with an ominous tone to his voice.

"It has to be some kind of holographic communication device." Josh said.

"We can use it to prove we have the device and then hand it over to them without anymore casualties." Styne said hopefully.

"Once we're on board we can take them out from the inside."

"Are you mad. All you'll do is provoke a more violent response if you fail to destroy them. We have the opportunity to end this peacefully." Styne looked away, his body language suggesting he was having a struggle to keep calm.

"We should try and get onto the ship and then assess things once we're on board." Josh said firmly. "After all we have no way of destroying them that we know of."

"How do you know that they won't just kill you and take the device?" Kolinsky pessimistically asked.

"We might not be able to destroy them but I'm betting it wouldn't be too hard to destroy the device, so we threaten them with that."

"You've got to have a clearer plan than that of what you'll do if you get on board." The General complained.

"Has anyone actually seen an alien?" Moore spoke up. They all stood quietly surprised by the question and to find that they had no idea what their enemy even looked like. "All we've seen so far are some kind of computer controlled vehicles and space ships attacking us, unless of course the aliens are invisible"

"There was that creature but we don't think it's the same alien as the ones who built that ship." Josh answered.

"So what's your point Moore?" The General asked

"Perhaps the aliens have all stayed on the main ship and if we manage to locate them we might find they're easier to kill."

"It sounds our best shot."

"Sir." A voice was coming over the Generals radio built into his wristwatch. "Eagle 1 here."

"Go ahead."

"I've spotted alien vehicles heading this way. Should be here in about an hour, judging from the speed they're travelling at."

"Keep track of them for as long as you can and then get back here."

"Will do sir."

"How's that working when we're inside the base and, I take it, this Eagle 1 chap is outside?" Kolinsky asked astounded. "You must have developed a way to bounce radio beams through solid rock."

"That's classified information," the General snapped, "besides which we've got more important concerns to deal with at the moment. It seems time is against us." He turned to Josh and Burnett. "See if you can make that call to the alien ship while I put together a team. I'll take you to the device those aliens are after first." The General marched back to the room they had previously seen the device in. Briefly he gave instructions to his personnel to allow them full access and then promptly departed.

Burnett made the hand gesture over the device and the blue light appeared, as before evolving into an image of the interior of an alien ship, identical to the command centre of the one underground. She looked across to Josh for help, unsure what to do next.

"We have the device," Josh hoped the aliens were listening, "as you can see behind me." Josh moved aside to give a clear view of the box behind him. "We are willing to hand over the device providing you leave this planet immediately and never return." There was no response. "Can you understand me?" Sparks of colour appeared on the image, fluctuating wildly as a synthetic sounding voice began to speak.

"We agree. Hand the device over at once."

"First you must agree safe passage for our vehicle into your ship or else we will destroy the device. We will be attaching an explosive to it and one false move from you will set it off." The voice remained silent, contemplating its options.

"Very well."

"We will let you know when we are approaching." Burnett waved her hand over the box to end the communication.

"We still didn't see an alien." Burnett sounded disappointed.

"They must have been blocking their image for some reason. Perhaps they really do have a weakness they don't want us to know about."

"I'm sure we'll run into one before long." Styne added.

"We'd better find the General and tell him." A uniformed soldier had entered the room and now spoke.

"The General's ordered that we all meet him by the airlock and bring this device with us. Arrangements have been made. This way."

"Don't tell me I've got to go." Kolinsky looked mortified.

"Hurry up" was the soldiers only response.

## Chapter 50

The strange energy fluctuated slightly as it explored the possibility of passing through the metal door after the biological life forms. It still remained completely invisible to the naked eye, seemingly able to exist in the same space as anything as long as it maintained its fixed volume. It had travelled up the passageway trying to track them and now moved through the second door and into a chamber. Before it could progress further a warning light began flashing wildly in the roof as a voice spoke. It had been detected. A security guard rushed up and pushed her face to the window, looking all round. She cursed at the sight of the empty room, putting the warnings down to faults in the computers. After all they were always breaking and going wrong.

The energy fluctuated more faintly becoming matter in places for the briefest of moments. It moved on feeling sure its current state would not last for long. It wanted to unleash a destructive force of energy at the guard, at all life forms but it was incapable. It barely even existed.

The energy moved on undetected, determined to find the life forms that had been in the cave. It searched and searched until at last it found them all, and others, standing before another metal door. Its form would take shape and appear faintly more and more now but until it returned to its normal state it couldn't attack. So it waited patiently, following at a distance.

## Chapter 51

There was an array of confusion as Josh and the others arrived at the door, eyeing the suited military figures suspiciously.

"Did you make the arrangements?" The general asked Josh.

"Yes they're waiting for us now."

"Good." The general turned his back on them and addressed the suited soldiers. "You have your orders, good luck." The military personnel stepped forward to take the device but Burnett and Josh blocked their path, realising they weren't going to be included in the team.

"Wait a minute." Burnett said forcefully raising her hands to stop them. "We have to go too."

"I'm sorry but that would be madness. We have trained military people here. Thank you for your help but now leave things to us." The general nodded for his team to carry on.

"You don't understand, the aliens are expecting us to make contact with the device." Burnett explained, determined not to be brushed aside. She knew she would be taking on a huge responsibility by going and that did scare her but somehow the thought of not going and not having any control over what happened scared her more.

"The team I've selected can contact them."

"Are you sure the aliens will respond?" Josh pressed trying to ensure his own inclusion. The general looked apprehensive for a moment, full of indecision.

"You must know most of our shelters could be wiped out, all those lives resting on us" he muttered to himself. Everyone remained silent. Finally he sighed, pointing to the racks of suits. "All 4 of you get suited up." Josh, Burnett and Styne hastily pulled suits on, only pausing briefly to look questionably at Kolinsky who hadn't moved.

"I'm not going. Not again." Kolinsky voice was more a wail of despair.

"You were all present when you contacted them so you had better all be on board." The general intervened. "And you do know the most about these aliens, you've been inside one of their ships."

"What about us?" Moore moved forward, gesturing to Quigly who stood next to him. "I believe we were out of sight when they communicated but I'd still like to go."

"It's going to be conspicuous if we send too many." The general answered thoughtfully.

"Oh don't worry when this plan goes wrong you'll get to fight them then." Kolinsky shuffled into his suit defeated and resigned to his task.

"I'm not going to complain about not going" Quigly said relieved "but you ought to know when we attacked it, that ship had some kind of energy field surrounding its exterior that repelled and destroyed anything that came in contact with it."

"Josh is still recovering from the radiation though." Burnett said concerned.

"I'm ok. In fact I actually feel fitter than ever."

"You should do." Kolinsky commented.

"What do you mean?" Kolinsky sighed, pausing in his struggle with the suit to explain.

"The nanobots are programmed to repair any damage to your body and they don't stop once the radiation damage has been fixed. They carry on, repairing any muscle strains or slight bruises inside or out. To a certain extent you can over exert yourself while they're working and they will just keep everything in perfect condition."

"How long do they last for?" Kolinsky, fell silent but that was enough to make Josh realise he had no idea.

"Kip Davies and Jules Porter will also be going with you. They're trained to fight their way out of any situation." The General pointed to two heavily muscled men both of whom wore grim expressions. The General pointed to the airlock. "They're putting a heavy transport shuttle together on the surface for you. Once you're inside try to find a way of keeping the door open, then maybe we'll be able to send more teams in after you.

"No one managed to get in last time." Quigly said. "It was nothing more than a slaughter."

"This time it will be different. It has to be. Hopefully you will find some weakness or …"

"You'll blow us all sky high with that nuke you've strapped to the device." Kolinsky finished.

"Of course not. We …"

"Save it. We've heard it all before." Styne cut in. "We are obviously expendable."

"We have no intention of detonating any explosives."

"Let's go." Josh pulled Styne and Kolinsky away and headed for the surface.

The journey in the transport vehicle was very comfortable with enough room inside for them all to sit. Davies and Porter had taken their places in the driving compartment, although the computer actually did all of it. Through the small circular window they could make out the alien crafts, all motionless, in two lines to form an avenue that prevented them from straying from their route to the huge ship settled on the ground ahead.

"It's time." Josh motioned to Burnett who triggered the alien communication box. As soon as the blue light appeared Josh spoke. "We're approaching your ship now and as you can see we have the device on board." He motioned to the black box in the centre of the floor. "Any act of aggression and we will destroy it."

"We will not attack you so long as you bring us the device." Burnett shut off the communication.

"I suppose this is it." She said apprehensively as the vehicle came to within yards of the ship and its open door.

"Be careful." Kolinsky burst out, aiming his remark at the driver. "Remember what Quigly said about that field round it."

"They would have deactivated it." Josh said adding hopefully to himself. "They wouldn't want to risk destroying the device."

The transport lurched slowly to a stop in front of the door, surrounded on all sides by the smaller alien vehicles, which had gathered and lay presiding over the proceedings. The occupants of the transport were all aware that there was no escape if they chose to attack.

"Everyone ready." Porter moved to the back of the transport followed by Davies. Between them they hauled the device onto a flat piece of metal, underneath which were attached wheels and hidden somewhere in it was a microcomputer. As soon as the load was put on it the robot powered up, unseen clamps coming up to lock the box firmly into place but so gently as to leave no marks on the item. "Crawler 2, follow." The wheels immediately swivelled round in the direction of Porter's voice.

"Aren't the aliens going to object to so many of us going." Kolinsky grumbled as they all grabbed weapons.

"They don't have much choice if they want the device in one piece." Josh answered.

"So why don't we just tell them to leave Earth or we'll destroy it."

"Somehow I don't think they would agree to that one." Porter gave Kolinsky a gentle shove with the side of his gun. "Come on let's get going."

The whole party filtered out into the daylight. The alien ships huge size created a shadow that fell across them and cloaked the door in darkness. They walked up to it, behind Crawler 2 obediently followed, at first with some difficulty over the muddy grass but then with ease as it moved onto the hard surface of the ramp and then the floor beyond the door.

From what Josh remembered the outside shape looked different to the ship below ground, this one having less bulges on its round form, yet the first room looked identical, with its lack of furnishings. It had to be some kind of air lock. They moved through the second door to an indistinguishable deck where all the vehicles had been only this area was even more deserted. Only a couple of vehicles remained and there were no signs of any aliens. They took the lift up to the next level, with its similar maze of machinery covering all floor space and the narrow hazardous pathways in between them. The same strange scintillating yellow light ran round the perimeter of the deserted deck.

"We need to get to the control room, it was up there in the ship underground." Styne pointed to the next lift as the alien voice echoed out all around them.

"Leave the device and go." They ignored it, the lifts swiftly taking them up to what they believed to be the habitation quarters with its corridors set with a multitude of doors.

"Davies, Kolinsky." Porter said in hushed tones, surveying the situation. "You two stay here and make sure nothing follows us, the rest of you come with me. There must be an alien somewhere around here."

The corridor extended either side of their position, branching out in all directions. They tried the first door, a click resounded down the walkway followed by creaking as the door swung outwards. Aliens had to be inside, there wasn't much of the ship left unsearched. Cautiously they peered inside. It appeared to be devoid of life. The walls literally were splashed with a vast array of colours as if some brilliant décor had been attempted. The floor glistened spectacularly drawing the eye to it. The longer they looked the more they felt they were staring into a picture. As they entered they felt the sponginess of the floor, which was amazing considering it had changed and assumed the appearance of marble whilst retaining the captivating pictures in it. As they examined it closer the pictures seemed to come alive. Great caverns of rock jutting up, out of the sea, that they were now flying in between and their bodies even had the sensation of it. They swooped upwards towards the clear blue sky, catching a momentary glimpse of strange flying creatures. They tried to look closer but they were being taken back down and into the sea, their masses throwing up giant plumes of white spray as they entered the watery depths. Strange sea life swam beneath their feet and even the walls came alive with the same scenery.

"Leave the device or you will be killed." The alien voice broke the hypnotising trance they had all fallen into and they were jarred back to reality.

"What is it?" Porter whispered in awe barely moving his eyes from the floor, its picture temptingly close.

"Perhaps it's some type of entertainment." Burnett suggested.

"We don't have any animals like that and never have had as far as I'm aware." Josh added. "I wouldn't be surprised if that wasn't all images of the aliens home world or at least some other planet."

"Perhaps it's to stop them feeling home sick."

"Why don't they use proper holographic images all around us?" Porter said stepping out of the room.

"I don't know," Josh answered, "but I had more of a sensation of being in the image than I do with our own images."

"It's the floor, I'm sure it somehow moved." Burnett said as they opened the next door. It was stiffer than the first. They held their guns ready and peered in. The room was empty. The same garish colours covered the walls and this time the floor as well. A soft light emanated up the side of one wall, an object in it remained suspended half way between the ground and dark ceiling. Burnett walked over to it, finding the object nothing more than a metal ball. She couldn't resist reaching out her hand into the light to touch it, immediately experiencing a strange awareness of her hand lifting by itself, as she did so. It felt like millions of tiny bubbles were hitting her skin, creating a warm comforting sensation. She moved further into the light until at last she was completely encompassed by it.

"Don't." Josh shouted but it was too late. Burnett felt her legs lift off the ground and in one easy flowing movement she found herself lying in mid air with the sensation of relaxing warm water all around her through which the tiny bubbles continued to rise.

"It could have been dangerous." Josh scolded, coming over to help her down.

"I can't see why it has to be their living quarters."

They moved over to inspect the large items against the other walls. They appeared to be cupboards but they were all sealed tight with no apparent way in. Styne had tried to open one but his efforts were to no avail.

"You must leave the device now." The alien synthetic voice sounded like it was trying to radiate authority and convey threatening menace but it failed completely in its lack of emotion.

"We haven't got time for this." Porter glanced at his watch. "We don't know if the aliens are still looking for the shelters. The group reluctantly followed him out and into the next room all but identical to the last, as was the one after, and all with no sign of any aliens.

"I guess all the crew had the same accommodation

but with only slight variations to the decor." Burnett said as they retraced their steps back to Kolinsky and Davies.

"More to the point, where are all the crew?" Styne asked in annoyance.

"It's like being in a ghost ship, deserted like the one below." Josh said thoughtfully.

"I want you two to continue checking the rooms." Porter ordered Kolinsky and Davies on the way past. "Take out any aliens you find. We'll be up there." He pointed to the next level where the control room had been in the ship below ground. They all looked up apprehensively as the other two left to continue the search.

## Chapter 52

The unnatural energy form had followed the group at a distance, not wanting to give away its presence when its normal shape returned as it did briefly every so often and more regularly now. It had seen all the alien vehicles surrounding their path to the ship but it had paid no attention to them, they were nothing more than a construction of combined inanimate materials. It was life forms that were its goal.

The humans now disembarked from the vehicle and continued on foot into the ship. The energy paused as it materialised into solid matter and light energy for some minutes; its normal form. It would soon return to this state permanently but for now it had to make do with short periods. It transformed back to energy and continued its pursuit, warily exploring the familiar surrounding until at last it finally stumbled across the two life forms moving around in a maze of rooms and corridors. At present it could do nothing but follow.

## Chapter 53

Porter was the first to arrive on the command level where the navigation systems had been held on the ship underground. Crawler 2 obediently followed in the rear. Although the deck had the same layout, this one was lit up like a Christmas tree with a lot more holographic images all around.

"Good the device has arrived." They looked round certain the alien voice was in the room somewhere. "Go now." It echoed round but there was no sign of the alien.

"Where are you?" Porter asked. Various holographic images fluctuated, changing rapidly of their own accord as the alien voice spoke again.

"That is not relevant. All we want is the device.

"You're a computer aren't you?" Realisation dawned on Burnett's face.

"Why wasn't there one on the ship underground?" Josh asked astonished.

"There seems to be more systems working here all together." Burnett whispered as the alien voice began talking.

"I'm a database of the thoughts and minds of the crew with some programming routines and so yes I am what you would term as a computer."

"And there are no aliens here on our planet, are there?" Burnett continued. The rest of the group looked at her in surprise.

"The device." The computer said determined.

"You can have it once you tell us everything you know about it and your crew." Josh said, silencing Porter as he tried to protest.

"That is classified information. I cannot tell …"

"You don't have a choice." Josh interrupted. "We will blow the device otherwise.

"That was not our agreement."

"The agreement has changed."

"And if I comply the agreement will change again."

"If you don't there won't be anything to agree about." Josh pressed his hand onto the casing of the bomb attached to the side of the device." The computer was silent as if considering.

"You do seem to be a race with a propensity for self harm." The voice went quiet for longer before at last talking. "Our race lives millions of light years away from here. We had spread out colonising our galaxy and those nearby. We were a thriving race until war broke out amongst us on a large scale, with entire planets being destroyed at a time. We have been fighting for years and even now the cause for it all is somewhat uncertain.

Our spies learned of an enemy research vessel, which the ship, you speak of finding underground, was sent to destroy after first taking all research. They managed to evade all security in the area and incapacitated the research vessel. The enemy had no choice but to surrender or blow themselves up. They chose the latter option, although our side managed to board and retrieve the device and some research material about it first. What they had rescued was all that was left since all research had been contained on that research vessel and no second copies had been sent anywhere for security reasons. Our side informed our senior officials of their success and set about examining their find.

The last message they sent the government stated that the device appeared to be able to transport entire ships over millions of light years in seconds but not via wormholes or any other theoretical method. In fact they drew a blank on how it actually worked.

Our ship and crew were pulled out of a ground attack on a planet to aid them but just as we arrived their ship disappeared. It would seem that they somehow triggered it. It was impossible for any of our race to build another device since all the research material had been lost with the ship and the original scientists had all been killed, so we were ordered to retrieve it. All our ships have tracers fitted to them and though it wasn't registering at first it did briefly appear and so we travelled in that direction. We've been travelling in the same direction for approximately 120 million years with no more sign of the trace until 3 months ago."

"That's when the military team found the ship underground." Styne whispered to the others.

"We came to this planet but the signal had stopped by the time we arrived."

"But what happened to the aliens, I mean your crew?" Burnett persisted.

"Some of them had picked up an infection on the planet where we had been engaged in battle before being called away. We didn't realise until a week into our journey after the ship. We tried everything we could but all the crew died within a short period. Automatic procedures were started to disinfect the ship and the computer was assigned the task to continue with the mission, as I have done. I control everything and have the memories and mission objectives of the crew."

"Let me get this straight." Styne snapped. "All this bloodshed and death was over a device that could transport a ship millions of light years in seconds."

"From our communication with the ship before it disappeared their short research suggested that it was more than just that but we have no idea what."

"And you took it upon yourself to continue the search for this device for 120 million years."

"Of course, I had to complete the given task."

"What's the life expectancy of your race?" Josh threw in.

"On average 200 years." The computer answered.

"And when you get this device you will return the same way?"

"Yes."

"It will be about 240 million years before you

return. Do you really expect your race to even still be in existence, let alone waiting your return." The computer was silent.

"I must complete the given task before returning to acquire new objectives."

"If the crew had have been alive they would have given up long ago." Josh stated, sighing.

"All this carnage and death because a computer can't comprehend any more than its programming routines and given instructions." Styne snarled.

"We require the device now. That was the deal for the information." The computer continued. "I insist that you hand it over at once and leave."

There was a sudden explosion somewhere in the distance that rocked the very ground they stood on and they all had to fight to retain their balance. They looked at each other stunned as the floor continued to vibrate.

## Chapter 54

The mass of energy had felt its state of existence changing again and a more stable form returning. The two life forms stood in a room in front of it, easy targets. In its normal form it could now manipulate its surroundings, causing a surge of energy build up, creating a wash of static electricity in the air all around. The build up reached its maximum and with one easy movement the creature unleashed it towards the startled humans.

The bolt of energy caught one of them, slamming him back into the floor, the rest of its energy creating a slight dent in the alien metal that the floor was constructed out of. The other life form had already taken to his heels as the creature moved in to finish off the crumpled life form. The violence of its attack made the floor shudder and shockwaves continued rippling out as the creature's arms ripped at the still form before it ploughed its way after the other human. Its arms crashed down onto the floor as it continually gathered energy and momentum, determined to destroy all traces of alien life forms. The man was racing down the corridor, his breathing harsh as his head frantically turned, his eyes, behind the thick glasses, searching for a place of safety. It was gaining on him and soon there would be nothing left to chase. The man tried several doors, deciding against going inside. He looked back at the creature and saw with horror it was almost upon him. He couldn't outrun it; he had to hide. The creature steadily advanced.

The man disappeared through the door as the creature felt the static buzzing around it and a strong gathering of energy inside. It passed through the door, the only exit in the room beyond and the only way out for the life form. It had him cornered. The man was backed up against the far wall, frozen, just staring at the creature. It moved its arms, about to release the energy when suddenly its form dissolved, flickering in and out of existence, the bizarre energy form trying to take a hold on it and at last succeeding. It was stuck unable to attack, not even visible. The man needed no second bidding but raced out the door, thankful for his good luck but certain it was only a matter of time before it found him.

## Chapter 55

"What was that?" Burnett whispered as the echo from the blast finally died away.

"It's here." A voice over the radio screamed. "Help me."

"Kolinsky is that you? What's here?" Josh asked confused by everything that was happening.

"That creature. For heavens sake do something."

"It can't be I saw it disappear."

"Well it's back now, Davies body or what's left of it can testify to that. It tried to attack me but then vanished and now it's back again."

"Calm down."

"It's not you being chased."

"Don't worry we'll figure something out."

"Well figure faster." Kolinsky's strained voice faded into silence.

"I don't know how it survived, nothing seems to kill it." Josh said turning to the others.

"We've got to help him." Styne headed for the lift.

"Wait you'll just get killed to. We need to work out how to destroy it." Burnett grabbed his arm.

"Nothing makes sense about it." Josh's eyebrows knitted. "How is it able to change form and alternate between matter and energy? It would take vast amounts of energy to do, if it's even theoretically possible. And it seems to be able to create energy from nothing, which is definitely impossible."

"No it isn't. I've seen it do it." Styne barked.

"All I want is the device." The computer repeated.

"This creature sounds about as strange as that device." Porter added. "I mean how it's able to travel faster than the speed of light and not use wormholes."

"There is one radical theory that might explain everything." Burnett suggested timidly "only I can't remember it too well."

"We'll take anything at this point." Josh encouraged reassuringly. "We might be able to kill it if we know what we're dealing with."

"We can't stand here discussing theories, we have to help Kolinsky." Styne fidgeted impatiently.

"You go if you like but it won't help anyone." Josh turned back to Burnett, ignoring Styne's flushed angry face. "Carry on."

"I will kill you all," the computer interrupted "if you do not leave." They all faced the dancing holograms, annoyed at the intrusion in their discussion, then Josh's face lit up with an idea.

"There's some kind of life form on board this ship, can you track it?" he asked the computer.

"There's only one life form detected outside this room."

"It must have got Kolinsky." Burnett breathed as Josh tried the radio, hoping to contact him. Silence before at last Kolinsky's breathless voice confirmed he was still alive.

"You've made a mistake there has to be two life forms." Josh corrected.

"No there is only one."

"My theory is becoming more plausible all the time." Burnett said absently as Josh asked the computer another question.

"Can you detect any unexplainable disturbances in the ship, particularly near the life form?"

"Yes, I'm detecting a mixture of strange readings of matter and energy in a fixed volume that is moving towards the life form."

"Well that disturbance is here to destroy the device and will do if you don't stop it." The computer again paused to consider how to react.

"I have ordered the robots to attack it along with any life forms on board this ship, so I advise you to leave at once."

"Great now the robots are after Kolinsky as well." Styne cursed.

"All hells being unleashed down there. We'll never get out." Porter looked concerned.

"Your theory?" Josh prompted Burnett.

"It's difficult to explain and impossible to comprehend."

"Try us, please."

"Well." She paused trying to gather her thoughts. "Everything we know in our galaxy, the universe and space beyond it is made up of energy and matter and subject to certain rules. For example energy and matter cannot be created or destroyed but only changed from one form to another, and these rules apply to anything in our plane of existence.

There's a theory that suggests that there are other planes of existence, in fact an infinite number of them, only they are all different. In one plane there may be only matter and energy but a different set of rules apply, so it may be energy can be created from nothing. Then there are the more interesting planes that are made up of something we couldn't begin to comprehend. Our senses are geared to detect matter and energy and it's difficult for us to believe that anything could exist unless it was made up of these but these planes exist and are made up of components we could never understand. They exist without matter or energy but something entirely new and unimaginable to us." Burnett paused again, trying to get her own mind round the unthinkable.

"These planes all exist together. You could think of them as sheets of paper floating in space, only time doesn't exist in the space between them, nor does anything else and time within the different planes works differently, strangely. There is no correlation between them at all. It's believed that if two of these planes collide, a new plane is created or new substances such as matter created inside one of them."

"The start of a universe?" Josh queried.

"Maybe." Burnett shrugged.

"What's this got to do with the device?" Porter interrupted.

"If you could somehow bridge a gap between two planes it would be possible to jump out of one plane at a particular point, into the other plane and then back into the first at an entirely new point in a matter of seconds. In other words you could travel great distances in one plane, virtually instantaneously.

"Because time is mangled in the different planes?" Josh asked.

"I don't really know how it actually works I just know there is such a theory. I think it's mainly because of the way you jump between the planes and how you travel or even exist in the other plane, while you're there."

"And you're suggesting the device bridges the gap between this plane and another one." Josh gasped at the revelation.

"This is complete nonsense." Styne shouted, losing control of his temper.

"No it isn't." Porter put a hand in front of him before he could close the gap on Josh. "We translated some of the pictures and text on the device. It didn't make any sense at the time. It was just nonsense about bridges and expanses and an end of time but now it seems to fit the theory."

"And the creature?" Josh asked Burnett. "How does that fit into all this?"

"The alien ship we found underground obviously used the device to get to Earth." Burnett hesitated. "This is pure speculation on my part."

"Go on."

"We've got plenty of time for your delusional ramblings." Josh's glare silenced Styne.

"The other plane they passed into may have been one that was made up of something other than matter and energy. It may also have contained something that although it wouldn't fit our definition of a life form would fit its own laws and definition of life. The aliens wouldn't have been able to sense anything in the other plane since they would barely be able to even exist in it and certainly not in their true form. When they came back into this plane they might have accidentally pulled this life form through with them. It wouldn't have been able to exist in its true form, since the laws won't allow the components from its plane to enter ours. It would have been trapped here unable to return to its own plane and with only a distorted control over matter and energy, governed by a set of rules different to either plane. It may still retain some kind of link with its own plane and rules and therefore wherever it is in ours the laws break down to a certain extent. In essence it can bend our rules slightly, hence the unexplained amounts of energy it conjured up and the strange effect the radiation must have had on it. From what we've seen it can manipulate a fixed volume of matter and energy, although 10 percent of it appears to have to remain as matter all the time, which means it couldn't pass through matter."

"You mean I was the cause of it escaping from that cave!" Josh face whitened with shock.

"It vanished after it was irradiated, we can only

guess that was what allowed it to pass through matter, we don't know. It's not your fault. It may have escaped anyway." The silence lengthened.

"Why's it killing us all then?" Porter asked.

"As far as it's concerned it was the life forms that trapped it here in this plane. It probably thinks by killing them all it can return to its own plane."

"If I buy into this, then how do we kill it?" Styne conceded.

"We don't."

"What?"

"You can't kill something that doesn't truly exist here but only has control over a portion of matter and energy."

"So what do we do?"

"Take it back." Josh said confidently.

"You mean use the device and take this ship into the other plane?" Porter asked bewildered.

"Can you see another way?"

## Chapter 56

The various alien vehicles began to swarm towards the door of the alien ship, like a stream of ants returning to their nest. As the last of the vehicles entered, the door swung back into place, slamming tight and sealing everything inside. The edge of the ship glowed a soft yellow as the systems powered up, energy spreading throughout it. Its massive form began to rise slowly and gracefully upwards making no sound in the process. It rose higher, gaining momentum as it went until at last it was speeding through the biosphere and onwards into space.

Inside the alien craft made their way across the deck, most hovering on some unseen energy field just above the floor, whilst the stranger monstrosities waded awkwardly on two mechanical legs that ended at the top in a round flattish disc. All the time they were in constant communication with the main computer as they tracked the moving distortion of matter and energy, the smaller craft using the lift up to the next deck and the maze of equipment it held.

It was right behind him; he could feel it making the hairs on the back of his neck stand up. Kolinsky dived through doorways and down corridors, desperately trying to find a route down to the deck below. He had to get off the ship and away from it.

He swallowed hard as he heard the crackling just behind and knew a bolt of energy was about to strike him. He threw himself flat on the ground, his hands over his ears, narrowly avoiding the destructive force that roared above over him. Kolinsky scrambled up and round a corner, at last seeing the lift ahead. Within seconds he was on it but nothing happened. The creature loomed into sight, its arms of energy pulling its body of matter forward. He stepped off and back onto the lift as the creature came into striking distance. The arms shot out at lightning speed straight for him. For a moment Kolinsky's heart stopped but then he felt a jolt and the motion of the lift racing downwards. He ducked managing to avoid the arms.

He was safe now on the deck below. An arm and then the form of the creature appeared in the hole above making him jump. He wasn't going to risk it; he had to get off the ship and the sooner the better as far as he was concerned. There was a thud behind him and he turned to look upwards, immediately drawing back at the sight of the empty hole. The creature was gone.

In front lay the jungle of alien machinery, their gleaming metal surfaces reflecting the light and refracting it. Kolinsky walked towards the lift down to the lower deck. In a whipping of air, the creature's arm shot out, just missing him but cutting off his access to the lift. He ran back away from it, ducking under pipes and avoiding any jets of boiling steam, becoming more disorientated by the second. It was still hunting him.

The machine next to him whined and then a hiss of hot steam powered out of a vent into the creature, which seemed unaffected by it. Kolinsky turned another corner, stopping dead at the sight of the ungainly robot, sitting patiently on two legs, blocking his path. The round disc on top swivelled as if detecting his presence and it moved jerkily forwards. Kolinsky backed up but halted when he felt the wash of cold air hit him in the back and heard movements. He glanced behind to see the creature dragging itself into view. The robot the other side was gaining speed. Either side was a wall of machinery. There was just no way out.

Kolinsky took his only option and ran at the robot hoping a miracle would take place and somehow he would get past. The creature lashed out but missed, the robot responding to the motion. He held his breath as he took the next few strides but there was no reaction and he was past. Behind him the robot continued towards the body of matter and energy, a field of yellow light powering up around it. The creature paid no attention to it as they reached each other. A flash of yellow dispersed outwards as the robot began its attack on the creature, the light hitting it with no effect. Some kind of explosive was fired next but it only made a small impact on the central core of matter, that quickly replenished and grew back into its previous shape. One swift movement of the creature's arm sent the robot toppling to the deck as one of its legs was severed. The disc on top swivelled fruitlessly at its predicament. Another limb of light destroyed the robot, shattering it into pieces as the creature continued after Kolinsky, barely losing pace. More robots were approaching from all directions. He had to get away but one or other hostile forces had blocked off all the paths.

## Chapter 57

"Ok, supposing I do believe a word of this, how do we put your master plan into action?" Styne asked. "I mean do you even know how to use that device?"

"It's created by these aliens so it must be a series of hand gestures that activates it." Burnett said.

"Maybe the communication device had a simple one but this is definitely going to be complex. We'll never work it out." Styne protested.

"The aliens who stole the device already hacked any security in it." Porter said. "From our studies of it I think you need to locate it in the right place as well as the hand gesture."

"How do you know this?"

"There was alien pictures and text in the ship underground that explained about it. The man who came back brought a disc with the information on, which our scientists have been studying since. It gave details on the hand gesture to use but we couldn't get the device to work when we tried it and variations on it. The only explanation we could come up with was that the device needed to first be located in the right place in the power room. We think it needs a direct source of vast quantities of energy and so you need to plug it in directly to work."

"You know the hand gesture."

"Assuming we translated the text and interpreted the diagrams correctly." Porter nodded. "I can't be sure though till we actually try it."

"In that case we need to get this thing down there." Josh jabbed at the black box. "and see if your hand gesture actually works."

"So passing through this plane or whatever it is, will get rid of that creature just like that." Styne reiterated sceptically.

"It's our only idea unless of course you've got something in mind."

"Nope."

As they descended they heard the ricochet of bullets followed by horrific wailings and the crackling ripple of raw energy. It was coming from somewhere lower down.

"Where do we have to locate the device?" Styne asked.

"You said it needed to be tapped directly into a source of power?" Josh absently asked, his mind mulling over the possibilities. Porter nodded.

"That yellow beam seems pretty powerful, remember what it did to Evans's hand." Josh grimaced as he spoke. "All the vehicles seem to emanate a faint yellow glow as well, it's as if they draw their power from that beam."

"You think that beam is the main power source for

all this?" Porter asked. "Fine we'll have to get this thing over to the beam then." They took the next lift, the robot carrying the device obediently trailing after them. As the lift plunged down they could see the maze of machinery laid out below all the way to the yellow horizontal beam that circled round the inside walls of the ship. Over to one side of them, a short distance away, was the creature coming under a bombardment of alien robot fire. It paid little heed to them, considering them no more than a nuisance, as it efficiently dispensed with each one in turn.

"We'll have to place the device directly under the beam." Josh shouted above the noise of gunfire. "The beam would just destroy it if we tried to put the device in its path."

"How can that light have so much power?" Styne asked scornfully. There was no time for anyone to answer as the lift stopped at the deck and they were thrown into a surreal world of smoke and noise. Their vision became distorted, as though they were looking through water. Everything was out of place slightly.

"What the hell's going on?" Styne screamed.

"That creature must be manipulating the density and volume of the surrounding air." Josh yelled back.

"Has to be close then." Styne spun round searching.

"This way." Porter led them towards the outside edge. A whining noise made their eardrums feel like they were about to explode and energy sizzled through the air. Explosions resonated round in the confined space. They were aware of machinery moving and working but couldn't even hear the sound from it.

"Nearly there." Porter yelled as suddenly all the noise stopped save for the chug of the machines. It became eerily quiet.

"The creature must have finished destroying all the alien robots." Burnett found herself whispering, not wanting to draw attention to them.

An unexpected scream from behind startled them. They turned to see Styne on the floor twisting round, trying to fire at the creature that had emerged behind him. One of its arms of light had ripped a hole through his stomach, creating a gush of blood that pooled around him where he lay. Further back two alien craft appeared, firing a volley of lasers into the creature, which absorbed them without harm. Styne's gun went off, bullets ploughing into the central mass of the creature. Josh and the others rushed forward to help as another arm sliced into Styne's exposed body, gripping him and dragging him closer. A stray beam from the robots pierced through Styne's head sending a spray of blood back over Porter, who went white, paralysed with fear. Styne's body collapsed to the ground, his face pointing upwards and his eyes still staring in shocked, pained surprise.

The creature sent out a wave of energy that blew one of the robots to smithereens and sent the other spiralling out of control, before focussing its attention on the rest of the humans.

"Go, go, go." Josh urged, shoving them forwards.

Another alien vehicle appeared determined to destroy the strange mass of energy and matter. The creature briefly halted at its onslaught, turning to dispatch it with one strike.

The robot platform carrying the device trundled past, a rogue shot scarcely missing it, as it turned the final corner to arrive with the others at the yellow beam.

"It won't fit under on the robot so we'll have to take it off and manoeuvre it into position by hand." Porter shouted to the other two. Josh and Burnett had already begun to carefully ease the black box off the platform.

"It's coming." Burnett' voice was full of panic. Josh could see it approaching out the corner of his eye as he furiously worked the heavy box into position. A crackle of light flared out, striking Porter in the chest.

"No" Burnett screamed reaching for him as he fell back. Josh gave the box one final shove, to locate it under the sparkling beam. The creature was about to strike again, when they heard Kolinsky frantically shouting and waving from the other side of it. His actions worked and the creature turned to pursue him.

"How do we activate it?" Burnett was checking Porter's pulse. "He's alive." She shouted to Josh. Between them the managed to pull his unconscious form over to the box and prop him up into a seated position.

"What do we do?" Josh asked again, shaking him awake. Porter mumbled something unintelligible in his groggy state. "What do we do?" Josh repeated. Porter groaned as he reached his hand out over the device and then faltered. "Stay with us." Josh gave him another shake. With a strain of effort Porter moved his hand in a series of shapes, only just finishing before falling back dead.

The creature had returned, drawing close to within striking distance before Josh or Burnett had the chance to back away and nothing was happening to the box or them. There didn't seem to be anything they could do except die.

## Chapter 58

Out of nowhere another alien craft sped round the corner straight towards the creature, not even hesitating. The creature's arms flailed as if in protest as the vehicle careered into it, disintegrating into fragments as it hit.

"Look." Burnett murmured pointing to the device. Some kind of holographic projection had appeared above it, mingling with the sparkling light, capturing it. There was a jolt of the big alien ship and then around them a sea of colours erupted. It subsided to leave strange translucent patches, which light couldn't reflect off, yet they blocked it out from reflecting what lay behind.

Josh ran to the edge of the ship followed closely by Burnett, ducking under the beam. He stood in front of the small window beyond which lay space filled with stars but then it was consumed by a multitude of colour before fading into the same strange flares of light. The stars had disappeared, swallowed up by darkness save for the blotches of light. Josh looked back at the device to see the yellow beam bending down towards it as though it were trying to drain more power. An array of colour once more engulfed their vision both inside and out, covering everything. Once again it subsided but this time to leave a horrifying transformation. Josh found himself in a bleak, empty darkness. Everything had vanished even his very being. He glanced down and couldn't even see his own body. Perhaps they had managed to pass into the new plane where matter and energy no longer existed. He couldn't exist in his own form but instead could only have a bizarre unsettling presence, trapped in this scary state with only his own thoughts for company. Maybe he was experiencing something similar to the creature's, only it had had to endure millions of years of its equivalent to this depressing nothingness and perhaps they were all now trapped in the same way. It had to end soon but then again he had no concept of time now.

At last bright colours flared into being and he breathed a sigh of relief at the sight of the ship and Burnett. The creature was still approaching the yellow beam and their position beyond it. Once again the stars filled the vast chasm of space that lay beyond the window.

"It's still here." Burnett gasped recovering, not even wanting to consider the events that had just taken place.

"We'll have to go through again. Something must have gone wrong."

"Kolinsky here." The radio lit up.

"I thought you were dead!"

"I'm in the control room, seemed safer. Unless I'm

misinterpreting them, the holograms are showing really strange star patterns. I don't think we're in our galaxy anymore."

"Well where are we?"

"The creature." Burnett indicated its continued approach. Josh skidded across to the device, his hand moving about in a pattern as closely resembling Porter's movements as he could remember. He pulled his hand back just in time to avoid the creature's swift attack. It pulled its self forward as the holograms appeared. The creature would hit the yellow beam with its next move. Josh scrambled back, trying to put as much distance as he could between them. The colourful light erupted all around as the creature's arms shot out and it began to move its huge bulk into the beam. The colours and light were now fading into the nothingness of before as the creature made contact, the ferocious ensuing explosion lost in the enclosing darkness.

Josh found himself in the same lonely place, lost with only a strange sensation of the presence of something more but there was no way he could actually experience it. He wanted to scream and break free but he couldn't do anything. He had no idea where the creature was or if indeed anything were close to him.

At last colours flooded his vision, blinding him at the same time as he was thrown backwards by the force of the blast that was still taking place but had been suspended as if time had stood still. There was no sign of the creature though.

"What happened?" Burnett stammered. "What was that?"

The strange masses appeared everywhere, contortions of matter and energy trying to inadequately represent something more, some other substance and then they were gone, dissolving to leave behind the bright hues of stars in the blackness of space. Calm and peace spread over everything.

"Where is it?" Burnett asked.

"We must have got rid of it."

"How? Why didn't it go the first time."

"Maybe it blew up in the beam. I saw it enter it just as we went through to the other plane."

"Nothing could destroy it though."

"But maybe we were in its own plane at the time and that yellow beam had some kind of effect on it."

"That's it." Burnett said. "That's how it got brought through the first time. It must have got caught in the power beam, which caused that effect."

"And catching it in the beam again, caused it to switch back to its own plane?"

"It's only a hypothesis; I don't suppose we'll ever know for sure."

"Nothing in life ever is certain."

"We're home." Kolinsky's voice shouted joyfully over the radio. "I think."

"It was cruel leaving that creature in that dark place." Burnett shivered.

"It could probably sense things in that place, if we could have seen it, we may have found it was full of different life and beings. To that creature, our plane may have been like the darkness, only it somehow managed to sense enough to have an understanding of what existed here and know the difference between life and inanimate objects."

"Err, guys." Kolinsky's voice sounded strained. "We're coming in fast." Josh and Burnett exchanged bewildered looks as they made their way to the control room.

"How do you work this thing?" Kolinsky was flustering around the holographic projections of an Earth that was rapidly growing larger. Through the windows the stars flitted past. "We're going to crash if we don't slow this thing down."

"What are you doing?' Josh asked.

"Trying to save our lives." Kolinsky snapped, eyeing Josh as though he had gone barmy.

"I was talking to the on board computer that communicated with us before. It's controlling everything.

"Oh that thing. It was driving me mad with threats but then it stopped talking."

"When?"

"Not long ago."

"That creature must have fried something important in the machinery room that took the computer out as well." Burnett suggested.

"Just do something." Kolinsky said with growing panic. Out the window a fleeting image of Saturn went past.

"Hand movements." Burnett concluded and proceeded making random gestures through the projection of Earth and the line pointing into the sea, showing their current flight trajectory. "If we could just slow it down." Nothing was working. They would be passing into Earth's atmosphere within minutes.

"We're going to crash." Kolinsky reiterated.

"I can't get this to work." Burnett anxiously looked to Josh for help.

"Kolinsky, for once I think you might be right." Josh said his voice restrained as they neared the biosphere. "We need to go to plan B, come on."

The huge alien ship burned brightly as it entered the Earth's atmosphere, its outer skin trying to dissipate the extreme heat generated. It began to shake as it continued its plummet towards the ocean. Minutes passed before the heat reduced but it still descended at the same alarming speed. More minutes passed before it at last hit the water with a horrendous impact that threw up plumes of water, hundreds of feet high and sent huge tidal waves racing out in all directions. Not even the density of the water could slow it to a stop and it plunged lower until it hit the seabed some miles down. It settled there creaking and groaning under the immense pressures that tried to crush it from all sides. Another lost wreck entombing its secrets within it and condemning any occupants inside to death.

## Chapter 59

Any spectators would probably have missed the two tiny objects that flew out of the huge ship moments before it impacted the water. If they could have got closer they would have seen that they were two alien planes, inside which three human occupants were crammed. The vehicles stayed close together as they sped over the sea, towards their shelter and the remains of their city, leaving the huge waves in their wake, which were rapidly losing strength. Soon they had covered the distance to find a large gathering of people, clearing debris from the entrance to the base.

Josh and Burnett were squeezed into one of the planes, the soft spongy material moulding around their bodies and restricting all their movement. They needed to turn and land but Josh had no idea how to initiate the process.

His thoughts intensified, turning to surprise as the craft banked slightly towards the people. The ship lurched downwards, bouncing slightly as it made contact with the ground; its momentum carrying it shuddering along the wreckage before coming to rest. Kolinsky's craft fared little better.

Warily the three of them emerged through the

top of the craft, which slid back and up, immediately greeted by Hawkins before they had even got out.

"What happened? Where are the aliens?" Hawkins looked cautiously at the vehicles they had arrived in. Kolinsky and Burnett smiled weakly as Josh answered. "You'd never believe us if we told you and as for the aliens they never were here or at least not while we've been alive."

"I don't understand."

"The alien ship is deep under the ocean."

"What's been attacking us if it wasn't aliens?" Hawkins stuttered.

"It's a long story but they shouldn't be bothering us anymore." Hawkins looked satisfied with that, turning to the crowd about them.

"At last we can rebuild our cities on the surface and hopefully leave all this death and destruction behind as just a distant unsavoury memory." They cheered wildly as Burnett pulled Josh aside.

"We don't know that. Another alien ship could turn up any day and we don't even know for sure that creatures gone."

"It's unlikely they sent any more ships, they probably wiped themselves all out years ago." Burnett still looked concerned.

"We can't worry about what might happen, we just have to get on with our lives and deal with the problems when and if they do arise." He strolled across the wreckage that lay all about him, Burnett following. "It's going to be hard enough a task just rebuilding this place and putting our lives back together."

"What about what happened, that place and the darkness? How can you forget that so easily?"

"It's over now. We're safe." Josh looked hard at Burnett concern on his face. She relaxed slightly as she looked back, the noise of the others all about her.

"I don't want to ever leave this plane again." Kolinsky approached.

"You're forgetting one thing." He added. Josh glared at him, already knowing what he was about to say.

"Shut up Kolinsky."

"What?" Burnett asked alarmed.

"How do you know this is our plane. That this isn't some kind of illusion or trick of the mind inside the other plane. After all what really exists?"

# About The Author

Yvonne Arlott is a woodturning artist who lives in Cornwall, UK. She is the author of a woodturning DVD that has sold all round the world and both Yvonne and her wood turned art have been featured on TV and multiple times in newspapers and magazines.

She has always had a passion for science fiction and writing, both of which have aided her in the creation of her debut novel, Prelude to Annihilation.